D1345697

MURDER
Offscreen

A HENRY HOLT MYSTERY

A HENRY HOLT MYSTERY

MURDER
Offscreen

DENISE OSBORNE

HENRY HOLT AND COMPANY NEW YORK

Henry Holt and Company, Inc.
Publishers since 1866
115 West 18th Street
New York, New York 10011

Henry Holt ® is a registered
trademark of Henry Holt and Company, Inc.

ISBN 0-8050-3113-8

Henry Holt books are available for special
promotions and premiums. For details contact:
Director, Special Markets.

Designed by Paula R. Szafranski

Printed in the United States of America

Lovingly dedicated to Christopher James Osborne,
who knows writing is a real job,

for laughing when lesser mortals would have screamed.

ACKNOWLEDGMENTS

THE AUTHOR WISHES to gratefully acknowledge a few out of the many for assistance along the way, and in no particular order: my parents Alberta and Harry Barker; my sister, Diane Barker; Phil Osborne; Dee Osborne; Steve Osborne; Marilyn Hicks Fitzgerald; Sandra Hawkins; Dr. Alice Feldman; Merrill Sanders; Ned Hockman; Jack Bickham; Jeanne Hollenbeck; Earl Stam; Myra Recker; Rick Rescorla; Donna Canfield; Barry Pendlebury; Cosette Thompson; Tracy and Ava Smith; K-Pig radio in Watsonville; Avalon Visions; and both the San Francisco and Santa Cruz police departments.

Without my agent, Teresa Chris, I would not be writing these acknowledgements, and without my editor, Jo Ann Haun, you would not be reading them.

PART ONE

A man has only to affirm his conscious
aspiration; and the enemy is upon him.

—ALISTAIR CROWLEY,
Book 4

PART ONE

A man has only to affirm his convictions
… and the enemy … upon him.

ALEISTER CROWLEY
Book 4

monday

NOT YET TEN o'clock in the morning and already
Queenie Davilov's white T-shirt stuck to her like wet
tissue. Outside the stifling fourth-floor apartment,
she could hear the rats in the date palms screeching
angrily, their nests threatened by the swirling Santa
Ana winds. Like a blast from hell, the winds only exacerbated
the heat in the bowl of Los Angeles. For good reason, the locals
called it the Devil's Wind.

Anxiously she toyed with the long black braid slung over her
shoulder. Sapphire blue eyes glaring at the computer screen,
Queenie willed a third act to appear. Something brilliant.
Something with impact. Nothing like anything she'd written
and erased over the past two weeks.

On Saturday she would deliver the script to Eric Diamond—
which meant Friday was the last day she could register it with
the Writer's Guild, and at the current rate, she'd need every

nanosecond to meet the Friday deadline. Eric Diamond would not read an unregistered script—nor would any agent. And producers, directors, actors? They wouldn't touch material that didn't come from an agent.

The writing had gone so well in June and July. Then August blew in, forked tail swishing, and stirred up strange forces.

First the flies invaded. Hundreds had entered the living room from the wainscotting sending Clue, her white Persian cat, into a frenzy. Soon after, an elderly resident was found dead in an apartment below Queenie's, a casualty of the heat. It was chilling to think that her neighbor and the flies were related. And Clue, who normally regarded life as an endless summer day, retreated to the darkness of the bedroom closet.

Then came the call from her younger brother Rex, a rookie with the Boston Red Sox. Racing to catch a fly ball in left field, he'd smashed into Fenway Park's Green Monster, ending his season with a broken wrist . . . and just when he seemed a sure bet for Rookie of the Year.

Not the worst news, but no less painful, came last night from Dick Takahashi, the gorgeous result of genetic East meeting West. Queenie'd fallen instantly in love when he'd first poked a hole in her door while trying to maneuver his hardwood futon bed frame into his new apartment across the hall. For a couple of hours, the frame had bridged the two apartments while he found another door in the basement to replace hers. Nothing but friendship had resulted from the initial encounter, as she'd kept her feelings secret. Each had a key to the other's apartment. He fed Clue when she went out of town. She kept an eye on his place when he was away. Then last night he'd come over to tell her he'd be going to Japan on Saturday. She'd been about to tell him how much she'd miss him when he added, "To meet the family of my fiancée."

Queenie rose from her desk and slogged to the adjacent kitchen for more coffee. She eyed the bottle of Jack Daniel's with what she knew to be dangerous interest. At thirty-one she was still lean and strong as a teenager, but soon she'd have to take care lest the whiskey find permanent portage around her middle. Maybe just a splash to kick start the brain, she thought. As she was poised to serve herself, the phone rang. She tensed at the unwelcome interruption. *Pour, don't answer.* Then she thought of her brother. *Answer, don't pour.*

"Hello?"

Without identifying herself, Queenie's boss's secretary exclaimed, "You've got to get over here, Queenie!"

"Selma? What's wrong?"

Queenie listened while Selma Steinberg ranted incoherently, "... rotting flesh ... Jesus, the *smell* ... who would do such a thing?"

"Whoa! Slow down."

"Please! You'll see when you get here!"

"Get where?"

"The office!"

Twenty minutes later, Queenie pulled off Lankershim in North Hollywood, parking in the small lot beside an aromatic pepper tree. After grabbing her satchel, she hurried toward the offices of Hammon Productions, located in a strip mall with a dentist's office, a bar, a Laundromat, and a shop that sold Hawaiian shirts. Nothing, not even a plaque on the door, declared this to be the offices of Burke Lymon, one of Hollywood's most successful independent filmmakers.

Queenie tried the front door but found it locked. Feeling a little exasperated, she took a deep breath and knocked. Only after identifying herself did the door open. Queenie entered the cool office.

"Selma, what . . . ?"

"I'm keeping the door locked," Selma Steinberg blurted. A crowd of freckles danced across her nose extending to the hair line, the neat salt-and-pepper cap of tiny curls cut close to her head. Her café latte skin looked lighter today, but despite her distress she was beautifully groomed in a gray linen suit that matched her eyes.

After relocking the door, Selma scurried to the desk where a telephone receiver lay on its side. She picked up the phone, pointed toward the hallway, mouthed "bathroom," then resumed the conversation Queenie's arrival had interrupted.

Queenie crossed the beige carpet considering Selma's sanity. Maybe the Santa Anas had gotten to her. *Rotting flesh*, though, suggested something much worse.

She entered the bathroom reluctantly, half wishing she was still sweating out an ending to her script, that she'd not answered the call. But besides being Burke Lymon's script supervisor, Queenie was able to do special favors for him since she kept her private investigator's license current. Film industry work was too unstable not to have something to fall back on.

An aerosol can of air freshener sat beside the sink, the cap beside it. The air stank of roses—and something else. The lid and seat of the toilet were up. Obviously a man had been the last to use it. Lymon must have returned from New York. Queenie noticed something on the floor behind the pebbled glass of the shower stall. The door opened with a slight *click*.

Darth Vader gazed malevolently from a lunch box. Nearby Luke Skywalker and Princess Leia looked brave; Han Solo, sexy. A storm trooper pointed his weapon at Queenie.

6

I don't want to deal with this, she thought. Not now. None-theless, she dug a pair of gauzy editing gloves from a side pocket in her satchel. Squatting down, she began breathing through her mouth in anticipation of an odor, then carefully lifted the lid.

Growing up on a horse ranch outside Norman, Oklahoma, she'd encountered plenty of dead animals: squished on country roads, ripped apart by other animals, stillborn, and those she'd hunted herself. But never had she seen small body parts nailed to a wooden cross, nor what appeared to be a skinned squirrel's head, a mushy rift between the dead eyes where the small ax had fallen from the rotting flesh.

She examined the crudely made weapon and, though she couldn't smell it, felt she could taste the stench of decomposition. The ax head, a gobbet of flesh still clinging to the blade, appeared to have been fashioned from the lid of a coffee can. On a bloodstained scroll nailed to the handle was a message written in red nail polish: *Love, your most adooring fan* and below it, *Lucifer.*

She shivered, a response having nothing to do with the air-conditioning.

Queenie replaced the small ax, closed the lid, and crammed the gloves into her jeans pocket.

Selma now hovered just outside the bathroom door.

"Well?"

"Just need to find a demon who's a bad speller," Queenie said lightly. Selma didn't smile. Queenie filled a cup from the water cooler in the hall to wash away the foul taste. "Where's Lymon?"

Selma nodded toward a door at the end of the hall. "Not to be disturbed. He got back from New York last night."

Queenie swirled the water in her mouth then swallowed. "Has he seen it?" She tossed the cup in a nearby wastebasket. The taste still lingered.

"Oh, yes." Selma shook her head in disbelief. "Not a ripple of emotion. Jesus! Wish I had such detachment . . . but with the premiere on Saturday, it would take nine-oh on the Richter scale to move him."

"Did he ask you to call me?"

Selma snorted. "He told me to throw the damn thing away! But no. You were the first person I thought of. Queenie, I'm scared. I mean, we've gotten weird mail and all but *never* anything like this. And with Nessa and L.D. missing . . ."

Queenie thought of the nearby bar. "Want a drink?"

"No. Too much to do." Underscoring the point, the phone rang. "Just a sec," Selma said, and darted to the desk. Queenie followed, now noticing the newspaper clippings spilling from a folder on the desk. *Lucifer's Shadow*, the title of Burke Lymon's latest film, was written on the cover.

Selma discussed the menu with the restaurant catering the after-premiere party. Though obviously frightened, Selma still had a strong stomach. Having seen the remains in the lunch box, Queenie couldn't imagine choosing a meat to use in the ravioli.

Selma tapped the folder and pointed at Queenie, who picked it up and moved to a sofa backed against the window, the sheer curtains drawn.

As she flipped through the clips, Queenie didn't have to be reminded of the film's casualties.

The furor had died down after the film wrapped in May. But now, nearly three months later, with last week's disappearance of Nessa (no last name) and L. D. Barth, the film's principal actors, the sensational stories had resurfaced. DEVIL FILM DAMNED?

8

LUCIFER SHADOWS HOLLYWOOD PRODUCER, HORROR PRO-
DUCER CURSED? Most of the stories, with the exception of
Variety's reportage, were angled toward the supernatural.

Variety kept to the facts. The director of photography,
Harold Jonge, had had a history of heart problems. He'd died of
heart failure on a sound stage shooting a scene in which L. D.
Barth's character conjured up a demon while chanting inside a
circle of salt.

Jim Hernandez, a member of the construction crew, had
fallen off scaffolding surrounding the four-story tower house
built on location near Inverness, on the northern California
coast. He'd been drinking the night of his death.

Jean Bliss, a former New York stage actress, had been found
hanging from a tree in the salt marshes near the motel where
the cast and crew stayed. Her death had been the most sinister,
underscored by rumors that she'd cast a few spells to land a part
in the picture and revive an otherwise dead career. Her boyfriend, a stage magician, had been a suspect until his alibi was
confirmed. The night of Jean's death, he'd been performing at
a Lake Tahoe casino, afterward taking his act to bed with a
couple of showgirls. Then later, a suicide "note" was found—a
message Jean left on her own answering machine.

The latest reports concerned Nessa and L. D. Barth's disappearance. To Queenie, the affair sounded staged. While L.D.
had cut out and eaten Nessa's heart on screen, off screen they
were presumed lovers. They'd probably create a sensation by
showing up at the premiere, Nessa announcing that L.D. had
given her a last name. And both handsome unknowns would be
pressed firmly to the public's sympathetic, if fickle, bosom.

After a few minutes, she placed the folder on the coffee table
beside an arrangement of dried-up flowers, the unusual shapes
and sizes once an explosion of colorful protea. They'd arrived

one January day while Queenie and several others were in a preproduction meeting. Lymon had just informed them they wouldn't be going to Scotland to shoot *Lucifer's Shadow*. For budgetary reasons, they'd be shooting on the coast north of San Francisco.

"It's a lot like Scotland," Lymon had said, aware of his crew's disappointment. At that moment, Selma had entered with the fresh bouquet, saying that his wife had sent it from Hawaii for their tenth anniversary. Obviously Mrs. Lymon didn't have budget problems.

At the expense of sounding callous, Queenie mused, the sudden disappearance of the two leads should generate interest in the picture. She'd heard Hammon Productions was struggling and hated the thought of having to pound on doors again. *If only I could get an agent . . . sell a screenplay.*

Feeling restless, she caught Selma's eye and tapped her watch. Selma raised a finger, continuing her phone conversation. Queenie grabbed her satchel and began searching for tobacco and rolling papers. Then she remembered Selma didn't smoke. Her broad shoulders rose and fell in an impatient sigh as her eyes darted around the office, but nothing held her interest. She needed to *do* something. She considered stepping outside for a smoke—but no, it was too hot.

On impulse, she emptied the satchel on the sofa. She never went anywhere in California without it, even to dressy functions like the last two premieres she'd attended. Earthquakes could hit at any time.

She began returning the items: a change of lightweight clothes, vitamins, a transistor radio and extra batteries, toiletries, fishing line and hooks, a Swiss Army knife, a notebook, an automatic pencil and extra lead, a set of lock picks, the stopwatch she used to time scenes for Lymon, a box of condoms, wallet, passport, the tobacco and rolling papers—

"Sorry about the interruptions," Selma said, suddenly joining Queenie on the sofa. She picked up a packet of Red Man tobacco. "Is this yours?" she asked incredulously.

Queenie looked up. "Yes, Selma." She quickly took the packet and put it in a side pocket. She'd been chewing since age twelve but few people knew it. She confined the habit to stables and her study. Neither horses nor computers cared what she squirreled away in her mouth. "Listen, I think Lymon would be best served if you call the special celebrity division of the LAPD."

"You're busy?" Selma sounded disappointed.

"Frankly, I am," Queenie said, returning the remaining items to the satchel. "Don't worry about it, Selma. They deal with this sort of thing all the time. And *Lucifer's Shadow* isn't exactly a guarded secret. Someone's pulling a prank."

"A sick someone," Selma spat. "Damn. Lymon won't want me calling in the police. Too much to do!"

Both women were quiet for a moment. Then Queenie asked, "Did it come UPS or regular mail?"

"Regular mail."

"Of course. Pretty well assures them of anonymity. What about postmark and date?"

"I saved the box and wrapper it came in. Mailed Friday in Los Angeles."

That cuts the possibilities down to about seven million, Queenie thought. "Well, the police might find some prints, maybe even match them to a known offender. Call them. It'll make you feel better." She stood up, anxious to get home.

"You think I'm overreacting?" Before Queenie could answer,

she added, "Look, my mother was Creole. She believed in voodoo, in the power of—that thing in the lunch box."

"Believe me, that dead animal has no power." Except what you give it, she thought. In truth, she felt uneasy too, but wasn't about to share her distress.

Selma picked up the folder. "I thought the clips might be helpful. Give you a clue or something."

"Well, show them to the police."

The two women walked to the door.

Selma stared up at Queenie for a moment. "That ax, Queenie," she said softly. "I think that scares me the most." Tears welled in her eyes. "There's a god, Chango, his symbol is an ax. . . . I hate to admit being superstitious, but it's the way I was brought up."

Queenie wrapped Selma in her arms. At five-foot-ten she topped Selma by a good six inches. "Hey. It'll be okay."

The two women moved apart. Wiping her eyes, Selma said, "It's just that I trust you—what with the extra work you do for Lymon." Then she managed a smile. "And besides, cops don't give hugs."

Driving home through the filthy curtain of heat on the Hollywood Freeway, Queenie tried to push the mutilated animal and the crude weapon from her mind. Still, what Selma had said kept coming back. *That ax.* Yes, that scared Queenie too.

CHAPTER TWO

QUEENIE PARKED THE Plymouth, formerly an unmarked police car, behind an equally unimpressive Ford. In this, the underbelly of Hollywood, only a fool would drive something flashy. Too many vandals and car thieves.

Litter swirled at her feet as she trotted up the sidewalk toward the St. Albans, the four-story, brick apartment building where she lived. Mr. Dhootie was picking up trash in the courtyard. He looked up, eyeing her in a way she found disturbing. A recent East Indian immigrant, Mr. Dhootie had purchased the old building and moved into a first-floor apartment. He seemed to be everywhere, *lurking*, silently watching the tenants. Everyone had been edgy since he'd moved in, like a school of fish sensing the nearness of a shark.

Long ago, the St. Albans had been a hotel frequented by film people with business at nearby Paramount Studios. At least half the current residents were elderly. Queenie rather liked that.

They didn't play cacophonous music or sell dope or ask her to baby-sit. They lived quietly on pensions, a few on residuals and royalties. Occasionally someone peed in the elevator or forgot laundry in the machines, and they kept the front door open all day, which did little for security, what there was. But during this particularly hermetic summer spent writing, they'd been friendly whenever Queenie wandered into the spacious lobby to take a break. Emma Schultz in particular liked telling stories of people who'd stayed at the St. Albans during its glamour days.

As usual, the clusters of mismatched sofas were filled with elderly residents awaiting the mail, each sag and stain seemingly familiar to its owner.

Emma Schultz looked up as Queenie entered. One of the few not in a bathrobe and slippers, Emma wore a full-skirted pink dress with a white Peter Pan collar. A pair of white gloves rested on a handbag at her feet. She beamed behind the net veil of a white cloche hat. And she had reason to smile. A TV show in which she'd starred in the fifties recently had gone into syndication—which meant residual checks. Despite the heat, she dressed each day in outfits that reminded Queenie of Beaver Cleaver's mother, June.

From her end of an ugly green sofa, Emma greeted Queenie. "Hi, dollface!"

"Emma," Queenie said quickly. "Don't you look nice."

Emma hopped to her feet and smoothed the full skirt. "Like this dress? Forty years old and it still fits," she said with a chimelike laugh. "Wish you were smaller. I've got a trunk full of beautiful clothes, even some designed by Billy Travilla—he designed for Marilyn Monroe, you know." Then Emma's smile lost a few kilowatts. "Something wrong? El been acting up?"

El, short for Elena, was the ghost of a dancer who'd died in

Queenie's apartment in the thirties, according to Emma, murdered by her married lover.

"No biggie," Queenie replied hastily. At the moment, she felt too pressured and apprehensive for an extended chat. "Look, I gotta go."

"When's that brother of yours coming?"

"Uh, Saturday."

"Well you'd better introduce us. No secret I like younger men," Emma called after her.

Queenie hurried to the elevator unaware that Emma's eyes followed her until the doors closed. Then, turning back around, Emma produced a pack of tarot cards from a pocket in the folds of her skirt and began shuffling.

After locking the door to her apartment, Queenie rushed to the bathroom to scrub the taste of the dead animal from her mouth. If she had to pick a color for it, she'd expect what she spat out to be gray-green, not red. She reached for the hydrogen peroxide, attributing her bleeding gums to stress.

She quickly peeled off her clothes, set the showerhead to "blast," and stepped behind the mossy Norman Bates shower curtain, a prop she'd designed for a film she'd made in college. Like hot gravel, the water pelted the jagged rosettes of muscle lumped across her broad shoulders. Gradually the pain subsided. If only the shower could melt and wash away guilt. She probably should have agreed to find whoever sent the crucified animal, just as she should have invited her brother to visit when he'd called last week. But no, she'd asked him to wait until this Saturday. However, there were times when a writer had to be a mercenary, no matter how bad it made one feel.

She dried herself with a faded yellow towel worn down to the texture of fine sandpaper. Five years, she thought. Same apartment, same towels . . .

Right out of college, she'd hit Hollywood at a dead run—particularly painful considering all the closed doors she bounced off. No one was remotely interested in some Okie dreaming of a screenwriting career. Nonetheless, she kept writing while working first as a reporter then as a private investigator with a small detective agency. It was during the latter incarnation that she met Burke Lymon. For three years she did the background checks on his new employees, making certain he knew she was available for film work. Then when his script supervisor went out of sync and started missing essential details, Queenie had been invited to replace her. The door had opened a crack. But a crack wasn't good enough. She wanted *in*.

After gathering her smelly clothes, she padded into the bedroom and entered the large walk-in closet. Clue barred her teeth and hissed as Queenie switched on the light.

"Poor kitty," she said, dropping the clothes in a heap. Maybe it was the heat or memory of the flies, but *something* kept the cat in the closet. Funny things happened in the apartment from time to time, but never before had the cat been so spooked. Maybe El *was* acting up.

She grabbed a pair of clean underpants from the four-drawer file cabinet in which she kept underwear and T-shirts as well as old scripts, notes, and cans of 16mm film she'd shot in college. Then she slipped on a old sleeveless work shirt, mentally preparing herself for writing, washing her mind of all distress. She'd just switched off the light when the bedroom telephone trilled. Damn it, she thought irritably.

She stepped from the closet and abruptly froze. "Holy Mother," she whispered as goose bumps rose on her bare skin. The ornamental ax, an award for her work on *Lucifer's Shadow*, was gone.

The phone continued to ring as she glanced quickly around

the room to see if anything else was missing. But for several seconds Queenie heard only Selma's words: *That ax . . . it scares me the most.*

She moved hesitantly into the room. Then she saw it, lying on the floor, and exhaled hot breath. While standing at the closet, the bed had blocked her view.

Shaking slightly, she hurried to pick up the phone on the nightstand, regarding the ax with some concern. Had someone been in her apartment? Dick had the only key. No wait, so did Mr. Dhootie . . .

"Hello?"

"Q?"

The caller was Werlanda Josephine Burroughs, assistant to Hollywood's most lethal gossip columnist, Arthur Favor. Despite taking different career paths, they'd stayed friends since starting out as reporters for the same Hollywood newspaper.

"Joey. You just get back?" Last week Joey'd invited Queenie to spend five days with her at a friend's cabin near Emerald Bay at Lake Tahoe.

"Unfortunately," Joey snapped. "Look, I'm in a rush. What've you got on L. D. Barth and Nessa? The Prince of Poop's gonna shitcan me if I don't come up with something nobody else has. Did you talk to the police?"

Queenie absently picked up the replica of the Willendorf Goddess on her nightstand. "No, why should I?"

"Hell! You do Burke Lymon's background checks! You know more about his people than anyone."

Oddly Burke Lymon had not requested a background check on Nessa. L.D., yes. But, for some reason, Nessa had been excluded, a fact that in itself was significant. But Queenie wasn't about to tell Joey that. "That's confidential."

"Okay then, what have you heard?"

"That they're not around for interviews. Wherever they are, they must be enjoying the attention."

"Aren't you worried? I mean, what with all those other deaths."

"Joey, I really can't be bothered right now."

Joey sighed. "God, I forgot. Your last session with Eric Diamond's on Saturday isn't it? Guess I'd better try someone else."

"Sorry I can't help on this one, Joey. Make up something. We both know how that works."

"Sure. But if you hear anything, call me first!" Then she added, "You're still picking me up at six on Saturday?"

"I haven't forgotten. And do me a favor, don't be obvious. I'm taking you as a friend—not as a gossip columnist."

"Thanks for the promotion, but I'm still an assistant—"

"—to a gossip columnist. And please, for once dress conservatively."

"Jesus, Queenie! We're not talking about some backwoods pig roast. This is a Hollywood premiere!"

"A Burke *Lymon* premiere. The word is 'conservative.' "

Queenie hung up then looked at the squat little Goddess. Burke Lymon despised those who made gossip their business. She knew the risk of taking someone in the media to the premiere, but Joey had introduced her to several agents and Queenie owed her. She whispered a prayer to the Goddess and then moved over to the ax.

Fashioned after a ceremonial ax used in the film, the two-foot-long handle was of polished bone with an intricately carved death's head at the end. The wickedly curved, single-bladed ax head glowed with a certain lethal beauty. The handle was engraved with Queenie's name, from Burke Lymon and Hammon

Productions, and included the name of the film and the wrap date.

Flanking its former position were two other engraved awards: a trident for *Neptune in Scorpio* and the most valuable of the three, a silver stake fashioned by Reed & Barton for her work on Burke Lymon's most successful horror film to date, *Vampire Moon*.

She started to put the ax back on the wall when she noticed the hooks were bent nearly straight, the screws dislodged. The weight of the ax had caused it to fall while she'd been gone that morning. There's always a reasonable explanation, she told herself.

Then a thought struck her. The ax in *Lucifer's Shadow*, though a prop, was as much a character as the evil man wielding it. It wasn't general knowledge—only those who worked on the film would know of the ax's prominence, at least until the picture was released. Had someone she'd worked with sent Lymon the ghoulish package?

Let the police take care of it, she told herself, but the thought of possibly *knowing* who'd commit such a cruel act was unsettling. Still, it was probably just someone's idea of a joke. If Lymon couldn't be bothered, neither would she be.

She slid the ax under the bed and out of the way. When she had time, she'd build a better brace for it. Now, though, she had a script to finish. Saturday just might be one of the most important days of her life.

s a t u r d a y

IN VARYING STAGES of distress, the seven aspiring screenwriters sat around the glass-topped table on Eric Diamond's flagstone veranda. The three-story Spanish mansion protected them from the winds— from which even Beverly Hills was not immune—but not the chainsaw effects of the sun.

Twenty minutes earlier, a Filipino servant dressed in white had served sweaty green bottles of designer water on pink linen napkins. In the heat, paper would have turned to mush. He'd informed them that Mr. Diamond would be a few minutes late. Queenie equated "few" with single digits. Mr. Diamond apparently did not.

Out of several hundred screenwriters, these seven had been chosen by Eric Diamond to attend six Saturday morning sessions to pitch their stories to an imaginary producer. In other words, sell to an unwilling buyer, one with a notoriously short attention span. The precedent was the pitch that sold the immensely popular *Alien*: "*Jaws* on a spaceship."

It had been an unusual move for an agent, dipping into the vast ocean of struggling screenwriters to find someone with a fresh voice, someone without high-powered contacts needed to even get a script read, let alone produced. But the agent had grown weary of the same hackneyed stories written by the nephews, nieces, and cousins of friends of friends, and so, when one of his writers died, he decided to look for new life to fill the vacancy. And finding new life required some exploration. Today he would announce the result. At least that's what he'd said last Saturday.

Nervously playing with her long black braid, Queenie's eyes swept past the honeysuckle-choked hedges, the hand-shaped swimming pool with its sparkling fingers of blue, the old Japanese gardener tending the yellow roses, and came to rest on six stately old palms swirling and swaying in the strong winds. Like the trees, Queenie felt that her own flexibility was being tested. Bad enough to endure the wait while the sun's hot blade sliced through her skull, but worse to listen to Susan Fry verbally stone Burke Lymon.

". . . making the same film over and over. So *boring*," Susan continued then clamped shut her fissirostral mouth.

"Sounds like you're jealous," someone responded.

"Envy and greed! The fuel that runs Hollywood," Clayton Myer piped in. "Ever hear the evaluation of Fred Astaire's first screen test? 'Can't act, slightly bald, dances a little.' Obviously written by some no-talent crippled by envy."

Susan snorted. "Me jealous of a Z moviemaker? I have a master's from USC. What's he got?" Susan turned her narrowed eyes on Queenie. "What's he got, *Queenie*?"

"Twelve films," Queenie replied flatly.

When they met, Susan had said she once had a dog named Queenie. The relationship had deteriorated from there. Susan had to be the first person she'd ever met with absolutely no redeeming qualities. But then she'd never had to sit next to Josef Mengele or Pennywise the Clown.

"Horror movies—that's not filmmaking, that's exploitation."

"Special effects are omnipotent now," another writer added, "and characters are just along for the ride. That's why performances are so shallow and lifeless."

Queenie noticed Sandy, a stylish blonde, at the far end of the table engrossed in a book. Was she really that cool, Queenie wondered, acting as if Eric's decision meant nothing at all, as if he were simply going to reveal his shoe size or what he'd had for breakfast?

"I heard Burke Lymon's films are popular in France," Clayton said.

"So's Jerry Lewis," Susan retorted. "And the French, because they hate to bathe, have a thriving perfume industry. Think about it."

As had occurred often that week, a vision of the small ax that had been imbedded in the skinned and rotting animal head suddenly appeared. *Love, your most adooring fan.* Would that particular fan show up at the premiere tonight? Queenie wondered.

To shake off a rising apprehension, she imagined the ax deep between Susan's eyes. Did Susan remind her of a squirrel? No. Even skinned, a squirrel was cuter. Ah, she thought, a goatsucker. That's what Susan looks like. Not a pretty bird, a goatsucker.

"You know," Susan continued, "only one of us is going to be coming back here."

Out of the corner of her eye Queenie noticed the Filipino approaching the table. There was something different about him today . . .

"Yeah," Clayton remarked anxiously, "and I wish Eric would hurry up and tell us who."

"Well, I've got the best credentials," Susan said.

Clayton groaned. "Give us a break, Susan. Education is theory. Work is application—and Queenie's the only one of us actually *working* in the industry—"

He was interrupted by the Filipino. "Queenie Davilov?"

Silence fell as all eyes turned to Queenie. Even Sandy, the reader, looked up from her book. Envy joined the heat shimmering on the table.

Then with a high-pitched screech, Susan threw back her head. "Oh, that's rich! The Okie gets it! What'd you do, sleep with Eric?"

The servant smiled. "You have a phone call, Ms. Davilov."

Relief was expelled in heavy sighs and nervous snickers. The reader's eyes fell back on the printed page.

Queenie followed the servant to a sun room just off the veranda. Only Dick knew where to contact her and he certainly wouldn't interrupt, especially today, unless something serious had happened.

The Filipino handed her the phone on a table just inside the room. She felt her pores contract in the air-conditioning.

"Yes? This is Queenie."

"Queenie. Dick."

Her heart did a backflip. No matter what he had to say, his deep baritone would always affect her.

"Listen, I hate to bother you but—"

Then another, hysterical voice came on the line. "Miss Davilov, Miss Davilov! Your brother's running loose in the building! He's a madman! If you don't get over here and control him, I'm calling the police!"

"Oh, no!" she groaned. It was her landlord, Mr. Dhootie.

The servant hovering near Queenie vanished.

Dick came back on the line. "I'll see what I can do, Queenie, but if you don't want your brother to go to jail, I think you'd better get home."

"I'm on my way."

Just as she put the phone down the man reappeared with her leather satchel. She felt grateful for his sensitivity, not having the least desire to return to the veranda.

He saw her to the front door. She turned to him and said, "Please tell Mr. Diamond I had an emergency. And thank you, you've been very kind. If he wants to call me . . ." She let the sentence trail off, thinking she sounded presumptuous. Eric would call if she'd been chosen.

He nodded and Queenie started to move away. Then she remembered something and turned back. From her satchel she pulled out the script she'd worked so hard to have polished and shining by today. Yesterday afternoon she'd taken a copy to the Writer's Guild and registered it. If Eric didn't choose her, at least she didn't want him to forget her too quickly.

"If you'd give him this, please."

He took the script and smiled slightly.

Queenie hurried back into the heat to her car. As she started the Plymouth, she was struck by the thought that there was something quite different about him today. She glanced back but the front door was already closed. For a moment her eyes lingered on the mansion's elegant façade, the big colorful pots of red and orange geraniums, the neatly clipped hedges of orange-scented *philadelphus*. . . .

Then, feeling like an outsider, her face pressed against the insular glass of wealth, she turned and sped off down the drive.

She thought of Susan's malice while heading east on Sunset. As mother always said, "No matter what you do, there's always shit in the corner."

CHAPTER FOUR

THE LYRICS BARELY comprehensible, Rex belted out some country-western lament while two-stepping Emma Schultz around the sofas, only her smile visible beneath his big black cowboy hat. Her cloche hat was pinched on top of his head, the net veil reaching as far as his nose. On his left arm was a fiberglass cast. In his right hand he clutched a bottle of Jack Daniel's. Written across the back of his gray T-shirt was GO AND SIN NO MORE.

He should take his own advice, Queenie thought angrily as she entered the St. Albans, the hot stale air smelling strongly of alcohol and Emma's perfume.

Mr. Dhootie, in his uniform of black polyester pants and short-sleeved white shirt, appeared on the verge of spontaneous combustion. Dick had him cornered by the mailboxes. But the elderly residents seemed to be enjoying the performance, several even clapping in time.

"Rex, honey," she said, calming herself. "Let's go on up to my apartment."

Abruptly he stopped. "My pleasure, ma'am," he said to Emma, then grabbed Queenie. At six-four and weighing around two-twenty, his enthusiasm provoked by alcohol, she half feared he might crush her.

"Miss Davilov! I will not tolerate this sort of behavior in the building," Mr. Dhootie exclaimed, he and Dick coming up beside them as Queenie finally managed to wiggle out of Rex's grasp. "I'd be well within my rights to evict you!"

"The boy was just having a little fun," Emma declared.

"We'll take care of it," Dick snapped. Together, he and Queenie marched the singing cowboy toward the elevator.

Emma scurried up beside Queenie, giving her Rex's cowboy hat. "He can keep my hat, honeypie, sort of a souvenir. Maybe he'll watch my show while he's here." Then she tugged on Queenie's sleeve. "Remember what I told you—be careful."

"Please, Emma, not now." All week, Emma had been trying to talk to her about some tarot reading.

"But *death*'s in the cards!" Emma hissed. "You taking your brother to that premiere?"

"If he sobers up," Queenie said, stopping at the elevator door as Dick and Rex filed inside.

"That theater's a firetrap!"

Trying to control her annoyance, Queenie said, "Burke Lymon had it renovated. I've been to two premieres there."

"Burke Lymon's cursed, you know. Death's in the cards."

Queenie entered the ancient elevator.

"My cards are never wrong!" Emma continued, peeking around the door as Queenie began to close it.

"Talk to you later, Emma," Queenie said gently then pressed the button for the fourth floor.

Rex segued into Jerry Jeff Walker's "Up Against the Wall You Redneck Mother."

"What happened? Where's his luggage?" Queenie asked Dick. The elevator chugged slowly upward, unused to the extra weight of two strapping young men at once. The lyrics bounced off the walls as Queenie strained to hear Dick.

"Well, I heard this commotion in the hall," he began. Dick's apartment was directly across from her own—so close, yet so far away. "Your brother was banging on your door, Dhootie charging up after him screaming that he was going to call the cops. I told him this must be your brother, that you were expecting him. I tried to get Rex to come in my apartment and wait for you but he suddenly looked at Dhootie and yelled, 'Injuns' and took off down the stairs."

Dick laughed, deep dimples appearing on either side of his sensual mouth. At six-one, Dick added another one hundred and ninety pounds of solid muscle to the weight the rickety elevator carried.

"Anyway, I pulled Dhootie into my apartment and called you. Sorry, but I figured you'd rather not spend your afternoon bailing your brother out of jail. His bag's outside your door."

Together they got Rex into her apartment. While Queenie made a fresh pot of coffee, Dick stripped Rex and put him in the shower.

A short time later, Dick entered the kitchen, setting the bottle of Jack Daniel's on the counter. His thick shoulder-length black hair and clothes were soaked.

"Won't need the coffee. He's passed out on your bed. Got a beer? My refrigerator's cleaned out."

"After my brother's performance, I'd think you'd want to stay away from alcohol. But I think I'll join you."

He laughed and pulled the wet T-shirt over his head. "I put that silly hat on the VCR. Wasn't any other free space."

"Rather like the Augean stables around here," she said, thrusting a cold bottle at him. She tried to avoid the sight of his smoothly muscled torso as, with his right arm braced against the counter, he raised the bottle to his mouth and drank greedily. His magnificent body stood between her and the study. What the hell, she thought, following the course of the beer down his throat. Tendrils of hair clung to his broad shoulders.

"How'd it go?" he asked, wiping his mouth.

"With Eric? He didn't even show."

"Don't worry, it'll happen. You're too good to be overlooked."

"Sure."

He put down the beer and stared at her for a long moment. "I'll miss you."

Her eyes shot up to meet his. She was momentarily speechless. He smiled again, his dimples doing their usual job on her libido.

"Listen," she said, finally squeezing the words out. "I'm sorry you had to meet my brother like this." She imagined his prospective in-laws bowing and greeting him in a far more civilized manner. "Look, I really appreciate your help, but shouldn't you be packing?"

"Been packed for days. Traveling light."

Anxious to see his fiancée, Queenie thought, willing away the pain. "I see."

He took a step toward, suddenly serious. "No, I don't think you do."

Before she knew it, one hand gently cupped her jaw, the other moved around the back of her neck. Then his face blurred, the scent of him overpowering as she closed her eyes. Lightly and sweetly he kissed her. Then he pulled away.

"My father arranged this. Out of respect, I've got to at least meet the woman."

"Holy Mother! You've never even met her?"

His beautiful smile reappeared. He shook his head.

"Then why—"

He put his finger to her lips. "You're a *gaijin*, Queenie. Don't try to understand." His eyes locked into hers and he kissed her again, this time more soulfully, his hand moving down her back and stopping just inside the waistband of her jeans.

"But I do have to get going," he finally said. They walked to the door, his hand still pressing into the small of her back. "Take care of yourself. Especially tonight. That premiere's gonna attract every religious crackpot in L.A."

After he'd gone, the base of her spine continued to tingle with his energy. Would the magic of his touch last the three weeks he'd be gone? More than simple geography would separate them. *Gaijin*, he'd called her. Foreigner. Yet his Japanese father had married a *gaijin*, an Irish one.

As with Eric Diamond, she wondered if a relationship with Dick was beginning—or just ending. But maybe the trip was serving a dual purpose; Dick was writing a book about Yakuza, the Japanese underworld. She mumbled a prayer for his safe return—with a pile of research instead of a bride.

She took Rex's bag into the bedroom. After hanging up his clothes, she stood for a moment at the end of the bed watching him sleep.

More than just his older sister, at nine she'd assisted the midwife at his birth, had shared the responsibility of raising him while her mother kept the ranch going. She'd been the first to put him astride a horse, the one who'd played pepper with him—teaching him to swing a bat, catch a ball, throw a ball—had even taught him to read. And she'd followed his career as avidly as any proud parent, though lately she hadn't been quite so attentive.

The eyes of the baseball world had been watching since his first at bat in April when the manager sent him in to pinch-hit with the bases loaded. Boston fans groaned at the decision with the score 0–0 in a game that had already gone ten innings. Then on a 3–2 count fastball, Rex unloaded. Fenway Park went dead quiet as the ball climbed the invisible ladder over the Green Monster. First at bat. A grand slam. Life as Rex Davilov had known it vanished forever, crushed beneath the feet of the jumping, screaming, ecstatic fans.

The Green Monster giveth.

Rex's stats increased as fast as the national debt and comparisons to Babe Ruth evolved into what every baseball player hopes for, a nickname. From Babe Too, to Babe II, he became known simply as The Sequel.

Then came August and the fateful fly ball.

The Green Monster taketh away.

Sympathy poured in for the first few days. Then the grumbling began—only a seasoned player could deal with the Green Monster. Who did this rookie think he was, for Chrissake? The comparisons dissolved into derision as did the nickname: *The sequel's never as good as the original* . . .

All his life he'd either been walking on water or drowning. His first summer job, hauling boxes for a moving company, came to mind. On a Friday he'd been named employee of the week and given a big, juicy kiss by the owner's wife. On Monday, the owner fired him.

While quietly gathering the clothes she planned to wear that evening, Queenie considered calling Eric Diamond. On the one hand, her curiosity would be sated, on the other, the news might ruin her evening. She settled the matter by deciding to wait: if she'd been chosen he'd call her—and he did have that second script of hers to consider. . . .

Passing back through the bedroom, she glanced at her brother who was now beginning to snore. She'd planned a great night out and, no matter if Rex joined her or not, was determined to have a good time.

Some plans, though, were just not meant to be. But, of course, how could she know that another monster waited, preparing to taketh away?

FIVE YEARS IN Hollywood and this was Queenie's first time in a limousine. She'd driven herself to the last two premieres, but out of consideration for her two guests, Rex and Joey, had decided to splurge, opening the evening with a touch of glamour the Plymouth could hardly provide. Rex sat beside her in the backseat, the pale gray leather matching the color of his face.

He'd awakened around four-thirty and, obviously not wanting to hear a replay of his arrival, had dressed and then waited quietly while she got ready. After leaving her apartment they'd spoken briefly about his injury, just enough for her to learn that he felt "okay" and had stopped taking pain-killers which, he complained, made him "goofy."

"Look, I'm sorry," Queenie said, hoping to loosen him up a little. He sat so stiffly in the slightly wrinkled dress shirt and tie she wondered if his wrist was hurting him. "I mean, I should have told you to come on out when you called. It's just that I was working on this script and—"

"Drop the guilt trip, Q." Then he added less harshly, "It's only right that I visited Mom first."

The limo whisked up Western toward the Hollywood Hills.

"How's the writing?" he said, breaking into the silence.

"One damn word after another."

"That great, huh? Maybe you should stick to being a detective."

"It's something to fall back on—you need that in this town. Show business makes no promises, gives no assurances. There's no certainty."

"Hey! Hollywood didn't invent insecurity. Look at baseball—*The Show* business."

Damn, why hadn't he stayed asleep? "So how's Mom?" Queenie asked quickly.

Rex shook his head but managed a smile. "Been on a rampage. Khan's got a cough and she thinks one of the new hands hasn't been soaking the hay."

"Uh-oh. Heads must be rolling." Before feeding hay to the horses, it is immersed in water for twenty-four hours to remove spores that could damage the horses' lungs. And Genghis Khan, eighteen hands of sleek raven's black, was L.J.'s favorite stud.

"And she's quit drinking."

"Mother?" Queenie said incredulously. L. J. Davilov's affection for Jack Daniel's was legendary, and no one believed they weren't wed for life.

"Won't allow a drop on the ranch." Finally he turned and looked at her. "Think we could ask this guy to stop at the next liquor store? I could use a little hair of the dog."

"No."

Expecting an angry retort, she was surprised when he shrugged then smiled. "God, she's mean when she's sober. Kicked me out. I got a motel room and stayed drunk. Guess I wasn't much use to her what with my broken wing and all. She told me I was as useless as clothes on a fish."

Ouch, Queenie thought.

A silence passed before he suddenly asked, "Do you believe her?"

"That you're as useless as clothes on—"

"No, not that," he interrupted. "That our grandparents were Russian aristocrats who came to America to escape the Revolution?"

That had been L.J.'s favorite theme of her rare bedtime stories. "When I was little, I suppose I did. But being an orphan she could pretty well believe anything she wanted. If it helped her get through such a miserable childhood, then so what?"

The miserable childhood was true enough. At age three, Lillian Jeanette Davilov had been sent from New York on the Orphan Train, finally adopted by a poor farmer in Arkansas, not out of affection but, like most of the children, to work. Maybe she'd needed to dress a thoroughly unenviable beginning in regal robes. Whatever the case, she'd survived. *What's he getting at?* she wondered, knowing their mother's history wasn't bothering him.

Rex cleared his throat. *Uh-oh,* Queenie thought. *What's coming?*

"One of the sportswriter's found out I'm illegitimate."

So that was it. "Aren't we all?" she retorted quickly.

"He's making a big deal out of it. Now I'm Rex, 'baseball's bastard king.' "

This news she hadn't heard. She felt a surge of anger but

determined to play it down. "Look, honey, you have to ignore that kind of crap. In a couple of weeks the pennant races'll start to heat up. Until then, it's slow news."

Rex gazed moodily out the window. They were now climbing the narrow streets of the Hollywood Hills. "Where are we going, anyway?"

"Gotta pick up a friend. Look, you've had a great season—unfortunately, it was just a little shorter than everyone else's."

He was quiet for a moment. Then he said, "Don't you ever wonder about your father?"

For an instant she succumbed to childhood memories, playing in the red dirt of Oklahoma with her twin brother, Raj. While other kids dibsed things from Sears catalogues, Queenie and Raj used baseball cards to dibs fathers. Being twins, and therefore requiring the same paternal source, they'd often fought bitterly.

"All I can say is he's somebody with a Y chromosome. And probably not Mickey Mantle."

Rex's eyes glittered. "God, what if he was?"

"Oh, hell. Mother never hung out with baseball players. My father's probably some grizzled prune of a cowboy eating dirt in West Texas."

"Well, I'm sure mine isn't!" Rex said a little too seriously. The difference in their respective physical appearances pretty well confirmed different fathers. Like L.J., Queenie had coal-black hair and remarkable dark blue eyes with silver flecks that in certain light shone like star sapphires. Rex's eyes were light brown, his chestnut-colored hair curly. Further, his bone structure was less pronounced, his body mass meatier. Then Rex added, "Someday I'll put your investigative skills to work and hire you to find my dad."

"Don't be too disappointed if the trail doesn't end at Willie

Mays's door," she said, naming Rex's all-time favorite baseball player.

He laughed suddenly, releasing tension. "God, I can't believe the silly nicknames—'Rex the Wonder Boy' and 'The Sequel'! What the hell kind of name is that?"

"Hey! You love it. I thought a baseball player was incomplete without a nickname."

Rex laughed again. "God, Mother and her obsession with royalty."

"Yes, but don't forget we were also named after horses. Be thankful you're not stuck with Bucephalus," she said, naming Alexander the Great's war horse.

"Yeah. Could get some pretty dicey nicknames out of that one."

"Look," Queenie said, "starting right now we're on a vacation from our careers and we're going to enjoy a relaxing time together. How about it?"

"Yeah. Good idea. So, can't we stop for a drink? Just one beer?"

"Honey. My boss does not abide drinking at his premieres, and anyone who shows up drunk is promptly kicked out. He's the lone exception to the rule. While the film's being shown, he hides out with a bottle. Never even enters the theater. But it's his game. He makes the rules."

Then she thought of another rule, one that, by taking Joey, she would be breaking . . .

The press was never invited. Only cast and crew and a few of Lymon's business associates received invitations, and they were allowed two guests each. Some members of the Hollywood community considered this omission sheer insanity. However, it was the sort of insanity that revealed Lymon's genius.

Exclusive tickets were always the most coveted. And any hot

ticket in town always drew the most attention. By just saying no to the right people, Burke Lymon created a cornucopia of free publicity. In retaliation, the uninvited film critics, forced to wait for the film's general release and having to endure the "humiliation" of standing in line like everyone else, invariably panned Burke Lymon's films. And the ruder the critique, the more people flocked to the theater. This negative manipulation resulted in good box office. However, now more than ever, he needed box office *gold* for, if the rumors were true, Hammon Productions was drowning in red ink. These days even companies with a string of successful films could surprise everyone by suddenly going belly up; Orion was the noteworthy, and frightening, example.

The limo pulled into a short circular drive and stopped before a set of massive double doors. The driver jumped out.

"Who lives here?" Rex asked while peering out the window.

"The lead singer for Technicolor Yawn," she said, explaining that the name was an Australian euphemism for "vomit." "My friend Joey's housesitting for him while he's on tour. She's—"

If Queenie had prayed that Joey would not attract attention this evening, then the Goddess was certainly busy elsewhere in the universe.

Sheathed in the sheerest of black nylon, breasts and pubis piquantly covered by beaded starbursts, Joey bent over to enter the backseat, an antique beaded bag dangling from her wrist. On black nail polish were silver star appliqués. Before Queenie had a chance to move over, Joey was stepping over her to the empty space in the middle of the wide leather seat, one of her spike heels nearly impaling one of Queenie's conservative pumps. Queenie caught a glimpse of Joey's lightly beaded backside before it wiggled into position.

Rex regarded Joey as if he'd never seen a female with less than six teats.

Joey smiled brightly. She flung her hands around, the stars streaking before Queenie's eyes. "Don't worry, Q. You'll see. He'll think I'm auditioning for a role in his next picture. Believe me, your future's secure."

"About as secure as that dress," Queenie snapped, fidgeting with her satchel. She fought a strong premonition that the pleasant evening she hoped for was not to be.

"Who's this? You didn't tell me you were bringing a date."

"That's my brother Rex," she said. "Rex, meet Joey Burroughs."

Joey offered Rex an elaborately manicured hand. But Rex's wide eyes were on the nearest unfettered breast. Joey patted his thigh when a handshake was not forthcoming.

"Why didn't you tell me he's so gorgeous?" Joey whispered.

"If you followed baseball you could have seen for yourself," Queenie retorted.

"Uh, you're an actress?" Rex blurted, his circuits functional again, the brain sending messages above his waist.

"A writer."

"Jesus," Rex muttered.

"Yes, well, we come in all shapes and sizes," Joey went on pleasantly. "I work for a columnist . . . Arthur Favor. I see the name doesn't ring any bells."

"And that's the last time you'll mention it tonight. Are we clear?"

Joey made a little squeaking noise.

In a more pleasant tone, Queenie asked, "Find out anything about Nessa and L.D.?"

"Who cares about them? They're nobodys."

Queenie felt stung. She despised the simple way in which people's lives were so casually dismissed by the word "nobody." "Probably not after tonight," she managed to say.

"Got something better," Joey said in a conspiratorial tone. "Burke Lymon's getting a divorce."

Queenie frowned but remained silent, pondering this new rumor and what effect it could have on the future of Lymon's employees.

Of the little she knew of Lymon's private life, he and his wife, Frances, had been a devoted couple for a decade. But if it was true, a divorce coupled with the rumored financial trouble could mean disaster for Hammon Productions. Hollywood divorces, because of their inevitable public nature, could be professionally deadly.

"Why would she divorce Lymon?" Queenie asked. "He's older—but hardly an old fogey. Besides, he's rich, handsome, and, as far as anyone knows, doesn't mess around."

Joey licked her lips. "Queenie, he's divorcing her!"

Queenie experienced a modicum of relief. Under those circumstances, Mrs. Lymon might go quietly and job security, as his employees knew it, might continue its course. *Might.*

"Where'd you hear this, anyway?"

"The only source worth believing—other than Burke Lymon himself."

"Jo . . . ey." Queenie enunciated the name like a warning. "Please. For my sake, don't ask him any personal questions. Otherwise, neither of us will ever go to one of his premieres again."

Ignoring Queenie, Joey turned to Rex. "You know, I was on a waiting list for two years. Someone has to croak before you can get an appointment. But he's the most intuitive man. Just by the feel of a woman's hair, he knows what kind of problems she's having—he knows who's going to be filing for divorce before *they* do. Do you know what an advantage that gives me?"

Rex regarded her with a stone-blank expression.

"I sat in the chair, looked at him in the mirror and said, 'Gabriel, make my career!' He's absolutely to die for."

"Well, that's good," Queenie said, "because you just might if I hear you trying to confirm some rumor heard in a hairdresser's chair." The thought occurred to Queenie that Gabriel's surname, Tak, just might be a self-styled acronym for The All Knowing.

She took a deep breath. C'mon, Davilov, she scolded herself. You know better than to take rumors too seriously. But there was something about a beauty salon that made rumors much more adhesive. Maybe it was all that hair spray. . . .

Just then the limousine slowed and the scene outside drew their attention.

The driver joined a queue inching toward the canopied, roped-off Astroturf leading to the guarded doors of the Mikado Theater. Crowds of the cameraed and curious packed both sides. Though still too light for the dramatic frame of floodlights, a massing of people with cameras always created excitement. One never knew just who might show up on the other side of the lens.

They passed a group of white-robed picketers chanting "Beware Satan's return!" Queenie noticed a similar group across the street. Both seemed to be vying for vocal dominance, their signs bobbing in accompaniment. As Dick had foreseen, the religious fanatics had flocked to the premiere to stage their own peculiar productions.

A liveried doorman opened the rear passenger door. While Joey and Rex stepped out of the limo, Queenie stayed behind to tip the driver with a twenty-dollar bill. He'd been hired for a one-way trip. The jobless summer had severely dented her savings and besides, the after-party had been booked, as usual, at a nearby Italian restaurant that could cater to a large crowd. She couldn't see paying extra for the driver to spend the evening hanging around. They'd walk to the restaurant and taxi home.

Queenie slipped out of the car and thanked the doorman. His eyes quickly slid away from hers. There was something familiar about him, but it was too vague to demand her attention. He vanished from her thoughts as she took a few steps forward on the green tongue of Astroturf.

Her attention on the crowd's reaction to Joey and Rex, Queenie was stunned by the fastball tomato that smashed into the right side of her face.

CHAPTER SIX

WHILE SHUTTERS OPENED and shut with the speed and precision of the best Japanese technology, several rounds of rotting red missiles reached target. Queenie's face, hands, and white linen jacket were stained with juice and dripping seeds. Behind her, the doorman was busy extracting the latest arrival. With Joey and Rex drawing all the attention, a couple of long seconds passed before anyone noticed what was happening to Queenie.

Nailed by surprise, her right arm up to shield her face, she was keenly aware of the wrap-around noise: the incessant whirl and click of camera motors, the wolf whistles and shouts Joey prompted, the biblical chanting battles, the heavy *plops* and *splats*, the rustles and curses of the media jostling with gawkers for position, and the creak of the heavy limousine door opening behind her.

Finally attention shifted to Queenie. "Look!" someone yelled.

A few feet ahead, Joey and Rex swiveled around. A guard near the entrance took his eyes off Joey and came running. All at once, all heads and cameras turned.

"—bitch!" her attacker shrieked.

Queenie caught a glimpse of the woman's wild-eyed face, the coarse brown hair greasy and matted to her head. Then a bystander grabbed her from behind. The bag dropped and someone stepped on it. A runny sauce oozed out onto the Astroturf.

Rex clutched Queenie's arm and Joey the other, hurrying her toward the door.

Mirrored glass fronted the theater. Those inside could see out. Those outside couldn't see in. Queenie cringed when she saw her reflection. Her right side was covered in tomato gore.

A tuxedoed attendant took her invitation. He quickly checked her name off the list and with a sympathetic eye and, thankfully, no comment, pushed open the door.

Those of her coworkers and their guests who'd seen Queenie's undignified arrival regarded her with a mixture of startled surprise, curiosity, and amusement.

Leaving Rex at the candy counter to order complimentary soft drinks, Queenie and Joey hurried across the luxurious red-and-black Oriental motif carpet.

Though only about thirty minutes remained before showtime, Queenie noticed that the crowd seemed skimpier than usual. By now, the small lobby should have been packed. Surely the rumors hadn't kept the crew away! After all, they weren't suits tripping over their tasseled loafers to flee a failing studio.

"Christ, Queenie," Joey hissed in her ear, "who was *that?*"

Wiping away a glob of pulp sliding down her forehead, Queenie replied, "My predecessor. Amanda Martin."

"*She* was Burke Lymon's script super? God. That's one ugly woman."

Queenie felt a twinge of pity, suddenly reminded of the precarious position held by everyone involved in moviemaking. How odd, she thought while she and Joey made their way to the rest rooms, the open doors of the auditorium just ahead, that an industry that flourishes on the display of emotion scorns those who show it off the set. Amanda Martin's only fault had been falling in love with Burke Lymon to the point of distraction. And for a script supervisor, a person who must be aware of all the details during shooting, distraction means career death.

Immediately to the left of the auditorium were narrow stairs leading up to the projection booth. As they passed, Queenie spotted Burke Lymon coming downstairs. She rushed ahead, not wanting to confront him in her present state.

The west exit was directly ahead, its sign's red letters glowing eerily in the dim hallway. A seventy-gallon plastic garbage receptacle stood just inside the door.

About halfway to the exit, Queenie and Joey turned left and entered an alcove. A black marble water fountain in the shape of an open clam was set into the wall. Just to the left was the door to the men's room, the silhouette of a man's head with a top hat indicating gender. They moved to the right down a narrow hall and at the end turned left again into another hall. After about ten feet, they came to an open archway.

After passing through it, they entered the richly decorated women's lounge. A floor-to-ceiling mirror covered one wall, while the remaining wall space was done in Chinese-red silk. Indirect light spread upward from fan-shaped brass lamps spaced along the walls. Instead of the usual vanity found in women's lounges, there were groupings of comfortable chairs each with its own low, Japanese-style table upon which were hand mirrors, ashtrays, and tissue dispensers. Beside each table was a wastebasket.

Queenie caught a glimpse of herself in the wall mirror and groaned. Her right side, from head to hip, dripped pulp and seeds. Selma Steinberg and another woman looked up from one of the tables.

"Queenie! What happened?" Selma started to rise.

"*Attack of the Killer Tomatoes*," Queenie said flatly, referring to the campy horror spoof released in 1980. "Don't get up, Selma"—she waved the woman back down—"this shouldn't be a major operation."

In contrast to the lounge, the bathroom was small and designed for practical use. There were four gray metal stalls and two porcelain sinks above which was a wide mirror.

Queenie removed her jacket while Joey dampened paper towels.

"Shit! Out of towels," Joey said, cranking the dog-leg arm of the now-empty dispenser. A quick check of the cupboard beneath the sinks revealed only cleaning supplies.

"Bet there's plenty in the men's room. They never wash up after they pee."

Queenie wondered where that bit of information had come from, but before she could protest, Joey was gone.

Exasperated, Queenie vigorously splashed water on her face. She reached for fresh towels—but, of course, there were none. Hands gripping both sides of the basin, she leaned forward, listening to the dull thunk of water droplets sliding off her face and hitting the reddish water in the sink. For the moment, she'd have to drip dry.

Selma entered and, crossing her arms in front of her sea-green sleeveless silk sheath, leaned against the sink and looked at Queenie, a no-nonsense expression on her face. Her nod to frivolity were winking silver man-in-the-moon earrings.

"So who did this?"

"Amanda Martin ... would you get me a tissue or some-thing?"

Selma went around the nearest stall, her heels clicking on the tile floor, and returned with a wad of toilet paper.

"That woman scares me," Selma declared while grimly watching Queenie pat her face dry. "She's been in and out of mental institutions since Lymon fired her." After a pause she said, "You know, I thought she might have sent that—that thing."

Queenie leaned toward the mirror, turning her face to check for more seeds on her neck. "What did the police say?"

"This is just between you and me, okay? I took it in after work Monday. Lymon thinks I did like he told me and threw it away. He was emphatic about not involving the cops. Anyway, so far, *nada*. No fingerprints or anything. I feel better"—she hugged herself, rubbing her arms—"even though I still get chills whenever I think about it."

Queenie didn't mention her own theory, that someone close to the film probably sent it.

At that moment, Joey returned with a stack of towels. "Told you," she said triumphantly. "And I met Burke Lymon!"

Queenie introduced the two women, and before anyone could speak she added, "Selma's Lymon's secretary—and more than that, she protects him from people like amorous fans and *gossip columnists*." She cast Joey a warning glance.

Selma laughed. "Actually, he takes pretty good care of him-self. I'm more his buffer zone."

"He's got to be one of the best-looking men I've ever seen—for an older guy," Joey remarked a bit breathlessly. "How old is he?"

"Mid-forties, I'd guess. I always thought he looked like a cross between Paul Newman and Norman Jewison," Selma added. "Well, I'd better be off." She reached over and touched Queenie's bare arm. "I'll keep you posted if the police find anything."

Selma and Joey exchanged nice-meeting-yous, then Selma left the bathroom.

"If the police find what?" Joey started, but Queenie shushed her then peeked into the lounge. Selma and the other woman had just passed through the archway.

"What . . . ?"

"Damn you, Joey! I thought you were my friend. Why in the hell did you have to go traipsing into the men's bathroom?"

"I was just trying to help."

Queenie shook her head in exasperation. "You didn't tell Lymon who you are?"

"Jesus, Q! You think I'm going to tell a man who refuses to be interviewed that I'm here to interview him? Give me a break. I'm not that stupid."

"Let's hope you didn't embarrass him."

"He was just taking a pee," Joey said as if it were nothing.

Queenie was beginning to feel like a Wimbledon tennis ball, smashed from one emotional court to the other in a never-ending rally. "Just do me a favor, Joey. Don't make me regret bringing you tonight."

Joey's deep brown eyes flared. Her flame-red hair seemed to have ignited. "I'm a professional, Davilov!"

They stared hotly at each other for a moment. Finally Queenie sighed. "Just—we're here to see a movie. So let's just keep it that uncomplicated."

Queenie put on her jacket. The linen was damp and faintly stained but at least the gore was gone. She cleaned up the basin while Joey examined the jacket and slacks, occasionally flicking a seed with her "starry night" nails.

4 8

Queenie threw away the dirty towels. As the two women left the bathroom, she remarked, "You must have paid a fortune for that nothing of a dress."

"I borrowed it from a girl who wore it to the MTV Awards."

"A manicure too. How much did that set you back?"

"On the house," Joey said, glancing at her reflection in the mirror in the lounge.

"And the hairdo?" Queenie asked, examining the mass of red curls cascading down her back from just behind the crown of her head. A few wispy bits framed the porcelain-perfect skin of her lovely face.

Joey sniffed. "Two hundred."

"Pesos?"

"Dollars, you poot."

Standing at the candy counter, Queenie took the opportunity to study the crowd while Joey searched for well-known faces and Rex sipped a soft drink (obviously yearning for something stronger). Who, she wondered, had sent Lymon the poor beast in the *Star Wars* lunch box?

During her days as an operative for the late Ignacius Peter Friedman, "I.P. the P.I." as he liked to call himself, she'd learned that most criminal acts were perpetrated by someone who knew the victim through work, friendship, or family.

She looked at Billy Bright, the sound man. At six-three and over two hundred fifty pounds, he dwarfed tiny Sooch Bauer, the Cambodian cameraman who'd been elevated from first assistant cameraman when Harold Jonge died of a heart attack. The two men were chatting earnestly, Billy in his perpetual slouch, and Sooch with his head thrust back to look up at Billy's somewhat pasty face.

Like Queenie, they'd each been given replicas of the ax as awards for their work on the film. She wondered if either man held a grudge against Lymon. It seemed absurd.

The door opened, admitting a blast of hot, gritty air. Hec Cerutti, the construction coordinator, entered alone. Hec paused just inside and wiped his head and neck with a flag-size handkerchief. His nod to the evening's formality was a navy blue tie over a white short-sleeved shirt. Under each arm were half moons of sweat.

"Queenie!" he greeted, and moved next to her while stuffing his handkerchief into the back pocket of his jeans. "Jesus! Is it hot or what?" He then called to Alice Baldridge, working behind the candy counter. "Hey, Baldy. Gimme a Coke—lots of ice."

Alice glared at Hec, then moved in the opposite direction and disappeared into the manager's office. A haughty woman, Alice deplored serving the crowd at Lymon's premieres, considered it too demeaning for an assistant director. Maybe it was to bring her down a few notches that Lymon insisted she work the candy counter. Later she would run the projector.

"Bitch," Hec said without much energy. He walked around the counter and filled his own order at the soda machine. After a long drink and an "Ah" of relief, he leaned on the counter and said, "Got a minute?"

He moved his large round head in close but looked out at the crowd with small eyes set above fat cheeks. He reminded Queenie of baseball manager Don "Popeye" Zimmer. His eyes darted back toward the office from which Alice now emerged carrying a plastic bag of prepopped corn. Hec moved to Queenie's other side as if he suddenly found open ground between Alice and himself dangerous.

"You remember the night Hernandez fell off the scaffolding?"

"Well, the next day anyway."

He laughed. "That's what I like about you—always got to get the facts straight. Well, anyway"—he lowered his voice—"he'd been drinking, you know."

"Yeah, Hec. I know."

"Well, you see, he'd been drinking with *me*. I, uh, didn't say anything because I was afraid I'd lose my job. Hell, you know Lymon's rules. No drinking on location."

A rule that Hernandez broke to his ultimate peril, Queenie thought. "Hec, why are you telling me—five months later?"

"Well, there's two things, really. You see, he had this crush on Nessa, told me he used to listen outside her window to find out if she, well, let any guys in at night. Anyway, before we got together that night he said he overheard Nessa talking on the phone. That conversation made a big impression on him. He said Nessa was someone real important. He could see through the curtain that Baldy"—he nodded toward Alice—"was asleep. You remember they shared a room after Jean Bliss, uh, died. Oh, boy, was he excited."

"Go on."

"Well, when I heard Nessa and L.D. had gone missing, I started thinking maybe Nessa's identity had something to do with it."

"Okay. So who is she?"

Hec shook his head. "Hernandez said if I raced him up the scaffolding to the top of the tower house, he'd tell me if I won." He pulled out the handkerchief, wiped his brow again, and sighed. "He was just a stupid kid. Maybe if I'd raced him, I coulda kept him from breaking his neck . . . obviously he went on up there after I went on to bed. Shit. Anyway, he seemed to think she was someone important."

"Maybe we'll all find out soon," she said, and started to turn away.

"And the other thing is, well, Lymon's not renewing my contract."

Queenie reacted with surprise. Hec had been Lymon's construction coordinator for several years. "But why?"

"Beats me. Called me this week and thanked me for my good work but said he wouldn't be renewing my contract. Said he looked forward to seeing me at the premiere and hung up."

"When did he call?"

"Monday."

"And that's all?"

"That be it. No one could ever accuse the man of talking too much. Uh, have you gotten walking papers?"

Queenie shook her head.

Hec nodded his head with resignation. "I'll just bet he heard it was me drinking with Hernandez, and—"

Suddenly he straightened. Lymon and his wife were approaching the candy counter. Hec slipped a business card into Queenie's hand and whispered, "If you hear of any jobs, give me a call."

Hec smiled and patted her arm. "Good seeing you, Queenie," he said a little too loudly, and disappeared into the crowd.

Queenie might have suspected Hec, except that the timing was off. The dead animal arrived Monday, the same day Hec was canned . . . if he was telling the truth.

She dropped the card into her jacket pocket and smiled at Lymon. Then she reached out to shake his hand, wondering if her name was on a pink slip in his.

CHAPTER SEVEN

LIKE MANY HOLLYWOOD luminaries, Burke Lymon was surprisingly short and slender. With an appealing dishevelment and moody blue-gray eyes, he had the sort of looks that would have been legendary had he been on the other side of the camera. But he was totally committed to his craft, a man unaware of the effect his physical presence had on others—especially women—which was probably why men naturally liked him and women were automatically compelled to the challenge of attracting his attention.

Rumors emerged occasionally linking him with a variety of actresses. They smelled of wishful thinking and fizzled quickly. On the rare occasions he appeared in public, it was always with his wife, Frances. As far as Queenie knew, he was a man of two obsessions: his work and his privacy.

Frances Lymon stood beside him. A striking woman in her mid-thirties, she was taller than her husband, her height accentuated by a full-length, strapless tube of black satin and her signature cloche hat. Tonight the hat matched her gown and was secured to her chin-length blond hair by an iridescent black opal hat pin, the opalescent theme carried through by the tiny chips on the net veil covering her face. Queenie thought of Emma's veiled cloche hat now sitting on top of her VCR. On Frances Lymon the veil enhanced a mysterious glamour. Over her bare arm, she carried a shimmering black silk coat.

What, Queenie wondered, had this woman done, if the rumor had merit, to prompt her husband to divorce her? Given Lymon's penchant for privacy and the public nature of Hollywood divorces, it must have been a whopper.

Queenie introduced Rex and Joey. Frances regarded her with some suspicion when Joey mentioned meeting Lymon earlier.

"Ah, yes," Lymon replied with a slight smile. "The girl after the towels. Frankly, I first thought you were a reporter who'd sneaked in."

Queenie's heart stopped. She and Joey exchanged startled glances.

"We needed those towels," Joey blurted. "Uh, Queenie'd been pelted with rotten tomatoes."

Queenie felt her face go hot but at least her heart kicked back in. "It was no big deal, Lymon," she said hastily.

"Amanda Martin did it," Joey went on. "Your former script supervisor."

"Lymon knows who Amanda is," Queenie snapped. With a more pleasant expression she turned to Lymon. "How was New York?" she asked conversationally.

Lymon's dark expression told her he wasn't ready for the shift. "That's terrible, Queenie! I'm so sorry. I hope it hasn't spoiled your evening."

"Not at all," Queenie said with a little laugh. "It was just a harmless prank."

Frances Lymon immediately protested, zeroing in on Queenie. "Amanda Martin is far from harmless! She's a mental patient! I can't believe the state has released her and God knows how many more like her because of their damn budget cuts. We have to lock ourselves in while they roam the streets. Did you know she's been camping outside our estate? The police can't do anything. They haul her away, and she's right back again."

"Frances," Lymon said sternly, "I don't think anyone wants to hear about that."

But Mrs. Lymon wasn't finished. "And what about the dead squirrel? The one with the little ax in its head. Who's the most likely person to have sent that?"

"What squirrel, Mrs. Lymon?" Queenie asked. Queenie didn't want to betray Selma's confidence but she did want to find out what Mrs. Lymon knew. Maybe that little mystery could be solved right now.

"Someone sent me a dead squirrel in the mail. Had a crude little ax in its head."

"Frances, really—" Lymon began, but his wife wasn't listening.

"It came in the mail last week. I'm sure Amanda sent it!"

So, Queenie thought, both husband and wife received them.

"At least you burned it," Lymon said quickly. "And that's the end of that." He grabbed his wife's arm and started to pull her away. "You'll excuse us," he said stiffly. But Billy Bright suddenly materialized, blocking their exit. Mrs. Lymon shrugged off her husband's hand and slid around Billy's pillar of a body and into the crowd. Smiling broadly and in his own personable way reducing the tension, Billy wrapped his arm around Lymon's shoulder.

"Hey, Lymon! I guess those axes you gave us must be worth something. Guess what! Mine's been stolen!" From his tone of voice, he seemed more proud than concerned.

Billy jerked his head in Alice Baldridge's direction. "Hey, Baldy!" he boomed. "Still got your ax?"

Alice and L. D. Barth had also received the unusual awards. Altogether, Lymon had presented five on this picture.

Alice glanced up momentarily then, ignoring them, continued filling cups and setting them on a tray. Then she did something Queenie'd never seen her do before. Carrying the tray, she left the candy counter and began circulating among the guests.

Lymon smiled ruefully. "I don't think Alice even took hers. For all I know, it's still in my trailer."

"If it ain't an Oscar, Alice don't want it," Billy noted, then turned to Queenie. "Ah, Her Highness. How 'bout you?"

"Still got mine, Billy. You seem to be the lucky one."

"Are they valuable?" Billy asked ingenuously.

Lymon laughed. "I'd hope in a personal way."

Joey jumped in. She'd been quiet too long. "What about Nessa and L. D. Barth, Mr. Lymon? Have you heard from them? Do you suspect foul play?"

Queenie felt her blood pressure rise again—Joey sounded too much like a journalist. "Mr. Lymon's only just returned from New York, Joey," Queenie said quickly.

Lymon smiled. "I wouldn't put too much stock in rumors. Nessa and L.D. are quite fond of each other. They probably went off someplace to be alone."

"And miss their own premiere? Bet it would cause a stir if they showed up tonight," Joey speculated.

Just then Selma moved up to Lymon. "It's getting close to seven, Lymon," she said.

"All right."

Thank you, Selma, Queenie thought with relief.

Alice scooted behind the candy counter, her tray empty.

"Alice," Lymon said. "Time to roll."

"But not everyone's been served," Alice protested, and quickly began filling cups.

Queenie was again surprised by Alice's behavior. But the woman seemed to have changed sometime since Queenie'd last seen her at the wrap party in May.

Usually outfitted exclusively by Brooks Brothers, tonight Alice wore a voluminous East Indian–style dress, the thin, deep-purple fabric shot through with gold threads. The feminine attire prompted Queenie to wonder who Alice had dressed for. A lover?

Like most people Queenie knew, Alice was single; further, a lesbian. Anyone new on the set quickly learned three things about Alice: her tenure with Lymon (now ten years), that she was a product of the film programs at Columbia University and USC, and her sexual preference. To Alice, all three proved her superiority.

Alice had shown a spark of interest when Lymon introduced Queenie on the set of *Vampire Moon*. But the light went out when Alice discovered Queenie had gotten her degree from the University of Oklahoma. To a person with Alice's academic credentials, Queenie had all the glamour of a pig farmer.

Though they'd worked together on three films, Queenie could not recall a time Alice had ever responded with a simple "thank you" when, after each day's shooting, Queenie handed her the timed scenes. At times, such as when they were reviewing dailies, Queenie had had the urge to stuff a wad of Red Man in her cheek and spit, aiming for one of Alice's expensive shoes.

Maybe she's gone straight, Queenie wondered, noticing that Alice's normally unruly blond hair had been cut and neatly styled. She even wore makeup. Somewhere in her mid to late thirties, Alice didn't look any younger but she did look better. Queenie wondered if Alice herself had, after a decade, fallen under Lymon's spell.

"They're still clamoring for drinks! It's this heat!"

Lymon glanced around as if looking for clamor. "I'll take care of it," he said impatiently.

Her jaw set, Alice moved imperiously through the crowd. She was halfway to the stairs leading to the projection booth when Queenie saw her turn back around.

"I want some popcorn and a Coke," she said, more like a petulant child than a grown woman.

Lymon went around the candy counter and fixed Alice's soft drink and a tub of popcorn. Alice took the refreshments and, without another word, disappeared up the stairs and into the projection booth.

Queenie saw Lymon stoop down and lift a bottle of Scotch from inside a green-and-gold Harrods shopping bag. Pouring some in a cup, he tossed it back. Then, catching Queenie's eye, he raised the empty cup in a silent toast.

Queenie smiled then turned her attention to the mob flanking the green length of turf and wondered vaguely if her arrival would be included on the late-night news. She sincerely hoped not.

The lobby began to empty slowly as people filed into the theater.

Outside, Queenie saw the doorman—*where had she seen him before?*—stoop slightly to open the door of a long white limo.

Emerging from the interior was Phil Sykes, Burke Lymon's attorney. Once all six foot two inches of him was outside, he stood to one side fussing with the front of his tuxedo jacket. His smug expression told everyone there was more to come.

Sure enough, a pair of legs Lloyd's of London hoped would never wither shot out of the backseat. The appendages, as recognizable and better looking than many famous faces, created a roar of excitement that caused everyone still in the lobby to turn and look.

A pair of open-toed silver sling-back pumps planted themselves on the Astroturf while cameras purred in submission. The magnificent legs moved slightly in a just-so perfect pose. A slender hand, followed by an equally slender arm, was extended out the door. Completing the tease, Phil Sykes took the hand and helped the rest of Reeves Holloway, wearing a short shift of silver and crystal bugle beads, out of the limousine.

Lacking any real talent, Reeves Holloway always made a production of the two things she did well. One was getting out of a car. The other was sitting. Reeves was a talking head. In the simplest terms, she read a TelePrompTer for an audience of cameras. Later her taped image appeared in millions of homes as viewers switched on *Showbiz Nightly*, an entertainment broadcast that made "news" out of gossip. Reeves never wrote her own material, but, being a heavy on the social circuit, she often supplied tidbits others would expand for her.

"My God," Joey hissed, "and you were worried about *me*."

Queenie could scarcely believe Phil Sykes's audacity. She glanced at Lymon, wondering if he'd noticed. He had.

Meanwhile, Reeves squeezed hands, patted shoulders, and powered on her smile with the characterless precision and timing required of television production itself.

Queenie looked over at Lymon again. He leaned across the counter and said something to Selma, who then moved to the entrance door and had a word with the guard outside.

Back inside, Selma clapped her hands and declared, "Showtime, everyone. Please take your seats."

Looking back out the door, Queenie noticed that the doorman was gone. She moved closer, thinking Reeves and Phil Sykes were blocking him. The couple was halfway to the entrance, their full attention on the fawning fans and media.

The guard entered, along with the tuxedoed attendant who carried a stack of invitations and the guest list.

"Where's the doorman?" Queenie asked.

The attendant moved on into the theater. The guard shrugged and pulled a set of keys from his pocket.

"I mean, wasn't he hired for the evening?"

"Hell, I don't know. Probably went to get a drink, which is what I'd just as soon be doing." He locked the doors and jangled the keys. "All locked up tight, Mr. Lymon," he said, and sauntered toward the auditorium.

Suddenly Queenie realized what had just been done. Lymon had locked out Reeves Holloway and Phil Sykes! Oh, what a fun time they'd have turning around for that long walk back to the street . . . with no limo to duck in to. It had already slipped away into the evening traffic.

Queenie took Rex's arm feeling certain now that her tomato attack would end up on the news editor's floor. More deliciously newsworthy would be Reeves Holloway's ignominious lockout from the night's hottest event.

"Wait!" Joey whispered. "I've got to see this! Look! They still don't know what's happened!"

Out of the corner of her eye, Queenie noticed Burke Lymon duck into the manager's office. As she and Rex moved toward the theater, leaving Joey by the door, Lymon left the office carrying a folding chair.

"Aren't you gonna watch the movie?" Rex asked him ingenuously.

"Already seen it."

"Oh, yeah," Rex mumbled, embarrassed.

"Lymon," Queenie said, moving up to the candy counter. "The doorman—"

"Yes?" He unfolded the chair with a slight clatter.

"He looked familiar."

"Did he now?"

"Well, yes. Usually they come in and watch the movie. This one didn't. He just seemed to vanish."

"Does that bother you?"

"Well, it's just that there's something familiar—"

"Don't tell me that infallible eye of yours is fallible after all."

Queenie frowned.

Lymon shook his head and waved her on. "Don't worry about it, Queenie. That little mystery will be solved when the film's over."

Queenie shrugged, dismissing the doorman.

"C'mon, Joey," Queenie urged.

Joey backpedaled, unwilling to miss the humiliation of a television rival. Queenie and Rex moved through the auditorium's open doors, the only access to the lobby.

The small theater accommodated around two hundred fifty, though tonight only about half the seats were filled. The bulk of the seating was in the center. Two aisles flanked the central wedge and gave access to more seating angled to right and left of the screen. People scattered themselves around the theater, most choosing to sit in the middle section. In front of and on either side of the stage were two more fire exits.

Queenie took her usual aisle seat, last row, center section. She liked to watch audience reaction—it helped her writing. Having sat in the back for so many years, she was an excellent judge of mood—what people liked, hated, and, most important, what sort of scenes put them to sleep.

Farther down and to the right, Queenie noticed Frances Lymon sitting on the aisle, her coat draped across the adjacent seat. From what Queenie remembered of the last two premieres, Mrs. Lymon seemed to treat attendance as a duty. It was hard to imagine, but maybe the woman just didn't like movies. Grounds for divorce? Queenie wondered. Probably in Hollywood.

Rex sat to Queenie's left. A moment later, Joey scooted past them to the open seat beside Rex. As soon as she sat down, she pulled a small notebook and pen from her beaded bag. Then she reached over and squeezed Queenie's arm.

"Whatever you want, it's yours, Q! I've waited for those last few moments my whole career." Then she took out a tiny camera and shook it in Queenie's face. "Even got her on film—her face pressed to the glass while she banged on the door. She was screaming to be let in! Bet I can get twenty-five thou from one of the tabloids for that shot!" Then Joey turned her attention to her notebook and began scribbling a story.

A hush fell as the lights dimmed and Queenie wiggled in her seat. This was one of her favorite moments—the tingling anticipation before the vicarious journey began. While one could view the same movie on a television, there was nothing like the big screen to do justice to the depth and scope that light on silver emulsion deserved.

She wondered vaguely why Lymon chose to ignore such an experience. Surely he'd feel a rush of pleasure seeing all heads riveted toward the unveiling of his personal creation. He acted like certain playwrights who kept to the lobby or a nearby bar during opening night. Lymon was certainly idiosyncratic—but then common, predictable people didn't make movies.

The slow ominous toll of a bell began just as the curtains parted. Then, simply and without flourish, the title appeared. The opening credits followed, superimposed on a tower house being consumed from the foundation by thick fog crawling up its sides.

CHAPTER EIGHT

AT A CAMPSITE *not far from the tower, a couple makes love in a sleeping bag. The shadowy form of a hooded figure moves stealthily through the trees toward them. Something flashes briefly in the moonlight. It is the blade of an ax the hooded figure carries. He raises the ax.*

"Gotta go to the bathroom," Rex whispered. Before Queenie could turn to protest, her brother was gone.

Queenie returned her attention to the screen. While she enjoyed the moments before a film began, the pleasure of a story unfolding on screen had been irrevocably lost since she'd worked as a script supervisor. Films were not shot according to the logical sequence provided in the original script. What was on screen at that instant had been shot toward the end of filming in the middle of May.

The scene cut to Nessa's reaction, a close-up. Queenie's attention was on details peripheral to the expression of horror—was Nessa wearing too much lipstick for a woman disturbed in the act of making love? Was her hair too neat, her open blouse not wrinkled enough?

A dark figure blotted out the screen. Queenie shifted her legs to the right. "Joey!" she whispered. "Please don't—"

"Can't see," Joey whispered, waving her notebook under Queenie's nose, and vanished.

The ax crashes into the actor's back. Nessa screams—the first of many designed to prickle the hairs of an audience—and wriggles free of the bloody body of her lover, then runs for her life through the moon-washed forest. The scene cuts to the campsite. With his head cocked, the hooded figure (L. D. Barth) stands listening. He seems unconcerned that she has run away. After a moment, he drags the victim away in the sleeping bag.

For the next few minutes Queenie tried to concentrate on the film but found herself unable to do so. What was Joey doing? Was she really just going to finish her notes in the lobby, or had she gone to question Lymon about the rumored divorce? If the news hit Arthur Favor's column on Monday, Lymon would put two and two together and come up with a new script supervisor.

She checked the luminous dial on her watch. It was almost nine minutes after seven. Now she began to worry about Rex. Where the hell was he?

At that moment, Rex returned, ice tinkling in his refilled cup.

"Lymon's a real nice guy," he whispered, slurring slightly. "Did you know he's a Red Sox fan?"

Queenie turned to look at her brother. In the dim light, she could see he was smiling drunkenly. Rex raised his plastic cup. "Gave me some of his Scotch."

"I told you he doesn't like anyone drinking at his premieres! You had enough today."

"He offered!" Rex retorted. "Well, after I told him how I'd gotten this cast. Told him I prefer musicals, like *Oklahoma.*"

"Rex, please. Just watch the movie."

But Rex was in the mood for conversing. "You know, sis, I got the feelin' he's worried about somethin'. Maybe I should go back and keep him company. I don't like these kinds of movies anyway."

"If you don't like it, close your eyes."

A dark figure again blotted out the screen. It was Joey sidestepping across them to her seat.

Queenie leaned across Rex and whispered, "I hope you didn't—"

"No. I didn't!" Joey answered irritably. "All I did was get a soft drink from him. If it makes you feel better, I couldn't have talked to him if I wanted to." Her eyes shone angrily as she glanced at Rex. "He and your brother were busy bonding."

"I don't like this kinda movie," Rex repeated, squirming uncomfortably.

"Would you both shut up?" Queenie hissed. Then to no one in particular she said, "You've probably cost me my job."

She glanced to her right and saw Frances Lymon mincing up the aisle in that restrictive tubular dress.

Then she found herself contemplating a reel inside her head. At twenty-four frames per second, she watched herself on stage accepting an Oscar for Best Original Screenplay. As she began reciting her list of thank-yous, the statuette clutched in her right hand grew into a transmogrified version of a furious Burke Lymon who fired her in front of a viewing audience of two billion people.

"You'll never work in this town—or anyplace else in the world again!" he shouted.

Rex nudged her. The frightful image vanished.

"Where's this movie take place?" he slurred.

"Supposed to be Scotland."

"Remind me never to go there."

"Rex, this isn't a documentary," Queenie said with a sigh. "We shot it in northern California. Now just watch, okay?"

He sank deeper into his seat and stared at his drink instead of the screen.

Queenie caught a glimpse of Mrs. Lymon returning to her seat carrying a tub of popcorn and a soda. A couple of minutes later Billy Bright charged up the aisle but was soon back in his seat.

Finally everyone seemed settled. No longer distracted, Queenie studied Lymon's editing; the pace and subtle match cuts were excellent—and would be largely unnoticed by the average moviegoer who would leave the theater knowing the film was put together well but unable to explain why. For the next twenty minutes Queenie watched L.D. work his evil, killing two more campers and, after devouring their hearts, placing their entrails in a large copper offering bowl.

Lymon had promised to put her on the flatbed during the next film's postproduction work. She was thinking about this when the image on the screen suddenly jerked. She wondered if it was a bad splice or if Alice had accidentally bumped the projector. A faint buzz of sudden conversation could be heard. Those familiar with split-second infractions had been aware of the movement. Queenie marveled at the synchronicity of the moment—there she'd been thinking of working on the editing table when a jump in the editing had occurred. Then Emma's warning about the Mikado being a firetrap popped into her head. Half expecting to smell smoke, all her senses were on alert.

Billy Bright moved up the aisle again. Had he smelled smoke, he'd have been running. He returned shortly. Once he took his seat, Queenie noticed Mrs. Lymon again move up the aisle. Had she been alarmed, she'd have hiked her restrictive skirt and run. The sight of her mincing steps lent an air of normality to the situation. It was stupid to think there was a fire.

Queenie returned her attention to the screen, banishing her silly fantasies.

L. D. Barth and Jean Bliss, playing a hag, began to prepare a protective circle of salt inside which they would soon evoke the demon Belial.

Queenie remembered Jean Bliss talking about this particular demon during a story conference the day before the shooting of the scene.

"Belial is a Prince of Hell and, of the seventy-two, second only to Lucifer," Jean had said while the actors, Lymon, Alice, and Queenie conferred in the small dining room of the motel they'd taken over. Besides her supporting role, Jean had been the "occult consultant" and was listed in the credits as such. "He's to be *evoked*," she'd emphasized. "To invoke him will actually put me and L.D. in grave danger."

L.D. had said nervously, "It's only a movie, Jean."

Everyone except Jean had laughed.

"Demons *do* exist!" she'd retorted angrily. "Believe me, we must all proceed with the utmost caution."

The day after her last scene in the film, Jean was dead, apparently a victim of her own demons.

Out of the corner of her eye, Queenie saw Mrs. Lymon

hurrying back down the aisle to her seat. Maybe *now* everyone would settle down.

An enormous full moon dominated the screen. Rex was suddenly silhouetted against the silver orb. Queenie felt momentary annoyance then decided he was probably just going for a pee.

After Rex moved out of her line of vision, Queenie watched Nessa struggling down a rocky escarpment while beyond and below, lights winked in a small village. On the soundtrack, a foreboding Gregorian chant began.

Suddenly Nessa's scream pierced the theater. Even though she knew it was coming, Queenie still started. A hand had shot through the darkness and grabbed Nessa's arm. But it was only one of the villagers out collecting firewood.

An instant later, Queenie herself felt a hand brush her shoulder. She jerked around and found herself looking up at her brother. Anger flared then abruptly changed to concern.

He looked about to topple into the aisle, his feet wide apart in an unnatural, awkward stance. His breath was coming in little gasps barely audible as the Gregorian chant crescendoed.

"Are you all right?" she whispered.

Rex mouthed something she couldn't hear while motioning for her to get up. She followed him into the lobby.

In the light, he appeared confused and frightened, his face a mask of horror—exactly the reaction that sent Lymon to the bank again and again. But a strange dullness hid the normal liveliness of his dilated eyes. He seemed to be having trouble keeping his balance. Sweat rolled off his splotchy, flushed face. His shirt was sopping. Though the lobby was warm, the temperature wasn't high enough to warrant such prodigious perspiration. Yet he managed enough control to clasp Queenie's wrist in his clammy hand and pull her unsteadily down the corridor toward the west exit door. The big garbage container was no long there.

As part of the renovation, speakers had been set high on the walls in the lobby and rest rooms. That way anyone having to get up during the film could still follow the action through the soundtrack.

The Gregorian chanting charged the air with foreboding. At the moment, Queenie could have gladly done without it.

"What's wrong?" she kept asking. Either Rex wasn't able to talk, or he was determined to show her.

Someone rushed up behind her. Her fear now aroused, she spun around defensively.

It was Joey. "What's the matter?"

Queenie took a deep breath. "I don't know but I think more than the movie's upset him."

"He looks bombed."

The two women moved with him into the alcove. The smell nearly knocked them over. Someone—it was easy to guess who—had vomited in the clam-shaped black marble water fountain.

"Oh, shit," Queenie said, her shoulders sagging. "Is this what you wanted to show me?"

Rex leaned against the wall, his eyes rolling toward the ceiling. He shook his head and jerked his arm toward the men's room door.

Someone had put up a sign since she and Joey had left the women's room earlier: OUT OF ORDER. PLEASE USE THE WOMEN'S REST ROOM. WE APOLOGIZE FOR THE INCONVENIENCE.

"Lymon must have put it up," Queenie said to Joey. Then she turned to Rex. "Okay, so you couldn't make it to the women's room—"

"Braagh-throom," he said, trying to squeeze the word from the back of his throat and through his slack mouth. He rolled toward Queenie and tried to push her toward the closed door.

She jerked away from him, her anger returning. "Damn it, Rex!" Then she took hold of one arm. "Let's get him to the women's lounge then I'll clean up this mess."

With a sudden surge of energy, Rex pushed her away and again motioned toward the men's room door.

"I think he wants you to go in," Joey said.

Rex's eyes widened and he nodded his head. Finally his legs gave out and he began sliding down the wall. Queenie tried to catch him but again he pushed her away.

"Oh, hell! All right! Stay with him, Joey."

Though Queenie had seen numerous horrors in the course of her film work and had investigated two murders while working as a private investigator, nothing could have prepared her for what she was about to see.

CHAPTER NINE

QUEENIE ENTERED A lounge almost identical to the women's. Only the offerings were different. Here on the low tables were boxes of cigars, crystal ashtray and lighter sets, and copies of yesterday's *Variety, Los Angeles Times,* and *The Wall Street Journal.* Less frivolous provender for men, Queenie thought irritably. Then she spotted the glistening viscous pool staining the white tile floor beneath the bathroom's archway. Any concern about inequities immediately vanished.

Feeling a sudden surge of panic, Queenie drew nearer and uttered a small cry upon seeing a foot and an ankle, then trousers so saturated with blood they stuck to the legs like glue.

The mingled odors of copper-scented blood, alcohol, and feces stung her nostrils. For perhaps ten seconds she stood in shock at the edge of the bathroom.

It was as gory a scene as Lymon himself might have created. A man's body lay flat on the floor, an ax protruding from his face like a grotesque parody of Pinocchio's nose. He had been ferociously hacked.

Having seen many staged mutilations, she thought for an instant that maybe this was another—a stunt cooked up by some tasteless publicist. But she quickly realized this was all too real. Then the horror of it sank in as she recognized the clothing and the hands of Burke Lymon.

Blood splattered and smeared the sides of the stalls on the left and right and pooled thickly out from the body. And, as if he'd been dipped in it, blood covered all exposed flesh; his clothes were soaked.

As she reeled from the shock of the scene before her, something tugged at the corner of her mind. Then she had it: There were no footprints anywhere near the body. She moved closer. Peering around the archway, her eyes moved across the undisturbed pool of blood and up to the sinks. A message scrawled on the mirror brought an involuntary shiver. Her skin ached as if she'd been burned.

"Love, your most adooring fan" had been written in blood and signed *Lucifer.*

A clinging, tenacious chill slithered up her spine.

"Holy Mother." Queenie gasped, hoping for an instant that Lymon would rise up and with a great peal of laughter say it was all a joke.

Queenie glanced down at the weapon, the familiar death's-head knob grinning at her from the end of the handle. To read the inscription she would have had to stand beside the body. Of course, it might be another copy. Something told her it wasn't though, that this very ax had been presented at the wrap party in May. It wasn't hers, so it had to belong to Alice Baldridge, Billy Bright, L. D. Barth, or Sooch Bauer.

She felt the blood begin to rush from her head and knew, if

she didn't sit down, she'd faint. She staggered backward and literally fell into the nearest armchair. With her head between her legs, she tried to focus on action—*what to do and quickly!* For a moment though, as her breathing eased, she could only imagine the scene through her brother's eyes. How horrible for him—how horrible for anyone, for that matter. But he was her little brother. He should never have to see anything like this. It was enough to have sobered him up, and fast.

Suddenly she jerked her head up. That's it, isn't it! she thought. The horror of Lymon's mutilated body should have *sobered* him. He hadn't been drunk until—until he'd had a drink from Lymon's bottle.

Her mind clicked over.

"Oh, no!" she said, and rushed back to the alcove. Rex was slumped over on the floor. Joey had removed his tie and unbuttoned his shirt and pants. She was just returning from the women's room with some of the towels, now dampened, that she'd taken earlier from the men's room.

Queenie squatted down and checked her brother's pulse. It was weak but steady, his breathing shallow. She slapped his face.

"Wake up, damn it! Rex! Wake up!" She turned to Joey. "Give me a couple of those towels! And for God's sake, don't touch that vomit!"

"You think I'm crazy!"

After a few moments, his eyelids fluttered and he licked his lips. He started to move, used his good arm to push himself upright. He opened his eyes and stared at her groggily.

"Wha . . . ?" he slurred.

"Stay with him and keep him conscious," Queenie told Joey as she got to her feet.

"Where are you going?"

"To call an ambulance." She didn't add that she'd be alerting the police as well.

"You're overreacting, Queenie. Seriously. The man's drunk. He passed out. He just needs to sleep it off—hey! You all right? You look sick too."

She ignored Joey's comments. "Got any change? My bag's in the theater."

Joey's beaded bag still hung from her wrist. "All I've got are bills."

Queenie stuck her hand in Rex's pocket and pulled out several dimes and nickels. "And if anyone comes by just tell them he got sick."

"I don't think I'll have any trouble convincing anyone," she replied, glancing at the water fountain and grimacing.

Queenie ran to the lobby. If anyone saw her, she'd just say her brother needed immediate medical care, which of course was true. She hoped the sign would keep anyone who might come along out of the men's room, though it certainly hadn't worked with Rex. But she felt certain he was under the influence of some disorienting drug. He'd told her he hadn't taken anything for pain since he'd left Boston and she believed him. There must have been something in the Scotch Lymon gave him, something intended for Lymon alone to make the murderer's job easier.

The telephone was contained within an antique glassed-in booth in a corner at the front of the theater, privacy afforded by a black lacquer Chinese screen.

She rushed into the phone booth, not bothering to close the doors. But then, no one was in the lobby to overhear her conversation.

Without hesitating, she punched in from memory the numbers of Lieutenant Joseph Patric Fitzgerald's pager. As she waited for the beep, then entered the phone booth's number and hung up, she prayed that she was doing the right thing. She had no time to contemplate her action. The telephone rang within seconds.

"J.P.?" she said immediately.

"My God, is that you, Davilov?" He sounded more startled than surprised, as if she'd caught him thinking about her.

Quickly and without embellishment, she informed him of the murder and Rex's immediate need of medical attention. After instructing him to use the west alley, she added, "—and we've got over a hundred suspects here quietly watching a movie so—"

"Got the picture," he interrupted. "I'll send an ambulance—and don't leave! Paramedics'll take care of your brother."

Queenie hung up, her heart thumping steadily and loudly against her rib cage. A heavy bead of sweat coursed down the side of her cheek.

She hoped she'd taken the right action by calling him rather than risk the possibility of a delay by calling the overburdened weekend dispatchers. Hell, she thought, J.P.'s a fine homicide detective, one of the best in Hollywood. That they'd once been lovers had nothing to do with her decision, she told herself, and abruptly left the booth. She wanted to take a quick look around before he arrived.

Outside, the sidewalk was empty but for litter twirling across the length of Astroturf and a few discarded signs declaring the coming of Satan. Traffic was steady and she didn't see anyone across the street showing particular interest in the theater. For the moment, the Mikado was of little interest to the rest of the world. She pushed the bar on both doors, but there was no give. Both were still securely locked.

She quickly checked behind the candy counter where she'd

last seen Lymon alive. The folding chair was still in place. She peeked in the green-and-gold Harrods bag. The bottle of Scotch was still there. Using her jacket to prevent leaving prints, she tried the closed door to the manager's office. It was locked.

She rushed back toward the alcove. As she passed the stairs to the projection booth, she wondered if Alice had heard or maybe even seen anything. But she was not about to ask. Alice would want to know what the hell she was doing up there, and Queenie didn't have time for explanations.

Rex was still on the floor, slumped against the wall, the soggy paper towels scattered over and around him. Joey was gone. Queenie groaned. She had a pretty good idea where Joey had gone—and it wasn't on an errand to collect more towels.

Queenie propped open the west exit door then returned to her brother. As she strained to lift him, her thoughts were on Burke Lymon's horrific, blood-soaked remains; the indignity of strangers looking, probing, taking pictures, and smelling his blood and excrement, remembering him only as a mutilated corpse with an ax jutting from his head.

Holy Mother! What demon had perpetrated such an outrage?

Propelled by fury, Queenie half dragged, half carried her brother to the exit door. In the days ahead, she'd use that anger to fuel her pursuit of the killer. And if her brother should die, well, the killer would never see the inside of a courtroom.

CHAPTER TEN

A TERRIFYING, HIGH-PITCHED scream speared Lieutenant Fitzgerald and two uniformed cops, a man and a woman, as they stepped through the west exit door. Startled, the young male cop reached for his gun.

"It's only the movie," Queenie said quickly. She still trembled from the sudden anger that had torn through her like a ball of fire searing the meat of her emotions while the juices bubbled inside. "There are speakers set up all over the theater."

Only a moment before, paramedics had whisked Rex off to Hollywood Community Hospital. They'd refrained from using the siren when they'd both entered and left the alley—undoubtedly on Lieutenant Fitzgerald's orders. Back in the theater, she'd seen Joey run from the men's room and disappear down the corridor to the women's.

The lieutenant automatically touched a gold St. Christopher medal gleaming outside a navy blue T-shirt tucked into a pair of faded jeans. A denim jacket shielded the holstered gun tucked under his left arm. When working, he usually wore suits custom tailored to his unique proportions.

Exactly the same height as Queenie, he had broad, square shoulders, narrow waist and hips. Most off-the-rack shirts and jackets fit him as if they were still on a hanger. He'd once said the only thing that had ever fit him perfectly was her.

Unsure how to greet him after a year and a half apart, she simply extended her hand. "Lieutenant. I'm glad I got you." With other officers present, she didn't use his personal moniker.

He eyed her warily, his expressive hazel eyes rimmed by impossibly curly black eyelashes. His eyebrows, too, were black, in contrast to his heavy, dirty blond hair. Currently it was longer than regulation, with tiny, darker curls pressed damply at his hairline. Beads of perspiration glistened beneath his handsome nose.

For one fearful moment, she thought he was going to ignore her extended hand. Then he took it in his hard grip. The air seemed to crackle the moment they touched. He quickly withdrew his hand.

"Night off. I was in the station catching up on paperwork. So, where's the body?" he said gruffly, his eyes darting away from hers as he lit an unfiltered Player's cigarette with a brass Zippo lighter. She wondered if the engraving had worn off: "To J.P. from Q.," and a New Year's Day date over a year and a half ago. His thirty-sixth birthday. The lighter quickly disappeared into his pocket.

"Davilov!"

"Sorry, J.—Lieutenant, I—" She cleared her throat. "In the men's room. No one's come out of the theater since my brother—" She stopped just short of saying "found the body."

Quite often, the person who "found" a murder victim was the perpetrator.

"The paramedics just took my brother to the hospital," she finished quickly. "Really, I can't thank you enough. I was afraid—" Queenie started to fidget. "Hell. C'mon." She stepped toward the alcove, but the lieutenant turned to the policewoman who'd entered with him, her uniform tag revealing her as Sergeant Noble.

"When the photographer and the M.E. get here, have them wait."

He then spoke to the young male cop whose freshness and intensity marked him as a rookie, ordering him to guard the auditorium doors. "Anyone leaves, detain them, and under no circumstances let them back in. All right, Davilov, let's go."

The lieutenant flinched as he passed the clam filled with vomit.

"My brother got sick," Queenie remarked.

Queenie stood to one side while Lieutenant Fitzgerald paced in front of the archway examining the body and scene, his muttered Jesuses and Christs ironically defying the dialogue piped into the room:

"O Belial, mighty and powerful King, speak on my behalf to Great Lucifer in thy comely voice, that he may find favor with my deeds, that he know I humbly work in his shadow . . ."

"Any windows in here?" the lieutenant asked.

"No," she answered quietly. "None in the women's room either. The closest way in or out of here is through the west exit."

He looked at the message on the mirror then stooped down and examined the carpet. It was black and red, the same carpeting used throughout the theater, making it impossible to see if there were any bloody footprints. Forensics would have to discover that. But there weren't even any areas sticky with blood.

They left the men's room. Since no one else had arrived, he told her to give him the tour.

"That's the projection booth," she said as they approached the stairs. "Alice Baldridge, Lymon's assistant director, runs it. She might have seen or heard something." Instantly she thought of something important. "Lieutenant, there's a fire escape off a small bathroom up there. Maybe—"

"Wait here!" he snapped.

She watched him move stealthily up the stairs, taking the gun from his shoulder holster as he went. Then he was gone. She moved closer to the stairs, straining to hear voices, a confrontation, anything. But the damn soundtrack drowned out other sound. What if the killer was up there? What if he'd been about to exit through the bathroom halted in his tracks by the paramedics and the lieutenant's subsequent arrival? But if he was up there, there was little chance that Alice Baldridge was still alive.

Queenie's heart began to race again. She recalled the split second when the film had jerked on screen. What if, at that instant, Alice had fallen, bumping the projector, another victim of the ax murderer? Would there be another ax? Whose? And whose had been used to kill Lymon?

The photographer arrived, detained at the door by Sergeant Noble. Queenie glanced over at him, then back at the stairs.

This was the first crime in which she was personally involved, and she didn't like the feeling. The victim was her boss. Her brother found the body. The murder weapon might belong to a coworker who could well be the murderer. Last, and surely least, she'd stirred up old fires by bringing J.P. into it. Instinctively she knew what she'd be hearing in the days ahead. It would be the voice of her former boss, I. P. Friedman. "Before you start any case, honey," he would say, "send your emotions on vacation."

J.P. holstered his gun as he hurried down the stairs.

"Is Alice . . . ?" Her question trailed off as he hurried over to Sergeant Noble. Then he said something to the photographer, who rushed past Queenie and up the stairs. At the same moment, Joey wandered into the alcove scribbling in a small notebook.

"Who the—" the lieutenant started then abruptly stopped. Though Joey and J.P. disliked each other, for that split second when he was caught off guard, Queenie read his thoughts and felt the sudden flush of jealousy. Cool it, Davilov, she told herself, embarrassed by her reaction. This was neither the time nor the place for personal feelings. Besides, J.P. was history. Or was he?

Joey smiled but Queenie could see her friend's mind racing. "Hello, J.P. Fancy meeting you here."

"Put the notebook away, Burroughs," he said. Taking her by the arm, he led her to the south corner of the west exit.

"Going to arrest me?"

"And give you an excuse to make a phone call?" He turned to Sergeant Noble. "Sergeant, make sure the young lady doesn't move from that spot."

Joey's eyes flashed but she stayed put.

"How the hell did she get in here?" the lieutenant snarled as he and Queenie moved toward the main lobby. "Everyone knows Burke Lymon hated the press. Made a few enemies that way. Maybe Joey axed your boss."

"In that dress?" Then Queenie added, "She was my guest. Lymon didn't know her profession. But I owed her one."

"Bad call, Davilov. You coulda lost your job."

"Can't see that it matters now," she retorted hotly. "What happened to Alice—the projectionist?"

"Unconscious . . . and all in one piece."

"J.P., I think Lymon had been drugged." Unexpectedly, the lieutenant's scent, a combination of cigarettes and male musk, switched on a reel of memories. She forced herself to shut off the uninvited images.

"My—my brother was given a drink from Lymon's bottle," she went on, "that must have made him vomit. Having much more body weight than Lymon, it would take longer for a drug to affect him. You'll probably want a sample to test—"

"You don't have to tell me my job," he blurted.

"Maybe Alice was drugged too."

"With a length of lead pipe? It's by her body."

He stopped, the auditorium doors to his back, the lobby laid out before him. After a moment, he stubbed his cigarette in a sand-filled bowl atop a stainless steel cylinder, then moved to the left and, using a handkerchief, pushed open one of the east exit doors. Just beyond was a full parking lot.

"That reminds me," Queenie said. "There're two fire exit doors farther down and on each side of the theater. You'll want to post guards there too."

"Thank you," he retorted coldly. "If you care to look, you'll see I've taken care of it already." Without giving her a chance to see, he closed the door.

Another ambulance arrived. The lieutenant left for a moment to supervise the removal of Alice Baldridge and sent the photographer into the men's room. From where Queenie was standing, Alice appeared to be sleeping. After the lieutenant joined her again, they moved into the lobby.

"Lymon and the security guard have the only keys," she said as he examined the interior locks on the entrance door. Then they stepped behind the candy counter. Both Queenie and J.P. stared for a moment at the empty folding chair.

"This is the last place I saw Lymon alive," she said, her voice catching.

"What time was that?" he asked, studying the fixtures.

"About seven. Lymon likes to start promptly. My brother got a drink from him a few minutes after the movie started and stayed at the candy counter talking to him until about nine minutes past seven. Joey can confirm that. She was here too."

"Why didn't your brother take something with him before the movie started?" He walked around the folding chair and glanced into the Harrods bag.

"Frankly, he doesn't like horror movies. I suppose it gave him an excuse to leave the auditorium. The opening scene's pretty gory. And he never met Lymon before tonight."

"That the bottle?"

Queenie peeked in the bag. "I guess. But the last time I saw it, Lymon had it out. I didn't see him put it back in the bag."

The lieutenant tried the knob on the locked door. "What's this?"

"Manager's office, mainly used for storage. It's where all the candy, popcorn, and soft drinks are kept. Lymon would have the key. Alice too, probably."

"Any windows?"

She had to think for a moment. Lymon had taken her through the newly renovated theater the evening of the first premiere she'd attended as his script supervisor. "No windows."

"How many people were back here tonight?"

"Alice and Lymon. But I wouldn't know who came back here

before we arrived—which was around six-thirty. There's no reason for anyone else to go behind the counter. Alice takes care of serving. Hec Cerutti—he's one of the crew—was back there for a minute while Alice went to the office to get more popcorn. But I saw him. All he did was pour himself a soft drink."

"Who's he?"

"The construction coordinator. Oversees set building."

They returned to the main lobby area. From what J.P. said into the crackling walkie-talkie, she learned he was going to set up a headquarters inside the theater to fingerprint and question everyone in attendance.

For a moment, Queenie stared out the window at the passing traffic and littered sidewalk. Another ambulance went by silently. She felt a thickness in her throat.

They moved to a bench near the phone booth. He pulled out a notebook and lit another cigarette. Then, almost as an afterthought, offered her one. She took it.

While lighting hers with the brass Zippo he said, "Thought you gave up your two vices—smoking and me."

Their eyes met for an instant. Queenie shifted uncomfortably.

At that moment, the medical examiner entered the lobby and the lieutenant rose to speak with him. She smoked and waited, trying to think of nothing.

"All right. Tell me what happened," J.P. said upon returning.

For the next few minutes, Queenie narrated the events since her undignified entrance at the hands of Amanda Martin to the moment she'd telephoned him, with a flow that would have made Eric Diamond proud. Too bad she wasn't pitching the opening scenes of a script to a producer with a short attention span.

J.P. jotted notes, looking up from his pad to glance around the lobby or out at the street, probably reconstructing the scenes in his own mind.

"And J.P.," she concluded, "Lymon's wife's in the audience."

He cursed. That was one aspect of his authority he would gladly have delegated—informing the relatives, dealing with pain, or for that matter, any deep emotion. In the fifteen years he'd been on the force, he'd struggled to entomb his own emotions, though he'd never completely succeeded. Queenie had seen them explode too many times, usually in bed, and a few times when he'd had too much to drink.

"She left her seat twice—so did the sound man, his name's Billy Bright."

Finally she told him about the mutilated animal she'd seen, adding that Mrs. Lymon said she'd received one. The ghoulish message, *"Love, your most adooring fan,"* had been repeated in blood this very night. That was no coincidence. Was Selma correct in her suspicions of Amanda Martin? For that matter, Frances Lymon had all but directly accused Amanda.

Maybe she'd been lucky Amanda had had nothing more deadly than rotten tomatoes in her bag.

At the sound of a commotion in the corridor, the lieutenant jumped off the bench. A moment later, all was quiet again as a couple of police officers set up a folding table and chairs, fingerprint equipment, and a tape recorder at a right angle to the auditorium doors and just in front of the east exit.

"Look, I've got to get things rolling," he said, sinking down beside her. "As it is, I'll probably be here all night. Another thing—do you know where we can find this Amanda Martin?"

"Mrs. Lymon said she's been camping out at their estate in Palm Isle. But if she had anything to do with Lymon's murder,

I doubt she'd go back there. Maybe Selma Steinberg has an idea where to find her."

"Where's she's sitting?"

"Toward the front—"

"Get her for me," he interjected. "And bring the wife. Might as well get that out of the way. Then you can leave."

They both stood up. The lieutenant started to move away.

"Just one minute, J.P.," Queenie said coldly.

He turned and gave her an impatient glare. "What is it?"

Queenie took a deep breath. "Lieutenant, I can help a lot more than by simply being your messenger. Look, I—"

Suddenly he went very still. For an instant, the soundtrack, and hence the theater, fell silent. Then a faint, hollow chant began.

On screen, L.D. raises his arms inside his protective circle of salt.

As the chant gradually increased in volume, so too did the expression on the lieutenant's face alter. His lips pulled away from his teeth. His body became rigid, one hand curled into a fist. His eyes widened to accommodate what Queenie took to be building rage—then an image flashed into her mind of what was at that moment being projected on the screen:

Out of the flat darkness of a great void, two tiny points of deep purple light speed toward the camera.

The lieutenant took a step toward her.

The two points grow and distort, the colors changing as they move out of the dark side of the spectrum. Shape takes form. They are eyes, rolling up and down, left and right, looking for something.

The lieutenant cursed, the sound like a hiss.

The color stabilizes between red and yellow. The rolling eyes nearly fill the screen. Suddenly they stop moving and, narrowing, stare directly ahead, the skin around them scaly and lizardlike.

"I am here, Master," a surprisingly melodic voice whispered through the speakers.

Caught between the real and the reel worlds, Queenie found she couldn't move. Her mouth went dry and she forgot what she'd been about to say. Whose eyes were she seeing? The demon's or the lieutenant's? Or were they one and the same?

She felt he was going to attack her when she suddenly realized that he was looking over her shoulder. She turned and finally understood what had invoked his sudden rage. Then she broke away and hurried into the theater.

CHAPTER ELEVEN

THE SCENE HAD cut to Nessa bathing in a wooden tub in the villager's steamy kitchen, her wet breasts and puckered nipples drawing all attention as Queenie stood just inside the womb of the darkened theater, taking a moment to collect herself.

She wished she was still in the audience vicariously participating in a staged murder rather than actively involved in a real one and wondered if the killer was staring at the screen, munching popcorn, appearing entertained like everyone else. Or had he muttered some evil verse and vanished in a puff of smoke? Given the horror of the murder and the nature of the film, her imagination strayed toward the supernatural. But imagination or not, whether she had to capture him in a bottle or scour every square inch of Los Angeles to find him, this ... this *creature* was hers.

Her step unhurried so as not to alarm anyone, Queenie's

thoughts turned briefly to Lieutenant Fitzgerald and the ugly scene outside the theater.

The press had arrived. The anger she'd thought directed at her had actually been the lieutenant's reaction to a sudden cyclone of whirling bodies and cameras. She'd been so concentrated on the images in her mind, underscored by the soundtrack, she hadn't even heard the crowd impacting against the front of the theater. And when she'd turned around, she'd seen a gallery of distorted, ghoulish faces smearing the mirrored glass. Someone had obviously gotten the message, and the topless bar at the far west corner of the block had instantly been relieved of those patrons who usually waited until shortly before the film let out to return to the Mikado and wrap their stories.

Minicams bobbed as television and print journalists competed for position. A couple of policemen had disappeared as they tried to preserve the peace by pushing the crowd toward the street. Instead of her, the lieutenant had grabbed his walkie-talkie, spouting orders to block off the street.

Queenie crouched down and moved to the center of the third row. Selma slouched in her seat staring up at the screen through a pair of wire-rimmed glasses.

"Selma?" she whispered.

Selma abruptly turned. "Wha . . . ?"

Queenie put her finger to her lips. "Need to see you in the lobby."

"What's up?"

"Just come with me."

They passed up the aisle together, Queenie ignoring Selma's inquisitive glances, until they were on the other side of the doors. Then she stopped and braced herself for the next delivery.

She knew where Mrs. Lymon was seated, had seen her come

and go a couple of times. Perhaps Mrs. Lymon had seen something during the moments she'd left her seat.

Queenie squatted next to the aisle seat and whispered, "Mrs. Lymon, excuse me, but you're wanted in the lobby."

The woman twisted around. "What?"

"You're wanted in the lobby. It's urgent."

"Oh, all right."

The two women rose together. "Better bring your coat."

As Mrs. Lymon brushed past, Queenie noticed several people watching them curiously, their faces washed with the light reflected from Nessa's candlelight bath.

"Gee, no plumbing, no electricity," Nessa was saying on screen, her words coming out in puffs of hot air meeting cold. The scene had been shot on a near-freezing set, which, Queenie remembered, Nessa hadn't complained about. "I never knew Scotland was so primitive. Hard to believe you people invented golf."

Some laughter rippled through the theater, as the audience enjoyed a moment of comic relief, the last for a long time.

Queenie stopped at the last row to pick up her satchel and slung it bandoleer-style over her shoulder. With a sudden inspiration, she searched around the seats until she found Rex's cup. Holding it carefully, she returned to the lobby.

All but a small area by the east exit door had been cordoned with yellow police line tape.

General quiet still prevailed even with the addition of several more detectives. She saw one bagging a sample of Rex's vomit.

In relative isolation, Mrs. Lymon and Lieutenant Fitzgerald sat in metal folding chairs by the east exit doors and behind the table where Selma, her back shaking with sobs, was experiencing the indignity of being fingerprinted, the first step toward coming to grips with the reality of murder.

Queenie noticed Joey still standing across from Sergeant Noble by the west exit doors.

After quietly asking one of the detectives for an evidence bag, Queenie dropped her brother's nearly empty cup inside and set it on the table. Unsure about what to do and not wanting to leave yet, she heard the click of a tape recorder and the lieutenant ask Mrs. Lymon his first question. Curious about what the woman had to say, she stayed by the table. The lieutenant hadn't noticed her yet, but then his attention was fully on the recently widowed.

"Enemies?" Mrs. Lymon said incredulously. "Of course he had enemies. He was successful! Now where is he? I want to see him!"

Queenie felt a certain compassion for the woman. She sat straight in her chair and held herself with far more restraint than Queenie could have mustered under the circumstances. Mrs. Lymon's voice quivered only slightly, and it was impossible to tell if she was crying since the opal chip–studded veil now shielded her face. She must have pulled it back down when she left the auditorium.

"Mrs. Lymon," Lieutenant Fitzgerald went on, "what time did you and your husband arrive at the theater tonight?"

"We arrived separately. I hadn't seen him since he got back from New York . . . Sunday or Monday, I think. We spoke on the phone but he usually stays at his office before a premiere."

"Then, what time did you arrive?"

"Six—six-fifteen, probably. My chauffeur would know."

"After the show started, did you leave your seat?"

She didn't answer immediately. Finally she said, "Uh, to get some popcorn and a Coke. And, yes, later to use the rest room."

"Did you see your husband?"

"He gave me the Coke and popcorn."

"Anyone else?"

"Anyone else what?"

"Did you see anyone else?"

"No, I don't re—" She stopped, seemed to be thinking.

"What is it, Mrs. Lymon?" The lieutenant persisted. "Even something you think is minor might be important."

She took her time. "Well . . . the janitor was taking out the trash when I left the rest room."

Janitor? Queenie thought.

"Where?"

Mrs. Lymon nodded toward the west exit doors. "Out that way."

"What time was that, Mrs. Lymon?"

She shook her head. "Oh, goodness, I don't know."

"Would you describe him for me, please?"

"Tall, I think . . . he was wearing a baseball cap—blue, and a sort of uniform, you know a jumpsuit. I think it was blue too."

"Was he white, black?"

"I only saw him from behind," she said, cutting him off.

"What about hair color—straight, curly? Did you see his hands?"

"Wait. His hair was kind of long and straight . . . and dark. I think he was white."

"What kind of build?"

"Uh, not small. Good-size. Yes, he was a good-size man. He reminded me of someone. . . ." she said, letting her voice trail off.

"Oh?"

Mrs. Lymon shook her head. "Don't know."

"Tell me about this animal you got in the mail."

She appeared surprised. Then she shrugged and repeated what Queenie had already heard. She didn't mention an "adooring fan" message and neither did the lieutenant.

"Anything else? Any odd people here tonight you haven't seen before?"

"Most of the people at these functions are strangers to me. I only know a handful of my husband's crew members, those who've been with him longest."

Abruptly the lieutenant changed his line of questioning. "Who benefits from your husband's death?"

There was a long silence. Finally Mrs. Lymon said coldly, "If you're implying—maybe I should call my lawyer before I answer any more questions."

"Mrs. Lymon, I'm asking a routine question. If you'd prefer not to answer at this time, that's all right. Of course, we will get the question answered eventually."

Mrs. Lymon sighed. "I suppose I do. But you should also know I have my own money. Now, I'd like some answers—you said my husband's been murdered. Well, how did he die?"

"Mrs. Lymon, your husband suffered a severe blow to the head."

There was a sharp intake of breath. "Oh, my God." Queenie could see some of the woman's composure ebbing. The lieutenant helped her to her feet and slipped a business card into her hand, obviously anxious to conclude the interview.

"Call me if you think of anything. Your husband's body will be taken to the morgue—you understand an autopsy must be performed."

"No! You already told me you know the cause of death! I won't have him desecrated!" Suddenly she was on the verge of hysterics. This was the part Queenie knew J.P. hated, the part he had the most trouble dealing with.

"Mrs. Lymon, I did not say that was the cause of death. All we know is—look, I'll have an officer drive you home," he said. Mrs. Lymon was now shaking uncontrollably. The lieutenant motioned to the policewoman standing beside Selma. Then he spotted Queenie.

"No!" Mrs. Lymon shrieked. "Use your people to find my husband's killer! My chauffeur's in the parking lot. He'll take me home."

"All right, all right," J.P. said quickly. "But first we need your fingerprints. It's just routine."

While Mrs. Lymon was being printed, the lieutenant went to Queenie. "Davilov, help the officer take Mrs. Lymon to her car."

Spine-tingling shrieks filled the theater.

"Jesus! And go turn off the goddamn movie."

She started to move toward the projection booth when he grabbed her arm. "No. Wait. I don't want you going up there."

He called another officer over and said, "Go up and just pull the plug on that thing," adding that he wanted the house lights turned on. Then he spun around and put Queenie's arm on Mrs. Lymon's.

"Now escort the lady to her car."

"Lieutenant, that's the cup my brother drank out of," she said quickly. Mrs. Lymon looked at the cup in the glassine bag. Then, with Queenie holding Mrs. Lymon's right arm and the policewoman holding her left, the three women moved to the east exit door. Abruptly Mrs. Lymon stopped.

"I just remembered—" she said, and twisted around.

Selma was just sitting down in the folding chair, appearing stunned.

"Lieutenant, L. D. Barth! That's who the janitor reminded me of."

"Who's he?"

"He's starring in the movie."

The lieutenant looked directly at Queenie. "Is he here?"

"He's been missing for a week," she replied flatly.

Outside, a firestorm of red and blue flashing lights raged. Yellow crime-scene tape belted the Mikado from just beyond the farthest fire exit on the east side, to its opposite on the west.

It was still light outside, a sickly gray orange. The wind had died down, leaving the hot air almost viscous with noise: the crackling of squad car radios, the shouted orders between uniformed policemen, the yells and rumbles of the burgeoning mob, the growing cacophony of blaring car horns, and the *thwak-thwak* of rotor blades as a traffic control helicopter passed overhead.

Queenie saw at once that the street had been barricaded just beyond the parking lot—probably on the west side of the theater too, she reasoned. Squad cars and emergency service vehicles were scattered within the perimeter. A number of policemen struggled to contain the swiftly growing mob behind the barricades.

Too early, Queenie thought, for cold-blooded murder. The crime had been so blatant, so shocking, so bloody—and so *public*. Not only confidence, it took arrogance to even attempt such a crime. By all rights, the killer should be easy to find— someone soaked in blood. But there hadn't even been a footprint.

And why Burke Lymon? What had he done to inspire such horrible retribution? Did L. D. Barth really have anything to do with it? Or Amanda Martin? If anything happened to Rex she knew she'd seek retribution with a vengeance.

They approached the parking lot where police officers were taking down the license plate numbers of all vehicles. There was always the chance the murderer had left a car near the scene.

Mrs. Lymon's limousine was among the thirty or so vehicles in the small lot. Being the only one of its kind, it was easy to spot. Unfortunately, it was parked next to the street, in clear view of the mob.

The policewoman and Queenie hurried Mrs. Lymon toward the chauffeur, who dropped his cigarette the instant he saw them approach.

She was struck by the appearance of Mrs. Lymon's chauffeur as he rushed forward: male Caucasian, mid-twenties, dark hair, tall and well built. Aside from the age and his clothes, he fit Mrs. Lymon's description of the janitor. Had he murdered Lymon in the guise of a janitor then quickly changed clothes and returned to the limo?

"Shit," Queenie muttered, for a moment unaware of the shouts and small stampede. How many men of that description lived in Los Angeles? Thousands? Tens of thousands? Probably every other man I see will look like that, she told herself. But how many men of that description were close to the theater?

Suddenly Queenie was struck by something else—the lens of a minicam to the side of her head. The jolt caught her off guard. Losing her balance, she stumbled and fell to the ground. Alone now, the policewoman hustled Mrs. Lymon toward her sleek, black Mercedes. A female reporter with a microphone immediately took Queenie's place on Mrs. Lymon's right arm. The cameraman who'd knocked Queenie down reaimed, shooting Mrs. Lymon, while his companion reporter fired nonstop questions concerning Lymon's death.

Someone lifted Queenie to her feet from behind, then, taking her arm, rushed her back to the east exit door. It was a plainclothes detective she'd seen inside.

The detective knocked once. "Lieutenant? It's Jameson! I've got her."

The door was opened a hair and they squeezed inside.

Selma looked up mournfully from the folding chair as she clutched a smudged tissue in her right hand.

J.P. gripped Queenie's upper arm and ducking under the tape, he led her into the lobby to a place of relative privacy. He leaned close, his lips nearly touching her ear. "That message in the bathroom . . . the one signed *Lucifer*. I don't want you to say a word about it to anyone. *Anyone!* You got that?"

"Joey saw it too," she snapped, twisting her arm from his grasp.

"Fuck." His feelings about the press pretty well mirrored Burke Lymon's. He'd been burned by a columnist who'd been a suspect in a murder case J.P. had investigated. The columnist had instigated his own investigation into J.P.'s past, disturbing skeletons with salubrious tales to tell. That columnist had been Arthur Favor, Joey's current boss.

She turned to look at him. "And, J.P., Mrs. Lymon's chauffeur matches her description of the janitor: Caucasian, dark hair, and 'good-size.' "

"What about this L. D. Barth?"

"Supposedly, he and his costar disappeared last weekend. Mrs. Lymon might be throwing a curve, diverting attention from her chauffeur. Maybe there's something going on between them."

"All right, we'll check him out," he remarked, and lit another cigarette. "Now go on home."

"One more thing, J.P. Mrs. Lymon might also be an intended victim."

He took a deep drag, eyeing her suspiciously.

"She did get a mutilated squirrel—or said she did. And the other person to have gotten one is dead."

"You hard of hearing, Davilov? I said go home. We've got it covered. Now, get your butt outta here." He turned his back and started to walk away.

Queenie rushed up beside him, now remembering what she'd been about to say before she'd been sent to fetch Selma and Mrs. Lymon. "What do you mean, go home? I know these people. Let me *really* help. Let me hear what they have to say." She pointed toward the auditorium. "The killer might be in the audience!"

"You don't honestly believe the lunatic that turned your boss into dog meat is still here!" he snapped. "Look, this ain't your game anymore, Davilov. Leave it to the pros. You work in the movies now."

"My car's not here. I'd like a ride." The instant the words were out of her mouth, she felt foolish. Still, she stood her ground.

"You're no one's bereaved widow, Davilov," he said pointedly.

"Lieutenant, I wasn't outside five minutes before some idiot cameraman knocked me on my ass! It's a damn feeding frenzy out there."

"Use the west exit. There's squad cars blocking the alleys." For a moment their eyes locked. In that fleeting instant she could see, could *feel* the hurt she'd resurrected by calling him. It was doubtful he'd share any information about the case with her. Even so, he'd gotten the paramedics to the scene more quickly than she or anyone else could or would have done. In that sense, she'd done the right thing.

"One other thing," he continued. "Come into the station.

9 9

We'll need your signed statement. Oh yeah, I sent a cop to the hospital to question your brother and the projectionist. Neither will be released until we talk to them. And remember, you're not a P.I. anymore so stay out of this."

He spun around and went to question Selma.

Fat chance, Lieutenant, Queenie thought as she ducked under the tape and moved toward the west exit. Inside her, some of those bubbling juices of anger and adrenaline froze into crystals of determination.

The auditorium doors were open now, the lights on, the film shut down. A police officer was stationed in each aisle to keep anyone from leaving. Quite a few bewildered faces peered over the backs of seats and there was the low buzz of many conversations, many questions. Queenie was now glad not to be among them. She would have gone crazy waiting to be questioned and not knowing what was going on.

Joey still stood in the corner, catching the eye of all who passed by. She grabbed Queenie's arm.

"Where're you going?" Joey asked anxiously. "Ask J.P. if I can use the phone. Please, Queenie! Sgt. Bull Dyke won't let me move without his permission."

Queenie glanced at Sergeant Noble. She hadn't flinched; obviously she was used to far worse indictments.

Joey moved closer and whispered, "I've got to call in this story before anyone beats me to it!"

"Sorry, Joey. Just be thankful he hasn't told you to leave."

As the lieutenant had said, a squad car, its top flashing red and blue light, blocked the alley's south entrance. A couple of plainclothes detectives bagged empty bottles and other debris strewn about the west side of the theater and the two-story brick building across from it.

To the right of the exit door and about nine feet above, a

detective dusted the fire escape for prints. The small window into the projectionist's bathroom—nothing more than a sink and toilet, as Queenie recalled—was open. But it was the activity just beneath the fire escape that really sparked her interest. Now she was even more reluctant to leave.

CHAPTER TWELVE

A DETECTIVE WEARING rubber gloves was hunched over an institutional garbage container with wheels and a flip top. It was identical to the one Queenie had noticed earlier inside the exit door.

Though his back was to her, Queenie recognized Zachery Mihalovich by his curly black hair and the slugger-size biceps threatening to rip the short sleeves of his extra-large, sweat-stained T-shirt.

Soon after she started working as a private investigator, he'd arrested her. She'd been immersed in the garbage of a man being sued for divorce. Vitch had been investigating a series of burglaries in the same neighborhood. Later, when he learned she was of Russian extraction, he'd become an instant friend, even going so far as to speculate that through some distant peasant, they might be related. She hadn't bothered to tell him that, according to her mother, the Davilovs were aristocrats.

Their paths had crossed often after that, the venue almost invariably garbage. And it was Vitch who had introduced her to J. P. Fitzgerald.

"Find anything interesting?" she asked.

Vitch spun around. His usual scowl changed to a wrap-around smile, his slightly slanted eyes sinking into his high cheekbones. "Princess! Why am I surprised to see you? Anytime I'm up to my neck in garbage, you show up."

"I could say the same thing."

"What are you doing here?"

"My boss was murdered," Queenie began, then her voice caught.

"Jesus." For an instant he appeared sympathetic. But only for an instant. "And you offed him 'cause he wouldn't give you a raise. You're a born killer, Princess." And he added with a smirk, "More a cop killer, though."

Uh-oh, Queenie thought, and moved up to the garbage bin before he shooed her off.

A detective across the alley turned angrily. "Hey, Vitch. Cut the horse shit."

"Suck a corpse, Jackson," Vitch retorted.

Queenie peered inside. A heavy garbage bag was opened, revealing theater-type debris: popcorn; small, large, and behemoth popcorn containers; soft drink cups.

"Davilov, this is *my* garbage."

"Look how clean it is," she observed. "Pull out that cup."

He brought out a soft drink cup that had never been used.

Taking a pair of editing gloves from her satchel, she quickly pulled them over her fingers and began examining the containers.

Vitch looked at her hands. "Hey! Where'd you get those?"

"They're editing gloves. I always carry several pair. They're more comfortable than rubber."

"Come here!" he said, and led her to a cleared space on the other side of the garbage can where an evidence bag lay. In it were thin white cotton gloves, just like hers. "They were behind the garbage can." Then he said in a low voice, "I suggest you get your butt outta here, Princess."

"Vitch, this is Hollywood. And the factory here is filmmaking. Thousands of people use these gloves. They're as common as film stock."

Jackson stopped collecting debris and straightened up to watch them. "Vitch, I mean it! The lieutenant'll have our asses if you don't get that civilian outta here."

Queenie looked over Vitch's shoulder back into the garbage receptacle and noticed several other bags. But he clasped her wrist with his big gloved hand and pulled her away.

"Come on, I'll give you an escort."

He led her north toward another alley parallel to Santa Monica Boulevard where she could see more red and blue lights flashing on dingy brick.

"Look, Davilov," Vitch said, his tone now somewhat apologetic, "you know what a bitch it is being under J.P.—no pun intended. He won't be happy unless he can haul someone in yesterday. Which is fine with me as long as he's got the right person. Hell, if he let you go, *go*. Frankly, I'm surprised he didn't arrest you just for breaking his heart."

"Hey, I'm the one who called him tonight, Vitch. I could help, you know."

"Yeah, I know. You were always a good garbageman. For a woman."

They reached the end of the theater where the second alley ran behind it. "Can you get to your car okay from here?"

"My car's at home."

He shrugged. "Just as well. You'll probably make better time walking—" Abruptly his attitude changed. "Hell, you shouldn't be walking alone around here! Especially with an ax murderer on the loose. Shit. C'mon.

"... damn Irish bastard," Vitch snarled as they hurried toward a squad car blocking the east end of the alley. "I mean, I can understand him being pissed when you started working for that movie producer—and dumping him at the same time—"

"The parting was mutual," Queenie said defensively.

"That's not what he said. And you know how proud he is. He'd have to be telling the truth to admit he got dumped. But letting you out on the street tonight, well, that's too much!"

Queenie glanced at him, seeing anger throb in a vein protruding dangerously at his temple.

She touched his arm, which was slick with sweat. "Vitch, it's okay."

"Can't blame you for wanting a better life. No woman in her right mind ever marries a cop. And I should know. I've had three crazy women to prove it." He laughed suddenly.

Two cops leaned against a squad car blocking the alley. Vitch told one of them to get on the radio and call a cab. The cop didn't question his reason or authority. Then Vitch moved out of their earshot.

"Listen, Sunday services at Callie's, say ten o'clock?" He glanced at the squad car then back at Queenie, raising his eyebrows expressively. "*Ponimaesh?*"

Queenie smiled. It had been a long time since anyone had spoken Russian to her. "Yeah, Vitch. I understand. And thanks."

With that, he hurried back down the alley to his garbage.

"...and I'm not the least bit impressed by professional ath-
letes. In fact, they're often the worst. They've got money for
drugs."

Since the cab dropped her at Emergency, Queenie had been
explaining Rex's situation to the attending doctor, a handsome
woman in her early thirties who refused to let her see Rex.

"Whatever he got hold of," Queenie went on, "it was
accidental. He told me he's not even taking anything for
pain."

The doctor eyed her skeptically. "Look, I've got a busy night
ahead. Go home. We'll call you if there's a change in his condition. As I told you before, we know what we're doing."

During the ride home in a second cab, Queenie thought
about what the doctor had said about the staff being first-rate
drug experts. In Hollywood, they'd have to be. It eased her
mind a little. She just hoped the doctor wouldn't neglect Rex
because he was an athlete.

Her own knowledge was limited to marijuana. She'd never
even snorted cocaine and figured she had the only virgin nose
in town. Being poor did have advantages; drugs weren't in the
budget.

Queenie let herself into the still, all-too-silent apartment. After
quickly turning on a lamp, she glanced around. Something had
changed, as if all energy had been sucked from the room. She
went around and touched her Goddess icons, straightened books
on the shelves, and looked at each Native American art print—
all for spiritual reassurance. Then she reminded herself that

Rex was in the hospital, Dick was somewhere over the Pacific, and her boss had been horribly murdered ... and J.P. had reentered her life.

Stop it, Davilov, you've got a killer to catch.

She went into the bedroom and changed into a sleeveless black leotard and a pair of cutoffs, leaving the linen suit atop the heap on the closet floor. Clue slept on the closet shelf. Queenie would have liked to cuddle the kitty, but didn't want to disturb her.

She switched on the bathroom light, intending to wash her face. But the mirror's reflection startled her to immobility. Something within her had vanished forever, something that had heretofore rounded her cheeks, given her skin freshness, and brought soft light to her eyes.

Suddenly, in a moment of perfect clarity, she realized she looked like a burned-out cop. And after so long, she finally understood J.P. He was just a man aware that his darkening spirit was in danger of vanishing forever. Like a black hole, L.A. was eating his light.

With shaking hands she washed and dried her face, then returned to the living room. As she sat in her cracked leather chair, she rolled a cigarette, an act that helped focus her mind. Then she rolled another.

For a few moments she smoked, closing her mind to the swish of the billowing curtains, the night sounds drifting through the open windows, and, more important, the white noise of fear. She'd never investigated a murder alone. What she needed was a place to start. After that, she could find her way no matter how often she groped or stumbled. It was like writing a screenplay.

Where to start?

She lit the second cigarette from the first, forcing herself around the choking thought of failure. That would only freeze her mind, as it always did when she tried too hard to write something really good.

You can do it. It's not beyond your ability. But she had no grand success as a measure. Still, she fought her own demons as her eyes wandered around the room.

Finally they came to rest on the television, the VCR on top. She checked her watch. It was still early, just after nine-thirty.

Tools, she thought.

After inserting a fresh tape, she programmed the VCR to record the late news. Then she went into the study and sat down in front of the computer.

Start with your tools.

CHAPTER THIRTEEN

AFTER CREATING A new file, called BLM, for Burke Lymon Murder, Queenie began ruminating on the keyboard under her first heading:

DRUG

Whoever killed Burke Lymon wanted him knocked out first, otherwise he would have put up a fight that could well have brought help.

Use of a drug also underscored premeditation. It would have taken considerable time for Lymon to drink enough untainted Scotch to be so drunk he couldn't defend himself against the murderer. And he'd been killed sometime after 7:10 and before 7:30, when Rex found the body.

Use of a drug implied that the murderer knew Burke Lymon's habits, knew that he sat and drank behind the candy counter during his premieres—information not available to a casual, "most adooring fan."

So who had access to Lymon's Scotch?

Frances Lymon stated she hadn't seen her husband since his return from New York. The bottle could have been purchased anywhere. He never took it home because he never went home. He'd been staying at the office—if Mrs. Lymon wasn't lying. Was it someone who visited him during the week? Yet the person wouldn't want him drinking from the bottle *before* the premiere.

At the office, Selma Steinberg would have had the opportunity to tamper with the Scotch; at the premiere, Alice Baldridge. Hec Cerutti had been behind the candy counter—but only briefly and Queenie watched him do nothing more than get himself a soft drink.

So why was the bottle still there?

Queenie went into the kitchen and grabbed a cold beer. Then she sat back down and stared at the screen. Why did the murderer leave the bottle? Had he overlooked it?

Then she thought of something else. Lymon had not been expected to share his Scotch. Usually at his premieres he drank alone. However, this time, he'd taken an interest in Rex. . . .

"Hmm." After setting down the beer bottle, she resumed typing.

The murderer didn't plan on Lymon's body being discovered until much later.

Had the evening followed its normal course, the moviegoers would have left the theater around eight-thirty. With the media waiting, it would probably be nearly nine o'clock before everyone finally settled in at the Italian restaurant. At that time, Lymon's absence would be noted and someone sent to look for him— and Alice Baldridge, if anyone missed her. Once the body was found and by the time the police arrived, nearly two hours would have elapsed since Lymon's death. Precious time to a killer.

Which brought up another point.

After each premiere a private firm cleaned up the theater and hauled away the trash. They normally arrived around 8:30 and finished by about 8:45. While cleaning up, *they* might have discovered the body, provided they entered the men's room. But Queenie figured the OUT OF ORDER sign would have kept them from going in. All they were hired to do was pick up loose trash and vacuum, not clean toilets or fix plumbing. Thus the murderer would count on the garbage being taken away before anyone could have checked it for evidence. Further, that fact indicated that the murderer knew about the regular cleanup, again information not available to the general public.

So what was a lone janitor doing taking out the trash, only a short time after the film began? There was only one answer: Frances Lymon had seen her husband's killer.

And if Mrs. Lymon's impression was correct, was it L. D. Barth? Or was she shielding her chauffeur by suggesting L.D.?

Queenie saved what she'd written then swiveled around in her chair, her back to the computer. She looked at the map of the world tacked on the wall, her wish map with countries she wanted to visit outlined in green. Her thoughts, however, were much closer to home.

Lucifer's Shadow was L.D.'s first picture with Lymon, and as far as Queenie knew, he'd never been to one of Lymon's premieres. She'd done his background check and knew he had a criminal record, that he'd done time in Colorado for assault. Still, L.D. seemed an unlikely suspect, if only because Lymon had given him that dreamed-of, elusive big break.

She got up and retrieved her tobacco and papers from the

living room. Back at her desk, she rolled a cigarette as she put herself in L.D.'s place. Say Eric Diamond did become her agent. (She *hoped* she'd have the chance to say.) Would she brutally murder him after he sold one of her scripts?

Not bloody likely.

Dismissing L. D. Barth and Eric Diamond for the moment, she typed a new heading:

MOTIVE

For several minutes Queenie puffed on her cigarette and stared at the otherwise empty screen. It was a big word, MO-TIVE, and one to which she could not adequately respond. Aside from the fact that she couldn't imagine anyone, not even Amanda Martin, who would go to such pains to remove Burke Lymon from the list of the living, she knew very little about the man himself. His wife could help, but to question her now would be grossly insensitive.

Other than a filmmaker, who was he? Where was he from? Had he gone to college? How did he meet his wife? Had he ever been married before? Did he have any kids stashed away? Why did he make horror films?

The irony of their relationship hit her. While she knew the personal histories of a number of his employees, Burke Lymon himself was a mystery—like the Mikado's mirrored glass doors, he could see others but no one was permitted to see into him.

Then it hit her. To find a killer, you have to know the victim. Maybe Burke Lymon himself could best supply the motive for his own death.

So who was Burke Lymon? she asked herself as she took a long pull on her beer. The act brought to mind her brother and how helpless he'd looked—then she remembered something and sat a little straighter.

When he'd come back from the candy counter, Rex had said Lymon was a Red Sox fan! That must have been why Lymon gave Rex a drink in the first place. Did that mean he was from Boston?

Not necessarily, she thought. Rex himself had been a Red Sox fan . . . and a Giants fan, a Royals fan . . . a Dodgers fan, and so on into baseball fan infinity.

And most Bostonians had accents; Burke Lymon didn't. *Hadn't.*

Deciding she needed a break, Queenie saved what she'd written and wandered into the living room.

Lymon's death brought to mind another unpleasant fact— she was out of a job. While she'd received a decent salary, between films she spent everything she'd saved on living expenses while she wrote. By the time the next project went into production, her bank account was as green as the moon. Like now.

Truth was, she couldn't afford to be investigating Lymon's murder. Instead she should be looking for work.

If only Eric Diamond had come through! Then she reminded herself that even if he had, remuneration from an option or a sale could take a long time. Feeling discouraged, Queenie was beginning to think she had as much chance of selling a screenplay as Miss Moneypenny did of marrying James Bond.

She whispered a prayer to the Goddess. She needed strength, not self-pity.

Of course, there was the chance that Hammon Productions would continue under someone else's leadership, especially if *Lucifer's Shadow* had a good box office. Hell, with Lymon's death the box office might go supernova. . . .

She felt a twinge of guilt for such a mercenary thought. But after a moment of mental flagellation, her instincts kicked in.

What if someone else had thought of that? *Counted* on it.

She stared out the window at the now-illuminated HOLLY-WOOD sign attached to the landscape like some funky oracle. Maybe if she stared at it long enough, it would give her a sign. *A sign within a sign.*

She'd once read where the secret meaning of words could be found by rearranging their letters, clues even discovered phonetically.

Holy, lowly, wooly, dolly, ly (*the phonetic of lie?*) Her thoughts shifted to Lymon . . . *Ly-mon* (my lie?) . . .

The telephone rang, interrupting the fanciful exercise.

She hurried into the study, her thoughts turning to Rex. Did the hospital have news?

"Yes?" she answered abruptly.

"Queenie! Oh, thank God you're home!"

"Selma?"

"Listen, can you come over to Lymon's office?"

"Lymon's office? Why? Where are you?"

"I'm at the bar next door. Please, just come! I'm scared to death!"

CHAPTER FOURTEEN

BURKE LYMON HAD made his money on a pile of thrillers, the sort that Joe Bob Briggs, drive-in movie critic, delighted in. An element of the supernatural usually tempted the obedient and virtuous and punished the rebellious and oversexed. The themes were consistent: You pay for your sins. *Lucifer's Shadow*, though, was the first to feature a true demon as the central character, and further, one that triumphed over good.

Merging onto the Hollywood Freeway, Queenie listened with increasing contempt to the bulletins interrupting the country-western radio station. It wasn't so much the breaks into the songs but the sensational messages they relayed that bothered her: Burke Lymon had finally paid for his cinemagraphic association with that earthbound terror variously know as the devil, Satan, Lucifer, the Prince of Darkness. . . .

If there is such an entity, he must be delighting in the free publicity, she thought.

She pulled off the freeway at the Barham exit. She crossed Barham to Lankershim Boulevard but did not go directly to the office. Like nearly everyone involved, Selma Steinberg was a suspect, albeit a weak one—what motive would a devoted employee have to destroy such a lucrative meal ticket? Still, Queenie used caution.

She parked at the all-night restaurant on the west side of Lankershim. Through the rear window, she examined the arc-shaped shopping arcade across the street.

A number of expensive European cars were clustered outside the Casting Couch, the red and blue lights above the bar's door staining the shiny hoods. Opposite the bar, the Clean and Dry Laundromat was still open, but no one was spending a Saturday night engaging the machines. Both the dental clinic and Hawaiian shirt store were closed. In the center of the communal courtyard was a small Spanish-style fountain. Selma was pacing alone in front of it, looking far more frightened than murderous.

Queenie reversed the Plymouth and at a break in traffic shot across the street. She parked in her favorite spot by the overhanging pepper tree.

From the glove compartment, Queenie took an aerosol can of Mace and slid it in her pocket. She owned a Smith & Wesson .45, but out of respect for the neighborhood vandals, she never left it in the car. If they ever broke in, they could do less harm with Mace than a gun. She hadn't carried the gun in over two years and then only when I.P. suggested it. At the moment, the .45 resided in a strongbox in her closet.

She stepped out of the car and locked it. The air had cooled at nightfall and she breathed deeply, somewhat refreshed by the tangy scent of pepper from the nearby trees.

But for the traffic on Lankershim, the constant rumble from the nearby highway, and the faint hum of music from the bar, it was relatively quiet.

Selma immediately stopped when Queenie entered the tiny courtyard. Since the drought, now officially ended, the water in the fountain hadn't been turned back on.

"Oh." Selma sighed and smiled wanly. "Thanks for coming."

"What's all this about?"

Selma explained as the two women approached the door where boxes were stacked. "I got home just a few minutes ago. After talking to that cop, I had to stop for a drink. Anyway, there was a message on my machine to call Mrs. Lymon."

Queenie remembered that Selma owned half of a duplex only a few blocks away. She always walked to work.

"So I called. She said she was afraid whoever killed Lymon might vandalize his offices, and she wanted *me* to come over! She'd send some people to cart the stuff away but she needed me to open up and start packing."

They each picked up boxes and stepped inside. Selma switched on the lights.

"I take it Mrs. Lymon doesn't have a key," Queenie commented.

"Just me and Lymon. Got these boxes from the Casting Couch. I don't know where in the hell she expected me to find them at this time of night," Selma said, her strained voice clearly edged with exasperation.

Selma moved out of the reception area and turned on the hall lights. Queenie followed. They passed the bathroom, an editing room, a screening room, and a small room that housed the free-standing custom-built refrigeration unit where raw stock, copies of all Lymon's films, batteries and such were kept, then entered the conference room at the end of the hall.

A long, scarred table where Lymon gathered his actors to informally read their parts, where preproduction work was discussed, and where Lymon wrote his scripts dominated the room. Papers littered the surface more or less leading to a neat stack beside a manual typewriter. Queenie glanced at the top sheet. At the top left margin of the page she read: FADE IN: WINDEMERE, 1620. Below followed the description of the opening scene, a witch-burning. Typical Burke Lymon stuff, she thought, and continued a quick examination of the room.

A cheap do-it-yourself computer desk, home to a personal computer and dot matrix printer, was against the wall at the end of the table. Along the left wall were bookshelves. On the opposite wall hung large sheets of newsprint segmented for storyboarding—sketching individual shots. Finally, beside a calendar displaying the copper sky of Cape Cod at sunset, the door to Lymon's private sanctum stood ajar.

"Would you mind packing books while I get my stuff together?" Selma asked as she took a green plastic box from the computer desk.

"Whatever," Queenie mumbled while thinking, If Emma Schultz's tarot cards had said I'd be in Lymon's office packing his books instead of getting bombed at the postpremiere party, I'd have never believed them. What had Emma said? *Death's in the cards.* Next time maybe she'd listen.

Lymon owned a decent occult library. Queenie pulled out several volumes by Arthur Edward Waite and Eliphas Levi and put them in the box, then moved down to an area of greater interest to her, Lymon's film books.

Somewhat reluctantly, she began packing them, wondering if perhaps Mrs. Lymon would sell them to her. After nearly filling two boxes, she came across a worn copy of *Independent Film-making* by Lenny Lipton. She pulled it off the shelf and riffled the pages. Nostalgia tweaked her. She remembered the day she'd given her own well-worn copy to another film student. She recalled feeling like some aging wizard reluctantly passing on a priceless alchemical manual to a young apprentice.

On impulse, she dropped the book in her satchel. Hell, she thought. Why not? Mrs. Lymon wouldn't miss it. Let the master pass the book on to another apprentice—even if indirectly.

Queenie filled two boxes then carried them out to the hall, not wanting them carted away with the others. The theft wouldn't matter if she bought the lot.

Before resuming her task, she stopped at the door to Lymon's sanctum and peeked inside. It would be her last opportunity to see how Lymon had lived the last week of his life.

Just inside the door was a brass lamp on an end table. She turned it on and entered. In the past, her familiarity with the room extended only to brief glances from a seat at the conference table.

The room was small and intimate, a comfortable bachelor's den furnished simply and tastefully. There was a sofa/hide-a-bed, a coffee table, another end table, and a cracked oxblood leather armchair much like her own.

Across the room beneath a large oil painting of a cold, gray seascape was a well-stocked drinks cart and an adjacent closet. The only items missing were an Irish setter and a fireplace, the one stretched out on a hooked rug in front of the other.

She didn't think his films represented the man, nor his estate in Palm Isle. But this room seemed to. There were no pretentious photographs of Lymon shaking hands with the rich and famous, just that single painting. She crossed the room and examined it. On the surface, it looked like nothing more than rocks piled at the edge of a gloomy sea. But on closer inspection, the color variances and individual textures emerged, giving each rock a separate and deeper existence. The simple irony of the painting suddenly struck her: That individual being is so easily disguised by a façade of familiar form; that, from a distance, things look alike. She sensed that Lymon often sat and stared at the painting. What sort of images did it evoke for him? Then, she wondered, was Lymon's killer disguised by familiarity?

In small, precise letters at the bottom right-hand corner she found the artist's signature, the single name, Holly, and made a mental note of it.

She peeked in the closet. Along with Lymon's familiar working wardrobe—jeans and T-shirts—were slacks and dress shirts, a set of undistinguished Samsonite luggage with the JFK-to-LAX tags still on the grips, a basket of dirty clothes, and a Harrods bag containing expensive cashmere sweaters that appeared to have never been worn. On the shelf were pillows and a comforter.

She closed the door and examined the bottles on the drinks cart. The seals were broken on all of them. They represented either someone with an eclectic taste in alcoholic beverages or someone who entertained. Did Lymon have a vodka friend, a bourbon friend, a brandy friend, and so on? Or were those bottles simply facets of the man's own varied tastes? There was no Scotch. Queenie lifted the lid of a silver ice bucket and tested the inch or so of water inside. It was warm. The glasses beside it were clean and dry. Presumably Lymon hadn't mixed himself a drink before leaving for the theater.

She knew Lymon kept all his personal files in this room but saw no cabinets of any kind. Keeping in mind his secretive nature, Queenie glanced around the room thoughtfully, finally moving to the center of what appeared to be a solidly paneled wall. Under the slight pressure of her questing fingers, two doors snapped open to reveal a solid line of file cabinets, ten in all, a total of forty drawers.

Some of the drawers must contain detailed files on the cast and crew members who had worked on Lymon's films: their special abilities, habits, foibles, personal lives, and residences since the age of eighteen. Queenie had sometimes thought that getting a job with Burke Lymon would qualify anyone for at least a "secret" clearance. She had compiled a number of those files herself both before she'd been hired as script super and during her tenure as such. Possibly something in these files could point to whoever had killed her boss. The rest of the drawers, she surmised, probably held Lymon's scripts, research notes, and personal files.

She was about to reach for the drawer marked *Lucifer's Shadow—Cast* when Selma charged into the room.

"Queenie! Get out!" Selma grabbed her arm and pulled her back to the bookshelves, where she shoved an occult book into her hand. Then she spun around just as a man entered. Queenie turned and recognized him as Mrs. Lymon's chauffeur.

"Who's this?" he demanded.

"A—a friend of mine," Selma stammered. "I was scared to be here alone what with an ax murderer loose and Mrs. Lymon telling me she was afraid the murderer might—"

"All right, all right," he interrupted, and led two Hispanic men into Lymon's den. Both pulled dollies. "She can leave. We'll take care of everything now."

"Go!" Selma hissed in her ear, taking the book back, dropping it in a box, and shoving Queenie toward the door. "I'll meet you at the Casting Couch."

Selma was certainly acting strangely—she'd been so glad to see her before and now was so glad to see her leave. The "strange," though, was rapidly becoming commonplace.

A glowing cigarette machine greeted her in the dark-paneled alcove entrance to the bar. Immediately to her left was a black vinyl couch on which reclined a mannequin wearing only a wide-brimmed hat and sunglasses, unless you counted the autographs tattooing the body. Above the couch and its resident, a wide window overlooked the parking lot. Queenie paused to read a couple of the unnoteworthy signatures then moved around a partition into the bar.

Clusters of men in business suits and a few women in cheap cocktail dresses sat in the red vinyl booths and around small tables. The men appeared to be older executives from nearby Universal Studios, those preferring *not* to be seen. White lattices choked with dusty plastic ivy separated the booths. A dance floor large enough to accommodate a couple of pairs of shoes was pressed against the back wall. Beside it squatted an illuminated jukebox now belching a vapid '70s disco tune.

Figuring the phone must be in back, Queenie hurried around the bar.

"Hey!" the woman bartender called out. "This isn't a public toilet."

"A beer, please. Kirin if you have it," she said without stopping.

"No Jap beer. Becks, Heineken—"

"Heineken," Queenie said, swallowing her irritation.

The pay phone separated the sexes in the back of the bar, "Producers" to the left, "Starlets" to the right. Queenie amended the designations to "Weenies" and "Women" as she dropped in her quarter and called the hospital. She gave the duty nurse the number of the pay phone and asked to be called if there was a change in Rex's condition. The conversation lasted barely half a minute, accompanied by strident screams coming from the emergency room.

At least Rex got in before the rush, Queenie thought ruefully as she slid onto the nearest stool.

The bartender approached with a bottle, her thin blond hair the texture of cotton candy. Too many home perms in forty plus years, Queenie thought, still peeved. Since Dick had entered her heart, she took exception to the term "Jap."

"A friend'll be joining me in a few minutes. I'd like to run a tab."

"No tabs."

"Fine." Queenie pulled a ten from her wallet and handed it over. She noticed there was no television. "You work nights?" she asked when the bartender brought her change.

"It's night, isn't it?"

"I'm wondering if you've noticed anyone visit Hammon Productions after hours this week."

"You checking up on somebody?"

"Burke Lymon. You know him?" She thought about shocking the surly woman with the news of the murder but didn't really want to unless she had to.

"Look, if you're trying to get discovered, go hang out on Hollywood Boulevard."

"I'm interested in information, not insults," she replied evenly, no longer concerned about sparing the woman's feelings. "Burke Lymon was murdered tonight."

The woman's face turned the shade of her hair. At that moment, Selma entered, on the verge of tears. She ordered a double Scotch and a pack of cigarettes, then said to Queenie, "Let's get a table."

Queenie picked up her beer and all of the change. Never tip

anyone who insults you. She joined Selma at an isolated table near the front.

"I thought you quit smoking," Queenie said when they were both seated.

"Three years ago," Selma replied matter-of-factly, then glanced around the room. "You know, I've never been in this place until tonight."

"Neo-sleaze," Queenie commented. "Did Lymon come in here much?"

"Sometimes for ice," she said absently. "All these years working just a few feet away, and I've never been in here. . . . Did you know I grew up in Washington, D.C.?"

"No."

"No, you wouldn't know that. I was here long before you started doing Lymon's background checks. . . . Lived in D.C. till I was twenty-one. And you know what? I never went to any of the memorials." She looked up. "Think I might have gone to the Smithsonian—only because some teacher dragged me there on a field trip." She shook her head.

"The Casting Couch isn't exactly a national monument, Selma."

"No, but you see what I'm saying . . . taking things for granted, slaves to routine, missing ninety-nine percent of what's going on around us." She stopped and took a deep breath.

The bartender brought the drink, cigarettes, and change. She frowned at Queenie and then looked at Selma. "You work for Burke Lymon, don't you?"

"Yes," Selma said flatly.

"There's people taking stuff out of his office."

"I know. Please, just leave us alone," Selma said.

The bartender moved to the window to watch the movers.

Selma lit her cigarette with shaking hands. Then she downed

half her double Scotch. Queenie realized she was having a difficult time composing herself and waited.

"Got something for you," Selma finally said. With her cigarette dangling from her mouth, she reached into a large shopping bag.

Inside the bag, Queenie could see a fluffy sweater, a healthy ivy plant, a plain coffee mug, a box of Kotex, one of Kleenex, and a bottle of hand lotion.

"Two things actually," Selma amended. "Can you believe it? That bastard actually checked the shopping bag and my purse before I left? Hadn't had that done since I worked as a sales clerk at Garfinkle's ... but you know us black folk, we steal anything that ain't nailed down."

She pulled out the Kotex box and handed it to Queenie under the table. "Can you fit it in your purse?"

Queenie opened her bag wondering why Selma wanted to give her a box of sanitary napkins. "It's too big."

"Okay, then just take the six on the bottom." She scooted her chair around closer to Queenie's. "Here, let me do it."

She removed the first six pads, squeezing each one, and set them in her lap. The remaining six made crunching noises when pressed. These she gave to Queenie who, mystified, stuffed them into her purse. Then Selma pulled out computer disks that had been placed along the sides. Finally she returned the other pads to the box and dropped it back into the shopping bag.

"Thank God he didn't look in the Kotex box, but what man would?"

Queenie shuffled the disks. There were ten, each labeled with a number and a short list of film titles.

"Put them away," Selma hissed, and turned around as if expecting the chauffeur to enter and make a citizen's arrest.

Queenie tucked the disks in her satchel, eager to know what stolen goods had just joined the Lenny Lipton book.

Selma moved her chair back to the opposite side of the table. "First," she began, "no one knows about that stuff except you and me. The disks contain the personnel files for almost everyone who ever worked for him. Lymon finally got me a computer, and I've spent the better part of this year transferring information in the files onto disks. You compiled a lot of the info yourself, but there's still plenty from before you did his background checks." She suddenly jerked forward. "You do have a computer, don't you?"

"Sure. An IBM PC," she said, wondering what exactly Selma was leading up to.

"What program do you use?"

Queenie named a popular word processing program.

Selma heaved a great sigh. "Great! Everything's compatible. And you won't have any trouble with the file names. They're pretty self-explanatory."

"You want me to go through the disks, right?"

"I'm hoping you'll go further than that. In each pad is a thousand dollars."

"What?" Had she heard correctly?

"Lymon always kept 'emergency' money in the office. Remember, he pretty much lived here several months out of the year. And before he'd leave to go on location, or like this summer when he went to New York, he'd up the ante a couple grand, in case I suddenly needed cash. Hiding it in sanitary pads was his idea—said he'd had a patient once who hid money that way in case she ever wanted to run away."

Queenie pulled out a notebook and, rather than interrupt, jotted down *patient* and *run away*, making a mental note to question Selma more fully about this. She wished she'd thought to bring a tape recorder, especially since her hand shook. She'd never had six thousand dollars in her purse. Had the Goddess really been listening?

"Well, this is an emergency," Selma continued. "I want you to find his killer." She glanced down at her lap. When she looked up again, her eyes were pleading. "You're the best person for the job. You have your investigator's license; you know everyone. Please, Queenie! I can't bear to think of Lymon as just another unsolved murder in the police files. If that's not enough, I've got savings."

Queenie forced herself to stay calm. Six *thousand* dollars. "One thing though, wouldn't Frances Lymon know about this money? It's a lot of cash, Selma."

"Hell, she doesn't know diddly about the office. Why do think she had to call me to open up? Only Lymon and I had keys—you don't hand out passes to your sanctuary, except to the caretaker. And anyway, even if she did suspect there was some money around, what's she gonna do if she thinks I took it? Fire me?"

"She could tell the cops."

Selma shook her head. "Huh-uh. That lady doesn't like cops. If she's that scared of somebody vandalizing the office, why didn't she call the cops in the first place? There's a crazed killer loose and she calls me and sends over her chauffeur and a couple of her underfed Mexican gardeners."

Selma shook her head again, adding quietly "All those years and not so much as a 'thank you.'" Then she straightened. "Anyway, consider yourself working for Lymon. It's really his money."

Both women were quiet for a moment as Queenie absorbed this most welcome development. Then: Get on with it, Davilov, she told herself.

"So, Selma. How long have you worked for Lymon?"

"Fifteen years next month," she said, her voice faint. She suddenly looked tired.

Queenie leaned forward. "Look, Selma, maybe we should just finish our drinks and talk tomorrow. Go home and get some sleep."

"Sleep? Are you kidding?" She stood up. "Order me another drink. I just need a minute to get myself together." She started toward the rest room then pointed a finger at Queenie. "Time you started earning your pay, girl!"

Queenie moved back to the bar and ordered another round.

"Like I said before, seen anyone visit Hammon Productions this past week?" Queenie asked while the bartender filled the order. This time she'd shown her investigator's I.D.—which she should have done in the first place, but it had been a while since she'd needed to.

"He was really murdered?" the woman asked contritely.

"You can read about it tomorrow."

The woman placed the drinks on the bar and leaned close, lowering her voice. "Usually gets dull in here after about eleven o'clock." She nodded toward the occupied tables. "When those guys go home to the wife and kids."

"Go on."

"Well, sometimes there's nothing to do except stare out the window. I mean, this must be the only bar in L.A. without a TV."

"Go on."

She studiously avoided Queenie's eyes. "It's not like I spy on people or anything. Okay, Monday night this girl goes into his office. I recognized her from the ads in *Variety* for *Lucifer's Shadow*. Blonde—"

"I know who she is," Queenie interrupted. It had to be

Nessa. Out of the corner of her eye, she saw Selma return to the table, a tissue wadded in her hand.

"Well, she went into his office around eleven-thirty. Left about fifteen minutes later."

"That's all? Anyone with her?"

"Well, there was a guy. They were on a motorcycle. He didn't go in."

"Can you describe him?"

"Dark hair, kinda big. Didn't see his face, his back was to me. He just stayed on the cycle smoking a cigarette."

Queenie remembered that L.D. both smoked and owned a motorcycle. As part of the insurance policy taken out on the actors, he'd had to agree not to ride it until his work on the film was completed.

"Were you aware that she'd been reported missing?"

"Hell, I figured it was some publicity stunt. Her being around pretty well proved it—to me, anyway."

"Do you know who L. D. Barth is?"

"Yeah, he's her costar."

"Was he the man on the motorcycle?"

She shrugged. "Couldn't say. You know, guy had his back to me."

Queenie picked up the bartender's pen and wrote her name and phone number on a napkin. "Call me if you remember anything else."

She returned to the table with the drinks.

"I need to know everything you can tell me about Lymon," Queenie began as she pulled out her chair and sat down.

"Sure. Where do you want to start?"

"How about the beginning? And I want to know *everything*."

CHAPTER FIFTEEN

SELMA LIT ANOTHER cigarette, taking a moment to assemble her thoughts. She inhaled deeply then began.

"When I first got to town, I registered with a temp agency. I'd been traveling around for quite a while and wasn't really sure where I wanted to settle down. Well, my first assignment was with Lymon. He was a bachelor then and lived in an apartment in West Hollywood. I worked in a tiny room off the kitchen. My job was only scheduled for two weeks—just to get the production company set up. So, after two weeks I left and took another assignment." She paused to sip her drink.

"Well, about six months go by and the agency sends me back to Lymon. He'd requested me. His first picture, *The Necromancer*, had been released—he'd made it in something like twelve days—and he was actually making some money.

"He asked if I'd consider quitting the agency and working for him full time. He said conditions would improve when he had the money to lease an office. Of course, I said yes. Frankly, I was a bit hooked on him myself."

"What about his social life? Did he have any trouble with creditors?" Queenie asked.

"None that I know of. He always paid his bills first then he bought food. That apartment was studio, office, living quarters. He was very conservative where money was concerned. As for socializing, he was a workaholic, just like now." She froze a bit after saying "now."

"Where was he from?"

"Back east, I think. But he never talked about his past—family, school, or personal life. It's kind of funny since he wanted to know everything about the people who worked for him. It must be a kind of control thing. But it sure made him a good director. In fifteen years I never heard one person bitch about working with him. Actors, crew, no one. That's why it's so hard to believe . . . who in the hell could have killed him?"

"You mentioned a patient before."

"It was a long time ago, when we first moved into the offices."

"How long ago?" Queenie asked.

"Oh, gosh," Selma said, rolling her eyes toward the ceiling. "Must have been about two years after I started with him—thirteen years ago. That's when he brought in the box of Kotex and emergency money."

"So, thirteen years ago you moved into these offices and he mentioned once having a patient who secreted money in Kotex pads, but he didn't say anything more about that."

"Right. It was such a bizarre thing for him to say. I mean, he was never a doctor of any kind; I asked him. But he wouldn't say anymore about it. Except that the patient kept the money to run away. You think it's important?"

"Everything that tells us something about Lymon is important. For one thing, people don't normally plan on running away from hospitals. They might if they're institutionalized."

"Like in an asylum?"

"Hmm."

"You think some crazy got loose and came after him?" she asked excitedly.

"Selma, we could speculate all night. Just tell me what you know, any little detail you can remember."

"Okay."

Queenie began to roll a cigarette as she waited for Selma to continue. When she finished she noticed Selma appeared to be a thousand miles away.

"Selma?"

"Huh? Oh. I was just thinking about his bio, the one that goes in the press kits."

"Yeah?"

"Well, there's nothing to it, just his credits."

"How about the very first one?"

"It had bio sketches of the actors and a synopsis of the film. Nothing about Lymon except that he was an independent producer. With each update, we simply added the last film. His bio's just a list of films."

Queenie lit her cigarette. "What about money?"

"Lymon's always been careful with money, always goes after the best deal. I don't think his wife's that way."

Queenie remembered what Mrs. Lymon had said in her own defense to Lieutenant Fitzgerald: *"I have my own money. . . ."*

"She independently wealthy?"

Selma shrugged. "I really don't know. A lot of secretaries are friends with their boss's wife. I sure can't claim that kind of relationship. Take last week . . . she comes in on Friday afternoon with two shopping bags. Said she'd been in England and had some gifts for Lymon and would I give them to him. I mean, surely she knew he was coming back from New York on Sunday. Why not just wait and give him the gifts herself? And she calls me *Miss!* 'Excuse me, Miss . . . would you give these things to Mr. Lymon?' Hell, we've known each other since she and Lymon got married! After ten years, you'd think she'd use my first name."

"Did you happen to look in the bags?"

Selma regarded Queenie sheepishly. "Is it important?"

"Selma, I just said everything's important."

"There were some beautiful sweaters, some things from Dunhill, and several bottles of duty-free liquor."

"Any Scotch?"

Selma thought for a moment. "Yeah. Johnnie Walker Red, I think."

"Was the seal broken?"

"I don't think so."

"Can you be certain?"

"Actually, yes. He'd asked me to restock his bar before he got back since he was coming straight from the airport. So, instead of going out to buy anything, I just put out what she'd brought. None of them had been opened."

"Does he usually drink Scotch?"

"He drinks all kinds. I know he prefers vodka when he's writing a script, bourbon when he finishes. He always takes Johnnie Walker Red to the premieres."

"Has Mrs. Lymon been in this week?"

"Not while I've been in the office, which has been every day but today."

Queenie thought for a moment. Then she asked, "Did Lymon say anything to you about filing for divorce?" She expected a negative answer since Lymon didn't discuss his personal life with Selma. Still, she had to ask.

Selma's eyes widened. "Wow! That's the first I've heard about it."

"Did he talk to Phil Sykes?"

Selma suddenly perked. "Now we might be on to something." She leaned forward. "Phil Sykes is history. Lymon dropped him—or whatever they do to lawyers."

"How do you know?"

"Well, Tuesday, I think it was, he told me we wouldn't be doing any more business with Phil Sykes and for me to take his card off the Rolodex."

"Did he mention a new law firm?"

"No."

"If the rumor's true, I wonder who he planned on using," Queenie mused. "So he didn't say anything about a divorce?"

Selma shook her head. "But it's funny. Several times this week he acted like he wanted to tell me something. When I asked if something was wrong, he'd just look away and shake his head."

"Did he go home at all?"

"If he did it was in the evening and he came back. I've been waking him up every morning. Where'd you hear about a divorce?"

"A friend of mine heard from her hairdresser, Gabriel Tak," she said. If and when Selma discovered that Joey worked for Arthur Favor, she wouldn't be too pleased with Queenie for bringing her to the premiere. At the moment, it was best to avoid any ancillary complications.

Selma lowered her voice, becoming conspiratorial. "Queenie, Reeves Holloway goes to him—hell, she's the one who made Gabriel famous. Christ! You know what I think? I'll bet good money Phil said something about a divorce to Reeves, probably to get her in bed, and Reeves passed it on to Gabriel. Now, I don't put great stock in rumors, but you do know how word spreads in this town, often from a point of truth. It sounds like Phil too. He'd use confidential information to get a woman in bed. And from what I hear, it would have to be pretty sensational to get Reeves Holloway between the sheets. Cold? That woman could hire herself out as air-conditioning."

"Well, it would seem that Lymon and Phil Sykes parted friends. Otherwise, why would Phil come to the premiere?"

"He had an invitation. I know because I mailed them all. Of course, bringing Reeves was something of a stab in the back. Phil knows as well as anyone how much Lymon loathes professional gossips."

Ribald laughter from a nearby table drew their attention momentarily. Two buxom women in low-cut dresses were squirming awkwardly in their chairs while their male companions tossed dimes at them. The women jerked their arms, slapping their breasts together to catch the coins.

"Everybody's gotta make a living some way," Selma said with a sigh. "Which reminds me. I'm unemployed."

Queenie grabbed her satchel. "Look. Why don't you keep this money."

Selma propelled herself across the table, jerking the satchel from under her friend's nose. "Put that away! That money's to fry Lymon's murderer. No more about that." Then she sat back more calmly, straightening her clothes.

Queenie lowered her bag. "Okay. But if I find out you got a job catching dimes between your tits . . ."

They both laughed, then got back to business.

"What do you know about Nessa?" Queenie asked, wondering if Selma knew anything about the late-night visit last week.

"Hell, you could answer that one better than me. You were on location with her."

"Well, how was she hired? We both know I didn't do her background."

Selma took a drink and sat back, ruminating for a moment, her eyes shifting off to the left. "It was all very ordinary—which makes it weird. What I mean is, she came in with him one day, he introduces us—first names only: 'Selma, I'd like you to meet Nessa; Nessa, this is Selma.' He asked me to bring them some coffee then they went back to his sanctum."

Queenie waited for more.

"That's it?" she finally asked.

Selma shrugged. "That's it."

"When was this?"

"Sometime after New Year's."

"What was your impression of her?"

Selma's face suddenly brightened. "I remember now," she said, more to herself. "When I took them the coffee, I remember thinking they were hiding something. . . ." She trailed off.

"Like they were lovers?"

Selma frowned. "I don't know. Maybe. It was like they shared a secret or a private joke. I don't know. . . . Wait a minute! He asked me to get the key for the house in Castaic, the one used as a set in *Neptune in Scorpio*."

"Was he renting it to her? I mean, he rented it to L.D. when we got back from Inverness."

"No, I think she was just going to stay out there until you went on location."

"Did she ever come to the office in the evening, say just before you went home?"

"As far as I know, she only came to read with the other actors."

"And you haven't seen her this summer?"

"Queenie, I haven't seen that girl, in the flesh, that is, since you all went on location at the end of March."

"But you're not here at night, right?"

"Rarely past five. And since Lymon's been in New York, I come and go pretty much as I please." She paused. "Now I wonder. Those stories about her disappearing with L. D. Barth sort of take on a new meaning."

"How so?"

"I don't know. Maybe something really happened to her . . . to both of them."

Queenie brought the conversation around to the past week, asking about Lymon's visitors and who may have spent time in his den.

"There were a lot of phone calls—requests for interviews, people wanting tickets to the premiere, the usual crap. And, of course, that poor animal came in the mail."

"Was Lymon his usual self when he returned from New York? What was his mood? You said he acted like he wanted to tell you something. And why New York when it would be cheaper just to do postproduction work here?"

Selma lifted her shoulders in an eloquent shrug. "I don't have a clue why he chose New York. Maybe he was scouting locations or taking a working vacation. As to your other question, every once in a while he'd kind of stare at me and just when I'd think he was about to tell me something, he'd stop himself. But he was always preoccupied and distracted before a film's about to be released. I don't know, though, there was something funny about it this time."

Queenie noted Selma's eyes becoming heavy, her speech more deliberate as if she were straining to both think and speak. It was probably a combination of shock and the alcohol, and time to draw the evening to a close. "Maybe you're just reading more into it since I mentioned the divorce rumor."

"No, I don't think so. I think something happened to him in New York."

"Like what?"

"I really wouldn't know."

"What about an itinerary, the hotel where he stayed?"

Selma's expression lifted a bit. "Damn, why didn't I think of that?" She dug into her purse and brought out a leather business diary, then flipped through the pages. She stopped. "Here it is."

Queenie jotted down the hotel's phone number and area code and was about to return the notebook and pen to her satchel prior to leaving when Selma said, "Oh, and here's another one he gave me." She read out the numbers, closed her diary, and stuck it in her purse.

"Maybe you could call them," she said. "You never know, Lymon's killer might have followed him from New York."

"Selma. This area code's different."

"What?"

Queenie turned the notebook around. "The two numbers. The area codes are different. What's the second number for?"

Selma bent over, squinting at the notebook, fatigue obviously overtaking her. "Huh. You're right." She reopened her diary.

"What's the second number for, Selma? Another hotel in another state?"

Selma sighed. "There's no hotel name. Just the number."

Queenie put her notebook away.

Selma started to gather her things, obviously not wanting to stay and continue drinking. "I'm beat, Queenie. Maybe I'll be of more help after I get some rest. Now I think I can sleep."

Queenie considered using the pay phone to call information for the location of the second area code but figured it could wait. The bar's atmosphere was getting to her.

"You know what I think, Queenie," Selma said as she rose from her chair. "I think Amanda Martin might have done it. I told that lieutenant about the squirrel. Amanda's just spooky enough to murder someone." Then she frowned.

"What is it, Selma?"

"What about Alice?"

"How do you mean?"

"Maybe she saw or heard something."

"Well, we won't know until she regains consciousness. She was hit over the head with a piece of pipe. The police found her in the projection booth."

"Oh, Jesus!" Then: "Why would the killer bother with Alice? Why go up to the projection booth?"

"The only likely reason would be if he used the fire escape off the projection booth to gain entry into the theater."

"That must be it!" Selma said, visibly relieved. "That means none of us did it! I mean, no one at the premiere."

"Alice was acting weird, though. Did you see her serving drinks?"

"Oh, that. She was running late. Apparently her car's giving her fits. Just after I arrived, Lymon lent her his car so she could go over to the restaurant and check on things for the party. I could have gone, but you know Alice—doesn't trust anyone. Got to take care of things herself."

They passed the autographed mannequin. In the dim light of the cigarette machine, Selma looked exhausted. Emotional trauma could really play havoc with body and mind; one minute you were rocketing on adrenaline, the next feeling you were encased in concrete.

They stepped outside and stood for a moment watching the Hispanic men, supervised by the chauffeur, loading the pickup.

"They'll probably have to make several trips," Queenie commented, remembering Lymon's books.

"I certainly hope so. In fact, I hope they're up all night," Selma replied acidly.

"Want a ride?"

"Nah. The walk'll do me good." She took a deep breath. "Best thing about this town is the night air. Even the wind's died down." She squeezed Queenie's arm. "Talk to you soon."

Queenie walked slowly toward her car, taking a moment to study the chauffeur. He now wore work clothes though he didn't do any of the work. All he did was a lot of unnecessary pointing and gesturing. Busy as bees, the two workmen largely ignored him. The chauffeur, she thought, appeared too ineffectual to be a successful murderer. Still, you never knew.

She stopped a few feet behind him.

"Excuse me," she said.

The chauffeur spun around, startled—and frightened. The blue and red neon lights from the bar distorted his features.

"What do you want?" he snapped, his voice high-pitched.

"Actually, I was wondering what Mrs. Lymon plans to do with Lymon's things, his books in particular. I was her husband's script supervisor."

"Oh. Sorry," he said. "Guess I'm a little jumpy. . . . Uh, she just wants his stuff in a safe place."

His eyes darted toward the darkness where Queenie's car was parked, as if expecting an ax-wielding maniac to jump out of the trees and bushes.

"I'm interested in buying his books."

"Well, you'll have to talk to her. Now isn't a very good time though."

"Of course. Well, thanks."

She memorized the license plate number and jotted it down when she was in the car.

During the drive home, she wondered if fear of vandalism had really prompted the raid on Hammon Productions. Or was Mrs. Lymon afraid of something else? Something in Lymon's files?

sunday

 QUEENIE JERKED AWAKE, the phone by the bed blaring. The firey apparitions in her dream vanished into the abyss of sleep as she grabbed the receiver. It was Rex, sounding bruised and edgy.

"They're letting me out."

"Great! I'll be right over."

"No. Some cop's bringing me."

"When?"

"I'll call before we leave. Bye."

Queenie hung up and glanced at the clock. It was seventhirty. He didn't sound good but at least he was coming home.

In the kitchen, she prepped the coffeemaker then went into the living room and switched on the VCR. While the tape rewound, she stared out the window. The HOLLYWOOD sign stared back. The sky was almost blue. Less traffic on Sundays meant less smog.

When the tape was ready, she watched last night's news.

The female newscaster who'd been first on the scene opened the late broadcast live from the theater. The crowd had been contained but by no means dispersed. Behind police barricades gawkers watched the theater, some jumping up and down, waving at the camera. From there the scene cut back and forth between those happily arriving at the premiere and those leaving stunned, tearful, and some, terrified. Reeves Holloway and Phil Sykes had been left on the cutting room floor. At least for now.

Footage of Queenie being pelted by Amanda Martin's tomatoes had been left out too in favor of more poignant footage of Mrs. Lymon arriving at the theater match-cut to her departure with Queenie and the policewoman on either arm. Queenie replayed the sequence, not because it was her first appearance on TV, but to look at Mrs. Lymon. There was something different about her. Queenie replayed it again. What had changed? But maybe it was simply the obvious: Her husband was alive when she arrived and dead when she left. Still, something else seemed—

The phone rang. She turned off the VCR and answered in the study.

"On my way, sis."

"Great. I'll meet you downstairs."

With a few minutes before his arrival, she cleaned up the desk. Having locked the money in her strong box the previous night, she threw away the "empty" Kotex pads, in the process uncovering the Lenny Lipton book. She now doubted her chances of seeing the rest of Burke Lymon's film books again. It would be insensitive to bother Mrs. Lymon about them at the moment, and anyway, the widow would likely donate them to some institution, either the American Film Institute or a university.

As she casually flipped through the book, about to shelve it with her other film books, she found a gold sticker on the flipside of the cover: HAROLD'S CINEMA BOOKS, BOSTON, MASSACHUSETTS. Burke Lymon's signature was beneath it.

Instead of shelving it, she left the book out. On her way downstairs she paired that information with Rex's revelation last night that Lymon was a Red Sox fan.

Rex arrived shortly thereafter with, to her surprise, Lieutenant Fitzgerald, who practically begged for a cup of coffee.

The three of them jammed together in the elevator. Both Rex and J.P. seemed severely depressed. And J.P. obviously hadn't slept. The small space quickly filled with the men's sour smell, overpowering her own.

"How do you feel?" Queenie asked her brother as the elevator began its shaky ascent.

"Like I've been run hard and put away wet."

"Got hold of some methaqualone," the lieutenant said. "That plus the Scotch could have put him in a coma."

"Quaaludes," Queenie muttered. "That was fast."

"Figured the sooner we knew what knocked him out, the sooner he'd get the proper treatment. Sent that cup you gave me and a vomit sample straight to the lab . . . truth is, I took a 'lude once—before I was a cop. Talk about the living dead. Anyway, on a hunch, I told the lab boys to run the test for methaqualone first. Bingo. They called the results into the hospital."

"Thanks so much, J.P." She had done the right thing in calling him, at least for her brother's sake.

He blushed suddenly, like blood flashing beneath gray ice.

Then he looked pointedly at Rex. "Yeah, well, the question is where did he get it? That bottle of Scotch is clean. So far, *nada*. No methaqualone anyway."

"Look," Rex said coldly, "I told you I haven't even taken painkillers lately. And I'm not dumb enough to do horse tranqs and alcohol. Besides, how did it get in my Coke?"

"We'll have to wait for Burke Lymon's tox report. If there's a match—"

"Then the bottle was switched," Queenie interrupted.

At that moment, the elevator jerked to a stop, throwing them all forward.

Once in her apartment, Rex excused himself to take a shower. Queenie poured coffee and took it into the living room.

"Thanks for looking out for my brother," she said.

"Seems like a good kid."

"He *is* a good kid."

"And the last person seen with the victim."

Queenie stiffened. "He met Burke Lymon for the first time last night."

"*And* he found the body."

"Hey, you just said you know firsthand about the effects of Quaaludes."

"And you gave me that cup—won't know whose it was until I can match the prints. Maybe he spiked Burke Lymon's drink and the cups got mixed up."

"That's ridiculous! You're just hot to make an arrest." At least J.P. had brought Rex home instead of taking him into the station.

"Davilov, everyone I talked to last night said Burke Lymon did not drink with people during his premieres. So why drink with your brother?"

"Lymon was a Red Sox fan. Maybe he felt sorry for my brother, having his season ruined by the broken wrist."

"Maybe they knew each other in Boston."

Queenie stood up wanting no more of this conversation. "I really appreciate what you did and for bringing him home—"

"Sit down, Davilov." He didn't budge, regarded her wearily. "The reason I'm here . . . I talked to Alice Baldridge."

Queenie sat back down. "Oh. How is she?"

"Mild concussion. She's been released. Anyway, she said we should talk to you."

"Oh? About what?"

"L. D. Barth. His name came up again—on the murder weapon."

"Holy Mother," she mumbled. "Did Alice see him last night?"

"No. I just asked her what she knew about him."

"Did you tell her his name was on the ax?"

"Of course not." He snorted and lit a cigarette. "And don't you mention it to anyone either. She told me you continued doing Burke Lymon's background checks even after you were hired as his script supervisor. That you'd know about him."

"Hold on," she said, leaving the room. She turned on the computer and, from the disks Selma had given her, inserted the one labeled *Lucifer's Shadow*. The remaining disks she put in the bottom desk drawer.

In the directory she found TAL (for talent) and called the file on screen, scrolling down until she came to Barth, L. D. Then she called the lieutenant. He peered over her shoulder at the computer screen.

After the personal and credit references came the information that L.D. had a criminal record. While playing rugby for the Denver Barbarians, L. D. Barth had once severely beaten a competitor after a game, even biting off half his ear. L.D. might not have served time except that the man he throttled was the son of a United States senator.

"God, a rugby player. The guy's into violence." J.P. eyed Queenie pointedly. She knew he was waiting for her to take the bait; she'd played the game in college, used to wear her old red and white jersey to bed when they were lovers.

Ignoring his comment, she went on, "And this happened over six years ago. He was only twenty-one."

"Why would Burke Lymon hire an ex-con?"

"He's a good actor. And charismatic. A hot combination of sensuality and intelligence. J.P., a number of well-known actors are ex-cons." She recalled her own attraction to L.D., sensing that he was a person of destiny—but she'd thought in terms of the big screen, not the big house.

J.P. reached across Queenie and paged down. Several dates and addresses in Hollywood and Santa Monica appeared on screen.

"He still at this last address?" J.P. asked, pointing to the one in Santa Monica.

"No. He's up north—"

J.P. jerked back. "Then why isn't that information on here?"

"J.P., I did the background check last October, before he got the part." No more coffee for you, she thought.

He eased a little. "Okay, where does he live now?"

"Up north in Castaic. Lymon rented him the house used as a set in the picture before *Lucifer's Shadow*. Hammon Productions owns it. Lymon doesn't always pay well but he does— did—provide certain perks. Alice could have told you. Everybody knew he'd moved up there."

"You got a phone number and address?"

Queenie reached for her satchel and removed her address

book. The lieutenant picked up the phone and called in the information on L.D. with an order to have the actor's prints faxed from Colorado. After covering the speaker, he said to her, "If his prints match those on the ax, we've got our man."

"Then you can get off my brother's back," she retorted. With that she rose and went to check on Rex.

Queenie found him in her bedroom, propped against the pillows reading J.R.R. Tolkein's *The Two Towers*, Clue tucked against him. She was relieved that the cat had left the closet and, upon her first meeting with Rex, found him acceptable company.

"Hungry?" she asked.

He shook his head. "The lieutenant gave me a couple of his doughnuts."

"That's hardly breakfast." Still, she gave J.P. another star, though not gold, and sat on the end of the bed.

"Still reading the trilogy," she remarked. He was superstitious about those books, had been since she'd first read them to him when he played Little League. They'd become part of his baseball career. Good things happened while he read all but *The Two Towers*. And the rules decreed that he read them in sequence; he couldn't skip over the second volume.

"Don't poke fun, Queenie," he said defensively. "Wade Boggs eats chicken and look how many times he's been batting champ."

"I eat chicken and I've never been a batting champ."

Rex made a face. "You know what I mean. Two's my unlucky number."

The phone rang once, then stopped. J.P. must have answered it, Queenie thought.

She got up. "If you need anything, just ask." Rebutting someone with strong superstitions was a waste of time, especially a baseball player. Besides, she had a few superstitions of her own.

While returning to the study she envisioned Rex writing a master's thesis entitled "Tolkien and Baseball: The Effects of Hobbits and Wizards, Dragons and Dwarfs, Orcs and Elves on Slugging Percentages and Defensive Strategy."

CHAPTER SEVENTEEN

"Yeah, yeah, I heard. A tie. Fine." J.P. slammed down the receiver as Queenie entered the study.

A *tie?* "What's up?" she asked.

"Gotta go home and change. The frigging mayor wants to see me."

"Oh, there's something you ought to know," she said, taking her notebook out of the satchel. She gave him a brief account of last night's activity at Hammon Productions.

"Mrs. Lymon's concern's understandable but she should have called us," he said.

Queenie tore out the sheet of notebook paper on which she'd copied the license of the truck used to haul away Lymon's goods.

"You might want to pass that by the DMV, just to be certain that pickup came from Lymon's estate."

He smiled slightly. "Still playing detective."

Ignoring the remark, she brushed past him and went to open the front door.

"Oh, I took this," he said, waving the *Lucifer's Shadow* disk. "Don't get hot. I saved the information on your machine." He moved into the doorway, Dick's apartment behind him. "Look, I'll let you know when we bring in this Barth character."

"Question is, why would he kill Lymon on the biggest night of his career?"

He grunted. "You know how unstable actors are."

"But they're not stupid. That ax might have been stolen. Last night Billy Bright said *his* was stolen."

J.P. didn't seem interested. "Listen, your brother says he doesn't remember much about last night. Maybe you can get something out of him."

"If he says he doesn't, he doesn't."

"Try, Davilov. And I'll want you two to come in today or tomorrow and sign statements." He moved into the hall, then stopped. "I'm surprised," he said.

"At what?"

"The way you're living. You haven't changed." He seemed pleased.

She suddenly realized that was another reason for his appearance on her doorstep. Another officer could have driven Rex home and gotten the necessary information from Queenie. And J.P. could have simply telephoned. He wanted to see for himself if her life had improved since their breakup.

"Not everyone in this industry makes millions. I'm just a grunt."

When he'd gone she hurried back to the computer, peeved that he'd taken the disk. But he had saved the information. Then she reminded herself that they were both after the same thing—Burke Lymon's murderer.

There was still plenty of time before her ten o'clock meeting, "Sunday services at Callie's," as Vitch had said, so she called up Burke Lymon's file, BLM, and started entering thoughts as they came to her, to see what they added up to.

Boston Red Sox
office calendar—Cape Cod
painting—rocky seascape, artist "Holly"
Harold's Cinema Books—Boston
patient, run away (mental institution?)
Selma—works for Lymon 15 years
Married to Frances 10 years
Nessa and L.D. (?) at office Monday night—why?

Then she remembered the two phone numbers Selma had given her. She called information and learned that the second area code, 508, served Massachusetts. The operator hung up before she could ask what part. She knew 617 was the area code for Boston. She grabbed the phone book and discovered that 508 served central Massachusetts. So, Lymon had stayed in Massachusetts but not the Boston area.

She dialed the number, rehearsing what she'd say. She needn't have bothered. On the twelfth ring, she hung up. Had it been a hotel, surely someone would have answered. Maybe it was a bed-and-breakfast inn. But wouldn't they have an answering machine? She tried again, in case she'd misdialed the first time. Still no answer.

The call to the hotel in New York City merely confirmed Burke Lymon's stay from June through the first week in August. The manager added that Mr. Lymon had left for several days last week, returning a day before departing for L.A.

Then, using the disks Selma had given her, Queenie searched

for and found Amanda Martin's file, compiled five years ago by another P.I.

Like Susan Fry, Queenie's antagonist at Eric Diamond's, Amanda had a degree in film from USC, had even made several award-winning 16mm films before hiring on with Hammon Productions. Also noted was Amanda's live-in boyfriend, Greg Chapin, one of Hollywood's most daring stuntmen.

Queenie started. Two years ago, Greg Chapin and a debutante, the heiress to a canned goods empire, eloped only a few days after meeting at a party. Queenie remembered the uproar, mainly from prominent families who'd planned on *their* sons merging with the girl's fortune. Had Amanda been living with him then? Perhaps his sudden marriage had unhinged her and sent her rebounding toward her boss, Burke Lymon.

Amanda was nutty, maybe too nutty to commit a carefully planned and executed murder. Let the cops check her out, Queenie told herself; she would look elsewhere.

She located Billy Bright's file on another disk in the subdirectory for *Altar of Death*, a film Lymon produced six years ago. Billy had been hired as the boom operator, a job requiring him to stand holding the boom mike attached to the end of a long pole above the actors and out of the shot. It was a job requiring patience and upper body strength.

She was somewhat surprised to note that Billy also had a police record, and one far more extensive than L.D.'s. However, the reasons for Billy's many short-term incarcerations were quite different.

From Beaumont, Texas, he'd come to California to enter the USC film school but after a year, he'd dropped out to become a full-time activist protesting nuclear proliferation. He'd once had a file with the Atomic Energy Commission and, of course, the FBI. The address and phone number listed were out of date. She looked up his current number in her address book and telephoned him.

Billy answered on the first ring. "You come near me, asshole, even your momma won't recognize you!"

"Billy? This is Queenie."

"Oh. Shit, Queenie. Sorry about that. Howya doin'?"

"Are you all right?"

"Ah, just sittin' here with a shotgun in my lap. Some turkey called, tellin' me he wants to rip my heart out and eat it. Gotta be some miserable pro-nuke faggot. Hell, I'm used to it. Had people tell me worse before. Hope this bastard does come over. Do me a world a good to blow somebody's balls off. My name must have gotten on the news or something after last night and one a those bastards from the old days decided to harass me again."

"Is your phone number listed?"

"No way. But that's never stopped those people. Hell, the government's behind 'em."

"Wait a minute, Billy. This might have more to do with Lymon's murder, not your political activities."

Billy was silent for a moment. Finally he said softly, "You don't think whoever killed Lymon would be after me too?"

"You'd better tell the police about the call, Billy." Then she asked, "Is there anything you know about Lymon that might put your life in jeopardy?"

"What's to know? He was my boss. Hey, wait a minute! Could be one of the unions! Lymon hired nonunion people."

Queenie sighed. Given Billy's unique circumstances, he'd probably add two and two and always come up with a politically motivated four.

"He coulda been hit, you know. And all that 'adoring fan' crap just a decoy to—"

"Wait a minute! What did you say?" Queenie sat straighter in her chair. How did Billy know about the bloody message?

"He coulda been hit—"

"—the 'adoring fan'?"

"Well, that's what it said in this morning's paper."

Queenie's heart began to accelerate. Had Joey leaked that information? Damn her! Queenie thought. If so, her friend better hide from J.P.

"What does it say?"

She heard the rustle of paper, then he said, "I quote, 'adooring fan axes producer,' spelled adoring with two ohs. Musta been a late insert. It's not mentioned in the other stories. I found it in the sports section next to the baseball scores."

"Last night you said your ax had been stolen."

"Yeah," he replied defensively.

"Don't get me wrong, Billy. If you'd tell me how it happened, I might be able to figure something out here—including whether or not your life is in danger."

"Oh, well, musta happened sometime last weekend between Friday night and Saturday afternoon. Got a standing poker game every Friday night. It's at my girlfriend's place in North Hollywood. I always stay over."

"How many people—people we work with—know about this?"

"Shit," he said, his voice a verbal shrug, "I don't know. Been going on all summer."

"How about L.D.? Would he have known?"

"Hell, L.D.'s been coming most of the summer, except when he and Nessa disappear."

"Meaning that he didn't show up last Friday night?"

"Yeah. But it's no big deal. There's been several times he hasn't shown up. Usually if he lost money the week before."

Then she remembered something, though it was probably of little consequence. She mentioned seeing Alice Baldridge talking to him at the wrap party in May and asked what they'd talked about. Alice rarely mingled with the rest of the crew.

"Well, let's see. We was all pretty loose, Lymon finally lettin' us party and all. Gee, I don't know. Summer, I guess. I think we talked about what we were gonna do this summer."

"And?"

"And what, Queenie? What does that day on the salt marshes have to do with anything anyway?"

"Might be nothing at all. I'm just wondering who'd know about your ax and when you wouldn't be home."

"What's your interest?"

"I'm investigating Lymon's murder."

"Well, hell! Why didn't you say so?"

"Guess I'm just getting used to it myself."

"Look, if I think of anything I'll call you back. It's been nice talkin' to you but I'm a little preoccupied."

"Just one other thing, Billy. When you left your seat last night, where'd you go?"

After a moment he replied, "Who said I left my seat?"

Queenie sighed. "I saw you. You left your seat twice."

"I didn't kill Lymon."

"I didn't say you did. I asked where you went."

"You workin' with the police?"

"When it concerns Lymon's murder."

"And when it doesn't?"

"Then there's nothing to say." Queenie began rolling a cigarette. "Billy?"

"Yeah, I'm here."

"Whatever it is, you realize you might need an alibi."

"It's complicated."

"Always is, Billy," she said patiently.

"I don't want to talk on the phone."

"Okay. Look, I've got a ten o'clock appointment. Why don't I come over to your place, say eleven?"

He agreed but thought it safer to meet at the park near his Franklin Street apartment.

After concluding the conversation, she went downstairs. Not being a subscriber, she flipped through another tenant's Sunday *Times*, glanced at the front-page story and photograph of a body bag being loaded into the back of an ambulance, then found the sports section and the late insert, a short paragraph, near the box scores.

Once back at her desk she grabbed the phone and called Joey. After three rings, a groggy voice came on the line.

"Werlanda," she said sternly.

"Queenie?"

She heard Joey shift in bed and clear her throat. "What's up?"

"Did you call the *Times* and tell them about the message on the bathroom wall?"

"No!"

"What time did you leave the theater last night?"

"Around two-thirty, three."

The paper would already have been put to bed. That eliminated Joey.

"J.P. made me swear not to say anything about it. Hell, he never did let me use the phone. I called Arthur soon as I got home—but I certainly didn't mention that message—not that it matters anyway. He fired me."

"Arthur? What for?"

"Because I'm a shitty reporter—his words. Said if *he'd* been there he'd have gotten to a phone if he had to kill to do it." She sighed heavily.

"Well, if you didn't leak that message, and none of the cops did, there's only one person who could have done it."

"You."

"Wake up, Joey. The person who wrote it."

"Oh, yeah. But why?"

"To bring the freaks out. Every nutcase in the state will have a handle now. The cops'll be bombarded with confessions. It'll put a tank-size clog in the investigation. J.P.'s really going to be pissed."

"Shit," Joey said. "He gave me a ride home! Queenie, he knows where I'm living. I gotta go. I'll check into the Beverly Hills Hotel—no, that's where Arthur hangs out. Shit. What a mess."

"Hold on, Joey. He'll know you couldn't have done it."

"So what? He told me in no uncertain terms to put a lid on my story and everything I'd seen. Pretty cruel if you ask me. Deliberately makes me wait around all night, won't let me near a phone. Just plain mean, if you ask me. Course I did get to see everything that went on and how he works. Could be he was putting on a little show for me knowing I'd use it in any story I wrote. . . . Look, I've still got a good chance to sell this to one of the tabloids. We're talking *real* money. Plus the pictures."

"Pictures?" A heart-wrenching thought struck Queenie. "You didn't take pictures of the body?"

There was a pause on the other end. "Yes, I did."

"Oh, come on, Joey, give the man some respect. You don't want him remembered like that!"

"Queenie, I'm unemployed."

"As soon as I hang up, you'll never hear from me again. End of friendship."

"Over a photograph? I don't believe you."

"Look, maybe I could help with the story. I'm investigating the murder."

"You've got a client already?"

"Yes."

"Those pictures are sensational."

"Tasteless, Joey. *Worse* than tasteless! What about the photos of Reeves Holloway?"

There was a pause. "Oh, all right. Look, I'd better get a move on. Call you later."

Queenie hung up feeling sick, but reminded herself that tastelessness was just another ingredient in the rich mix that fueled show business.

CHAPTER EIGHTEEN

CALLIE MUNDAY'S AUTO leasing business took up half a block on a side street off Fairfax and a few blocks south of Santa Monica Boulevard. An old pink stucco gas station served as the office. Built in the thirties, the structure reflected a time when architectural style trained the eye to travel appreciatively across rounded arches and curves, when building materials had an earthy, comfortable texture.

Queenie pulled into a slot between a new maroon Jaguar sedan and a little white Hyundai. Callie carried most makes and models, with an emphasis on American cars to accommodate her biggest client, the LAPD, to whom she leased unmarked cars for use by plainclothes detectives.

Having just cleaned the car at a nearby car wash, Queenie locked it and removed the keys from her braided leather key ring as she approached the office, carrying a bag containing the items from the glove compartment.

When I. P. Friedman was alive, his detective agency shared the office with Callie. She was his sister and his ops were required to lease from her. The rule benefited everyone. Callie maintained her profit margins and, by frequently changing cars, working ops were hard to spot. Queenie remembered one "domestic" during which she'd changed cars twenty-one times in under three weeks. Now, though, she changed cars once every several months.

Because of her years doing business with the LAPD, Callie probably knew more cops than the chief of police did. Hers was a place detectives liked to stop for coffee, whether they were changing cars or not.

On the other side of the counter, Callie pecked at a keyboard while her neatly coiffed head bobbed from the computer screen to the keyboard and back again. Though the bells on the door heralded Queenie's entrance, Callie didn't break her rhythm. She was playing a computer game. A radio played sixties' tunes.

Callie had been widowed in her mid-thirties. For the past twenty years, she could be found on the premises at almost any hour. After her husband had been in the wrong place at the wrong time—shot during a liquor store robbery—Callie had plunged into work and never resurfaced.

Sylvester Stallone's naked chest and trademark grimace—which, Queenie thought, made him look like he'd had a stroke—wallpapered the office. The single break in the muscular monotony was a framed pen and ink, yellowed with age, at the end of the counter. It was I.P.'s face, partially in profile. An arrow pointed from an empty socket to an eye about two inches in front of the face. Below the sketch was the caption: KEEPING AN EYE OUT FOR YOU.

Using the car key, Queenie tapped on the counter.

"Be with you in a sec," Callie said without turning her head. A blue-green muumuu tented her abundant flesh.

"Yo, Adrian," Queenie muttered, mimicking Stallone.

Callie started. Her hand went to her heart as she swiveled her head toward the counter. When she saw Queenie, her body sagged beneath the yards of polished cotton.

"God!" she moaned. "The next time you do that I'll *really* have a heart attack."

"Maybe next time it'll *really* be Sly. Care to let me break in that new Jag?" Queenie asked, half teasing.

"Since when did you acquire a taste for flashy cars? Vitch is in the kitchen. Help yourself to coffee and cake."

Queenie lifted a section of the counter and moved into the adjacent kitchen overlooking the back lot.

"Princess," Vitch greeted from a Formica table, his mouth full of fresh-baked coffee cake. The room was redolent with the aroma. It was the homey feel of Callie's that attracted certain policemen. She always had plenty of French roast, always some goodie especially for them.

"Well," Queenie began, pouring a cup from the coffee maker. "Find anything interesting?"

"You bet. Thirty-eight twenty-four thirty-six, young white female, red hair, and, sweet Jesus, this dress . . ." He rolled his eyes.

"In the garbage, Vitch." She joined him at the table.

"And I'm talking about Venus on the half shell. You know her?"

"Yes, I know her. She went to the premiere with me." Queenie immediately tensed, sensing she'd opened her mouth too soon.

Vitch looked at her and smiled. He took a folded envelope

from his shirt pocket. Putting his arms on the table, he leaned forward. The envelope stayed beneath his hands.

"I want a date with her."

She *had* spoken too soon. "Look, you were going to share that information with me anyway, at least that was the impression I got last night. *Ponimaesh?*"

He shrugged and leaned back, pulling the envelope toward him. "That was last night. I don't know that your help would matter now. Looks like J.P.'s about to nail the guy." He paused. "She married?"

"No."

"Then what should it matter to you?"

"I don't offer up my friends in return for information."

Then Queenie reminded herself how Joey had nearly blown it for her last night, barging in on Lymon in the men's room, asking those potentially embarrassing questions in the lobby, then leaving Rex to take pictures of Lymon's body ... even considered selling them.

"She's a grown woman," Vitch went on. "Set up a date. If she doesn't like me, well ..." He trailed off, unable to believe such a possibility.

"Oh, all right," Queenie finally said, now deriving a sort of wicked pleasure in the transaction. More than likely, Joey would agree to a date, especially since Vitch was involved in the investigation. That particular Venus would do just about anything for a story. She wondered what she would have said if Vitch had asked for a date with *her*. Would she do anything for information? She laughed to herself. *Of course.*

Queenie sliced open the envelope with her finger and removed a page torn from a notebook. After unfolding the sheet, she began to read Vitch's list of evidence.

On the ground below fire escape:
1. Pair flimsy cotton gloves. Fingertips ripped.
Green Garbage Bag #1 (Inside Garbage Can):
1. Drink and popcorn containers, unused.
Green Garbage Bag #2 (Beneath #1)
1. Pair yellow household rubber gloves.
2. One Dodgers baseball cap. Size adjustment tabs separated.
3. Pair plastic-soled, black canvas Chinese shoes. Size 39.
4. One dark blue workman's coverall. Large.
Green Garbage Bag #3:
1. Pair opaque surgical rubber gloves. Bloody.
2. Pair black rubber boots. Medium. Bloody.
3. Large-size silver plastic jumpsuit. Elasticized wrists and ankles. Bloody.
Green Garbage Bag #4:
1. Half-dozen heavy-duty garbage bags, one inside the other. Two interior bags torn. Three bags very bloody. Traces of hair, tissue, and bone chips in innermost bag.
2. 25 feet clothesline.
3. Folded blue tarp.

Queenie glanced at Vitch.

"Well?" he asked expectantly. "Think it's worth a human sacrifice? What's her name again?"

"Joey. And yes. It's interesting. Just to be sure I've got this straight," she began, "you found the editing gloves by themselves, beneath the fire escape."

His mouth full of cake, he nodded and gave her the thumbs-up sign.

She looked at the list. "These things in the second bag—household gloves, baseball cap, shoes, and coverall. Any traces of blood?"

"All that stuff's being checked out in the lab. Even the garbage can. But from a visual inspection, I didn't see any."

"The tabs on the baseball cap were pulled apart so we can't figure the head size," Queenie said. "Any hair?"

"Like I said, Queenie, it's being checked out."

"Okay. Chinese shoes, size thirty-nine," she said, and brought out her own pair from her satchel. "Were they like these? Were they new?"

He took one and examined the sole. "Same brand. I forgot to write that down. White Dove. Yeah, they looked new." He handed the shoe back.

"Size thirty-nine is equivalent to woman's seven and a half American. They'd be too small for one of the suspects, guy named L. D. Barth. L.D.'s a big man who weighs about two hundred pounds. He could barely fit his big toe in those shoes."

"Maybe he didn't wear 'em."

"If you find carpet fibers, *someone* did. The blue coverall. No actual size, just large?"

"The label had been removed. And it wasn't new, not by a long shot. Looked to me like it would fit someone between five nine and six, six-one."

"A shorter person could fold under the sleeves and legs," Queenie commented. Then she asked, "What did it smell like?"

Vitch gave her a blank look.

"Did it smell of body odor? Or cologne? It was hot last night," Queenie said. "And this murder was strenuous work."

"Didn't notice." He shrugged, didn't consider the oversight important.

Queenie went on. "The order listed is the order found?"

"Yup."

"And it was beneath the other bags that you found the items with blood on them," she said more than asked and read aloud: "Surgical gloves, black rubber boots—knee high or short?"

"Knee high," he said, and got up to freshen his coffee. Hers cooled, untouched.

"And the silver plastic jumpsuit—"

"—with elasticized wrist and ankles. Bigger than the coverall."

"Zipped up the front?"

"Crotch to neck."

"When I was in college I remember seeing some football players running around in those things to get their weight down. Did it look like an exercise suit? New or used?"

"I'd say new. And yeah, probably exercise gear—fashion for the overweight and the homicidal."

"This last garbage bag," Queenie said, "the bags inside the bag . . . I take it you actually saw bone chips and hair?"

"Right. The lab'll make the match. But it's pretty evident they're from the victim."

"Was there a lot of blood in the bags?"

"No."

Queenie studied the list again. "Clothesline and, finally, the tarp."

"It was folded in the bottom of the bag. And those items could have come from any hardware or grocery store. That exercise suit might be easier to track down."

"How about a fifth of Scotch?"

"Not in my garbage."

Queenie checked her watch. She needed to get going if she wanted to meet Billy at eleven, and she needed to pick out a car. "I'll be back in a minute."

"Sure."

Once outside, she could smell the heat building, especially here in the lot full of metal. The Santa Anas agitated the air but, at the moment, she was indifferent to the hot wind and the dust motes settling on the surface of her coffee.

She examined several automobiles while her thoughts sifted through Vitch's "garbage."

The cops had indeed been lucky. The murderer must have intended for everything to be hauled away by the cleaning crew last night at about 8:45. Leaving evidence at the scene was either gutsy or stupid. And if the murderer had left the theater, why not just take it with him—throw the bags in the trunk of a car and dump them elsewhere? That it all remained at the scene suggested to Queenie that the killer never left the theater.

She moved among the cars, now and then stopping to examine both foreign and domestic—trusting neither very much. As she opened the door of an anonymous Ford Escort, she was surprised to see Vitch suddenly leave the office at a quick trot.

"Hey!" she shouted to him. "What's up?"

"Don't forget to set me up," he yelled, then jumped in his car and sped out of the lot.

Deciding on the innocuous Ford, Queenie hurried back to the office, gathering the list and her things from the kitchen.

"What's with Vitch?" she asked, moving back around the counter, the bazooka-bearing Stallone watching from the wall.

"His pager went off. Called the station and off he went."

Queenie told her which car she'd chosen. After finishing the paperwork, Callie handed Queenie the keys and walked her outside. The two women hugged.

As Queenie started toward her new car, Callie called out,

"You need any help on this one, holler. But just be careful. Ax murderers do it with gusto."

"Sounds like a bumper sticker."

"I'm serious, Queenie."

Billy Bright paced behind a park bench under a huge sycamore tree in the park. Nearby, a couple of bronzed teen-age boys played catch while a white dog patiently followed the ball like a spectator at a tennis match.

Queenie leaned against the back of the bench. Clearly, Billy was too nervous to sit. "So, what was it you couldn't tell me on the phone?"

He glanced around nervously.

"It's okay, Billy," she said soothingly. "Last I heard, trees still didn't have ears."

"Will you keep this out of it?"

"If it has nothing to do with Lymon's death."

"This summer, my, ah, poker nights have put a real strain on my finances."

"Go on."

"Okay, Queenie, but you gotta promise I'm not gonna get in trouble."

"Billy. I told you, if it doesn't have anything to do with the murder, don't worry about it!"

"It's my alibi."

"Okay, it's your alibi."

After a deep, audible sigh, Billy confessed his sin. "I left my seat to sell some coke."

Queenie shook her head. *That* was the alibi? "Who was your contact?"

"L.D."

Holy Mother. "Why two trips?"

"Well, I was nervous. We were supposed to meet at seven-thirty but I hoped he'd be early so I could get it over with. But he had to get changed and all. Second time he was there."

"Where?"

"Outside the west exit. I was gone only a couple minutes each time."

"Why didn't L.D. come to the premiere?"

"But he *was* there. He was the doorman."

CHAPTER NINETEEN

INSTANTLY QUEENIE REMEMBERED the face of the doorman who'd given his hand and helped her exit the vehicle and enter the red hail of tomatoes. She mentally removed the layers of appliances (the latex pieces that changed facial features), pancake makeup, hair, and colored contact lenses, scolding herself for not having recognized him last night. But the makeup job had been good: enlarged nose, weakened chin, age lines at the forehead and around the mouth, dark contacts to conceal his almost transparent blue eyes.

And Lymon had known! He said as much when she asked him before taking her seat in the theater . . . said something about her infallible eye. Then she remembered the last words she was to ever hear from him: *"That little mystery will be solved when the film's over."*

Of course! The last shot in the movie was of L. D. Barth's diabolical character, transformed and taking on the persona of a doorman at a posh nightclub, practically salivating as he helped a young woman from the back of a limousine.

Queenie felt an instant thrill. "That's right! I thought he looked familiar but he was too well made up. I doubt if anyone recognized him. But Lymon knew!"

"And so did Baldy."

"Alice?"

"Oh yeah, L.D. told me it was her idea."

Why, Queenie wondered, hadn't Alice mentioned it to J.P.? There was no reason for J.P. to withhold that particular tidbit, especially since he'd told her L.D.'s name was on the ax. Of course, Alice might not have been thinking clearly when J.P. questioned her at the hospital, and L.D. might have lied to Billy. Still, Queenie's suspicions were aroused.

"Go on," she said.

"Yeah, L.D. told me she arranged it a couple weeks ago, the disappearing act too."

"Did you tell the police last night?"

He shrugged. "Why? It's not really important and I sure as hell wasn't going to tell 'em about selling cocaine!"

"Okay, just tell me what L.D. told you."

"After working the door, he was supposed to come back to the theater around eight-fifteen with Nessa. Baldy told Lymon about the setup when he got back from New York. Lymon was supposed to let them in. After he worked as the doorman, L.D. went to change clothes. Later, he and Nessa were going to meet the press. It was supposed to be all a big surprise. That whole disappearing act was a publicity stunt. He said they'd been holed up in some motel in San Diego."

"When did he tell you this, Billy?"

"Late yesterday afternoon when he called about the coke. Said he didn't have enough left so Nessa could get high too."

"She was with him?"

"No, she was out at his place. She was going to drive in and meet him around eight."

"Where was he?"

"Some fleabag hotel downtown. He said he couldn't leave 'cause Alice was coming over with the makeup and costume."

"Why didn't he just stay at his own place?"

"Well, he said they got back Friday afternoon. Alice didn't want them seen together in L.A. You know, spoil the publicity stunt. He dropped Nessa off at his place then went to this hotel full of winos where Alice said he wouldn't be recognized. Said he shared most of his stash Friday night with a couple of junkies.

"You promised, Queenie. You're not going to tell the cops about my coke dealing?"

She didn't answer; the problem was, if Billy had access to coke, he could also have access to other drugs—like Quaaludes. Maybe Billy spiked the Scotch. But why? For someone else? For L.D.?

"Did you see Lymon—that is, when you sold L.D. the coke?"

"Didn't see anyone. Except L.D."

"No janitor?"

"No."

"How was L.D. dressed?"

"In regular clothes."

"Have you sold any other drugs lately? Barbiturates, uppers—"

He shook his head and looked away.

Queenie was silent for a moment, absently watching the two good-looking teenagers putting on their show. He's lying, she thought.

"Billy," Queenie finally said, "you're going to have to tell the police."

Suddenly he looked frightened. "And if I don't, are you going to?"

She stood her ground but didn't answer immediately. At the moment, she had a very bad feeling that they were all being manipulated by some diabolical puppet master.

"Consider this, Billy. You could be L.D.'s alibi."

His eyes widened. "Gee, I hadn't thought of that." He sighed deeply, some of the anger washing away. "I gotta think."

"You really should talk to the cops, Billy."

Queenie walked toward her car. Upon reaching the street, she glanced back. Billy was sitting on the bench with his head in his hands. Was he desperate—or guilty?

CHAPTER TWENTY

"PHONE'S BEEN RINGING off the hook," Rex snapped irritably, meeting her in the living room when she entered the apartment. He handed her a yellow legal pad containing a list of names and numbers. She wondered if he should stay in a hotel.. Things might get hectic and at the moment he needed quiet and routine. "Why don't you have an answering machine?"

"Never been that popular."

She glanced at the list. "Joey called three times?"

"Yeah," he snapped. "Seems to think my head got vacuumed last night. She's at the Ambassador, not the Beverly Hills Hotel," he said, mocking Joey, and stalked out of the room.

"Sorry you were bothered," she called out. He didn't answer. She went into the study and rolled a cigarette.

At the moment, she wanted to know who still had their axes. The murderer might strike again. If Billy hadn't lied about the theft of his ax, why would someone steal it if not to use it? Hers was still under the bed, and L.D.'s had been used. That left Alice's and Sooch's. Though she'd heard Alice didn't accept hers, still, the woman might now be concerned about its whereabouts. After all, it did have her name on it.

After finding Alice's number in her address book, she lit the cigarette and punched in the numbers. In two rings Alice's machine answered. Queenie left a message then called Sooch Bauer.

"Sooch?" she said when a male answered.

"That you, Queenie?"

"Yeah. How you doing?"

"All right, I guess." He sounded depressed.

"You still have the ax Lymon gave you at the wrap party?"

"No. Why?" Depression segued into suspicion.

"What happened to it?"

"I sent it to my mother in Thailand." Then he blurted suddenly and defensively, "You don't think I killed Lymon?"

"Of course not, Sooch, it's just that—"

"I don't kill anyone," he went on, his English quickly deteriorating. "Mr. Lymon give me break. I never kill him. See plenty killing in Cambodia. How you think that? I love States. Send all awards to mother. They have honor in her home! You think Sooch Cambodian, Sooch have no respect for life. Khmer Rouge, Vietnamese, they have no respect for life."

"Sooch, Sooch! I'm sorry, it's just that—"

"I talk police. Police watch me—Cambodians ignorant, kill people."

"No, Sooch, they don't think—"

"Now *you* hassle me," he declared. "No listen!" With that, the line went dead.

Searching through the computer files, she discovered that Sooch had started with Lymon as a film loader on *Altar of Death*, at the same time as Billy Bright. He'd been a cameraman for a television station in Phnom Penh, Cambodia, before his arrest and internment in the mid-seventies; had spent two years laboring in a death camp until he'd escaped to Thailand where, after a three-year search, he finally found his mother and one sister. They were the only survivors in a family of fifteen. He'd gotten a sponsor and come to the United States six years ago, changing his last name to that of his sponsor. Shortly after his arrival, he'd gotten work with Lymon.

Harold Jonge's fatal heart attack had given him a big break. Even so, Sooch's devotion to Lymon was beyond dispute. She couldn't imagine him harboring resentment for having to wait several years before becoming director of cinematography. Still, she'd seen him carry around some heavy equipment. If he could do that, he could swing an ax. She tried to remember if she'd seen him leave his seat anytime before 7:30, but her mind drew a blank. Of course, there was the possibility that he hadn't been in the auditorium when the film started, that he had waited somewhere else for Lymon and after killing him had *then* taken his seat.

Queenie took a deep breath and tried Alice Baldridge again, but the recording still did the answering.

Thumbing through the address book, she got an idea and placed a call to Paula Cyrk in San Francisco.

Paula was the nurse Lymon had contracted to work on location in Inverness. The conversation was brief. Did Paula recall anyone having the sort of infirmity that would require them to take strong painkillers, even Quaaludes?

"The cameraman," Paula replied without hesitation. "Suke, Suki—"

"Sooch."

"Yeah. Poor guy. Sixty percent disability—but you'd never

1 7 6

know it the way he worked. I understand he'd spent a couple years in one of those Cambodian death camps. Every bone in his body must have been broken at some time."

"What'd he take for pain?"

"Nothing, as far as I know. But the way you people worked, anyone on painkillers couldn't have kept up."

"Anyone else?"

Queenie listened to Paula think. Finally Paula said, "I used to give a lot of massages . . . oh yeah, that woman you called Baldy, the assistant director, she had back problems . . . but frankly, no one really stands out except Sooch. His little body was so knotted and scarred."

"If you remember anything, give me a call." Queenie gave Paula her phone number and rang off.

She glanced at the list of callers, most of whom were journalists, some she knew, some she didn't, and saw Selma's name and brief message: staying Westwood. The phone number followed.

She was about to call when the phone rang. "Yes," she answered, thinking about Sooch and how he would swim in those clothes Vitch found in the garbage.

"Quee-nie," said a chilling, eerie soprano.

"Yes?" She tried to sound casual, though she'd tensed immediately. She listened for any background noise that might give away her caller's location.

"I'm going to slowly peel the skin off those fine muscles. You'll be alive, of course. You see, I, Lucifer, simply adoore you!"

Queenie slammed down the receiver. She mumbled a prayer to the Goddess and took a few deep breaths to calm herself.

She walked back to the bedroom. "Honey?"

Rex glanced up from the book.

"Those calls you took while I was out—were any of them, uh, strange in any way?"

He frowned, seemed to be thinking. "Not really. Except a couple where the caller just hung up. Wrong numbers, I guess."

She didn't want to alarm him, but neither did she want him staying at her apartment. It might be dangerous. She went back to the study and made coffee. Then she called Selma's new number. Selma said she'd received a threatening call around ten and left immediately to stay with a friend. What frightened her the most was that her number was unlisted—whoever called had to be an acquaintance.

"It's probably some crackpot," Queenie said, trying to convince herself as much as Selma. "Still, you'd best inform the police."

"Okay. Well, I didn't just call this morning to give you my new number—I remembered something that might help."

"Oh?"

"You know that second phone number I gave you last night, the one with the 508 area code?"

"Yes?"

"Well, guess I was too upset to make the connection, but this morning I remembered. You see, Lymon used to go away every Christmas. And he always left a number where he could be reached—but only if there was an emergency and under no circumstances was I to give it to anyone. He never told me where or who he was visiting."

"It's the same number, right?"

"You got it. I called it this morning. If I'd had any sense in all these years, I would have looked up the area code and found that he was spending Christmas in Massachusetts."

"And?" Queenie prompted impatiently.

"And no answer."

Queenie didn't bother mentioning her own unsuccessful efforts.

"I'll keep trying, though. At least it'll give me something to do. I'll talk to you later."

Queenie didn't feel as discouraged as Selma sounded. This news represented one more arrow pointing to Massachusetts. Chances were good that Lymon had family there. From Boston she could pick up a trail. . . .

Queenie stood for a moment staring out the narrow window by the desk. The palms dotting the rooftop landscape were performing a contortionist ballet, choreographed by the Santa Anas, now back to their old dervishlike tricks. Thinking of the threats, she wondered if they were genuine or simply meant to dissemble. If the latter, then "Lucifer" wanted them all preoccupied by fear. If the former, well, she'd better get Rex to a safe location. As for herself, she just might be going out of town anyway.

She went to the bedroom. "How would you like to stay in a hotel?" she asked pleasantly. "It would be a lot quieter and less stressful."

He eyed her suspiciously. "What's up, sis?"

"I just thought you'd be more comfortable—"

"Bullshit! I'm not leaving you alone."

"Rex," she began, then finally told him about Selma hiring her.

"Okay," he said when she finished. "So you're working. I'm still not leaving. There's no one to look out for you. That cop'll be busy with his investigation. And that neighbor of yours isn't even in the U.S. That leaves—"

"Wait a minute!" Queenie went back to her desk. As she removed a key from the top drawer, she called to her brother.

After unlocking the door to Dick's apartment, Queenie

walked across the small living area and pulled back the curtains then opened the windows. The apartments on this side of the building were large studios facing the units on the other side of the courtyard.

"No view," she said, "but it's quiet and a little cooler. And you'd be just across the hall."

"And it's cleaner." He walked into the kitchen.

After yesterday's all-too-brief amorous encounter with Dick, she was more aware of their respective living habits. Dick was much neater, which didn't add any pluses to their compatibility rating. Nor did he smoke.

Don't be premature, she cautioned, reminding herself that he might not even feel the same about her upon his return.

"This might work out," Rex added.

While he set up shop in Dick's apartment, Queenie went back to the phone. She called Alice again then tried the Lymon home, not really expecting much. However, there was a chance that once Queenie told her she was investigating her husband's murder, Mrs. Lymon might be forthcoming. But as at Alice's, an answering machine was on duty. Understandably, she must be under bombardment by a hungry media.

She sat back for a moment and rolled another cigarette. It had been a productive morning and she wasn't ready to stop. Then she caught a whiff of her own scent.

"Jeez, Davilov," she muttered.

For a few moments in the shower, she allowed herself a fantasy:

The CAMERA FOLLOWS a woman running along an empty beach in the Seychelles—or maybe Sri Lanka. Her raven-black stallion canters in the surf beside her. They approach a beach house where WE SEE a man's muscular, naked back. He turns. CLOSE UP of the man's face, then the woman's face. (Dick Takahashi and Queenie Davilov.)

Queenie shut off the faucet and grabbed a towel. The six thousand dollars Selma gave her would more than pay for a nice vacation. Maybe she could meet Dick in Japan. . . .

Suddenly she stopped, her wet hair dripping, the towel hanging limp in her hand. *Money*. What if Lymon had been killed for money? Then a certain person came to mind.

As soon as she was dressed in clean jeans and a sleeveless blouse, she made a call. After grabbing her satchel, she left the apartment, stopping first to tell Rex she was leaving.

"Can I go with you?" he asked. "I'd like to get some food in—then I won't have to bother you when I get hungry."

"Sure. If you don't mind a detour. I've got an appointment with an accountant."

CHAPTER TWENTY-ONE

AFTER STOPPING AT a taco stand on Melrose, they ate on the way to Venice Beach, Rex hunched over a greasy bag, Queenie picking most of her food off her lap.

Queenie parked behind a rusted old Woody, stickers from Hawaiian, Australian, and South African beaches peeling on its back windows. After dusting bits of lettuce and tomato off her lap, she reminded herself to stick to hamburgers while driving and exited the little Ford Escort.

Once a world-class surfer, Alan "Chip" Ingram had been permanently beached by a surfing accident off the North Shore of Oahu. The money he'd made endorsing wetsuits, surfboards, and a line of men's beach clothing vanished as quickly as his "buddies" had, forcing him finally to use his accounting degree to support himself.

Queenie and Rex crossed a patch of dry grass and mounted

the tiny porch, the roof threatened by the weight of a huge wind chime constructed of iron pipes.

"Hell, it would take a typhoon to move that thing," Queenie remarked, and knocked on a dirty screen door. The interior door stood open, revealing a dark living room, the drapes on the front window tightly drawn. They could hear a woman singing Madonna's "Like a Virgin," the sound crescendoing as she approached them.

"Yes?" the singer said, her features indistinct behind the screen.

"I'm here to see Mr. Ingram. My name's Queenie Davilov. He's expecting me."

"Just a minute." She disappeared into the house, the song trailing behind her.

A moment later she reappeared and pushed open the screen door. "Come on in."

They followed a cascade of luminous blond hair through the dark house to the covered patio. Hanging from the overhead beams were baskets of pink and purple fuchsia.

Chip Ingram sat sunning himself by a Jacuzzi. His skin was dark and heavily lined, mapped by the years he'd spent in the sun on the oceans of the world. Below his broad bare chest, a thin Madras cloth covered his lap and fell to the footrests extending from his wheelchair.

Queenie had done his background check three years ago when Lymon had been shopping, considering independents as well as prestigious accounting firms. Lymon had chosen Alan because he had few clients, which enabled him to give better service. She doubted sympathy had anything to do with it—it never did in Hollywood, where money was always a concern.

"Sit down," he said. Rotating his wheels, he moved over to

a redwood picnic table. They shook hands. She'd already introduced herself over the telephone.

"My brother Rex."

"Jane?" Alan called out.

The woman who'd led them to the patio approached the table. Again, it was as if she materialized from the ether. Queenie experienced a momentary shock, having seen such beauty only in paintings or artfully produced on film. Her skin was perfectly bronzed and just a little lighter than her large amber-brown eyes. Blond hair rippled over broad shoulders and the smoothly molded torso of a swimmer. Her movements were fluid and graceful despite the impression Queenie had of awkwardness under scrutiny.

Ingram regarded her with flagrant adoration. Then Jane's eyes locked on Rex's. He had never bothered to master the art of concealing his feelings. But then, he had been taken by surprise. The French had a word for it. Three actually, Queenie remembered: *coup de foudre*. The thunderclap. Exactly what she'd felt when she first saw Dick.

"Jane's my—" Ingram started.

Jane flashed a smile, quickly finishing the sentence. "Neighbor. I help Chip out around the house."

"Beer, if you would, Jane," he said a little too abruptly.

Queenie sat down, her eyes urging Rex to follow suit. But her brother's attention was fully on Jane's backside; Ingram's attention was now on Rex.

"Mr. Ingram, as I said on the phone—Mr. Ingram?"

"Chip. Call me Chip," he said absently, his eyes shifting back to the doorway.

Jane reappeared with two cold bottles of Bud. She glanced at Rex, then at Ingram as she set the bottles on the table. Queenie wondered why she'd only brought two.

"You're out of bread, Chip. Want me to run down to the corner and get some?"

"Good idea!" He smiled broadly, no doubt glad of the opportunity for her to be safely away from Rex. "You know where the money is."

Then she glanced at Rex and the reason she'd brought only two beers became clear. "Wanna come with me?"

Chip's expression soured.

"Don't be long," Queenie called after her brother. Turning back to Ingram, she felt an urge to apologize for bringing her brother but didn't. Best to get right to business.

"As I told you on the phone, I'm investigating Burke Lymon's murder, and you probably know his finances better than anyone."

Chip grabbed the bottle of Bud by the neck but said nothing.

Give him a moment to cool off, Queenie thought. "You see, if money is a motive, you might be able to help me."

He took a long pull on his beer. Then he sighed, his shoulders relaxing. "He was dissolving Hammon Productions."

Queenie felt as if she'd suddenly been slapped. So the rumors were true, she thought. "Do you know why?"

He looked past her. "When he first hired me, I naturally had to look at the company's financial history. His books were a mess. No wonder, though, he'd been doing them himself. Anyway, to make a long story short, Hammon Productions—which essentially is, er, was, Burke Lymon—was in great shape until the eighty-seven stock market crash. Then it went belly-up."

"But it couldn't have. I mean—"

"I know what you mean. He's been making movies since then. All I know is that in a matter of months he recovered his losses and was able to continue, but not as easily. Hell, that's hardly unusual given the current financial climate."

"How did he do it? Did he take out a loan?"

"No loans on the books, didn't mortgage his house—rob Peter to pay Paul. And just for the record, he was a straight arrow; never asked me to indulge in anything, well, creative."

"What about his wife? Might she have given him money?"

"I don't know much about his personal—" He stopped, frowning. "No, that's not true. July of last year he started sending statements of his wife's accounts. Don't ask me why. I'd guess he wanted an outside source to have a record. Sometimes happens when people are thinking about a divorce. She's a heavy spender."

Queenie remembered the trip to Hawaii Mrs. Lymon had taken in January, the recent holiday in England, the expensive sweaters and liquor she'd brought her husband.

Maybe the divorce rumor was true too. "Just out of curiosity," Queenie asked, "what happens to the company now that he's gone?"

"I can't tell you. Talk to his lawyer."

"He fired his lawyer last week."

Chip drained his beer then looked at hers. "You gonna drink that?"

She smiled and moved it in front of him.

"Thanks." He raised the bottle in a toast. "Fired me too."

Queenie's eyebrows rose in surprise. "When?"

"Last Monday. Came over in the morning and we boxed up all his papers and he settled with me—in hard cash. Someone pays you in cash, they don't want you to know where the money came from . . . but it's a clean way to say *adios*."

"Did he seem upset in any way?"

"Burke Lymon never struck me as the sort of person who wore his emotions on his sleeve. If anything, though, I'd say he was anxious to conclude his business—like one part of his life was over and he was going into something new.

"And if you're thinking he might have been hit, well, he always paid his bills . . . vendors and employees first." He paused then regarded her thoughtfully. "You people must have really liked working for him 'cause no one on his payroll got rich."

"Anyone get points? How about on *Lucifer's Shadow?*" she asked, thinking that after all her time with Lymon, surely Alice Baldridge would have negotiated for a percentage of net profits—gross if she was ballsy, which she was.

"No one got points that I ever knew of. And hell, *Lucifer's Shadow* hasn't even been released yet. No one knows if it's going to make money or not. What are you getting at?"

Queenie sighed. "It's a long shot but his death *is* sensational—it'll draw attention to the film. Someone might have taken that into consideration before killing him."

"You mean, say you want to get rid of some producer *and* make money at the same time . . . pop him at the premiere of his own movie? Pretty hard core but it does put the movie on the map."

"I thought you might know who had a serious monetary interest in the film. For that matter, we all want the film to make money. But there might be someone—" She stopped. Somewhere between "I thought" and "someone" she'd lost him.

Chip looked at his watch and then toward the kitchen.

"Chip?"

"Huh?"

"Let me put it this way," she said, trying to regain his interest. "Who had the most to lose with the dissolving of Hammon Productions?"

"Hey, I wish I could, but I can't tell you who killed Burke Lymon." He was obviously getting anxious for Jane and Rex's return.

"Can you think of anyone?" How far away is that store? she wondered.

He didn't answer.

"Were you invited to the premiere?"

"Yeah. So what?"

"Why didn't you go?"

He slapped both arms of his chair. "I don't like to be fussed over. Especially in public." Then his expression darkened. "You think I sent someone to ax him. . . ." Then he laughed. "Better yet, I did it? They find tire tracks on his body?"

Before she could respond to the absurdity, Jane and Rex came through the door. The change in her brother was radical. This was the anticipated Rookie of the Year, not just another player on the disabled list. In about fifteen minutes, Jane had managed to lift Rex's color and mood from sea level to Denver.

Feigning no interest in their return, Chip turned, remarking too loudly "Anyone who worked for him. Could have been you. I mean, 'the most to lose' is relative to individual circumstances."

He backed his chair from the table. "Well, good luck. Hope you find who did it. Burke Lymon was a decent man in what's essentially the *Valley of the Gwangi*."

An interesting description of Hollywood, she thought, and gave him her phone number. "If you think of anything, please call me."

She started to leave.

"Look, if it's any help, I think he had money stashed someplace. He may have been dissolving Hammon Productions, but he had something to fall back on," he said.

Queenie stopped. "How do you know that?"

"Honey, I'm an accountant. I've got a nose for money. And Burke Lymon, while on paper he wasn't doing so hot, the man wasn't suffering."

"Meaning?"

"There's money someplace. But if he was murdered for money, you won't find it in Hammon Productions. My guess is it's hidden."

"But where?"

He smiled for the first time. "You're the detective."

Queenie slid behind the wheel. "You find your soulmate?"

"Whew . . ." Rex shook his head. "Only one problem," he said, awkwardly pulling the seat belt across his chest with his good arm.

"What's that?" Queenie asked, expected to hear that Jane was engaged or something.

"She's got a social disease."

"Oh!" she said, taken aback. "Well, at least she's candid. What is it?"

"She's a Yankees' fan."

CHAPTER TWENTY-TWO

DURING THE DRIVE back into the crockpot of L.A., Rex tucked himself into his own thoughts—easy to tell where they were—while Queenie rehashed the interview. While she had no reason to doubt Chip Ingram's veracity, a couple things didn't make sense.

For one, with money a problem, why would Lymon choose to do postproduction work in New York, where living expenses alone would blow his budget?

Further, if he was dissolving Hammon Productions, what about that script she'd seen in his office last night, *FADE IN: WINDEMERE, 1620*? Burke Lymon would not have written a new script just to have it gather dust.

As his assistant director, Alice Baldrige might have some answers. Figuring she'd be home recovering from last night's ordeal and letting her answering machine handle calls, Queenie asked Rex to locate Alice in her address book. With further help from her well-worn travel bible, the Thomas map of Los Angeles, they arrived about twenty minutes later.

Alice lived just east of Doheny, where it marked the border between Beverly Hills and the rest of the world. Only a few more blocks west and Alice would achieve the status she believed to be her due.

Her bungalow was one of seven units connected by a central walkway, three on each side, one at the far end. Ferns leaned limply against each façade, exhausted by the heat. Honeysuckle thickened the air with its sweetness while pink and purple crocus lent color to the tiny patches of garden in front of each bungalow.

Queenie and Rex stepped up onto the small porch of number two. Three panels of curtained glass were at the top of the door—an old version of the contemporary peephole. Queenie knocked and waited. Through the open window of the bungalow across the way they could hear a baseball game.

Queenie knocked again then moved through the shrubbery to the front window and pressed her face to the glass. Through thin nylon panels, she could see the living room. Heavier curtains affording greater privacy hung on either side.

"Can I help you folks?"

Queenie spun around. A man of about sixty, a beer can in one hand, had stepped onto his porch. Bare chested and clad only in the briefest of shorts, he proudly displayed a fit body with just the slightest beginning of a belly.

"Looking for Alice Baldridge. Do you know if she's in?"

"You got an appointment to see the bungalow?"

"Uh, yes." Queenie glanced at her watch. It was five to three. She improvised. "At three. I guess we're early."

"Just a minute." He snorted and reentered his bungalow. A moment later he reappeared and crossed the courtyard.

"Would have to come during the ball game," he mumbled irritably while unlocking the door. "Oh well, got a lot on her mind, I guess. Asked me to show it for her but didn't tell me anyone's coming this afternoon."

He pushed the door open and they stepped into a tiny foyer. Straight ahead was a dark hall. There were two rooms immediately to the right and left.

Leaving the door open, he aimed his beer can to the right. "In there's the living room. Got a fireplace, as you can see. No central air but the air conditioner comes with the place. These bungalows are real sturdy, though," he said, making an attempt at a spiel. "Built when people cared."

The air conditioner was in a window at the far end of the living room just left of the fireplace. It was turned off but the room was still slightly cool. Alice must not have been gone more than a couple hours.

In front of the small, stone fireplace was a grouping of expensive leather furniture. Behind the sofa stretched a handsome antique sideboard, a large circle and narrow rectangles on a thin patina of dust indicating where a lamp and several framed pictures had stood. Numerous boxes were stacked in the room. One beside the sideboard was partially open.

"How much is she asking?" Queenie inquired, maintaining the ruse.

"Have to ask her," he said and stood in a doorway. "But mine's been appraised for two twenty-five. These places got character."

She felt oddly disenfranchised, doubting that she'd ever be in a position to buy her own place, even a dump.

Rex followed him but Queenie lingered, catching a glimpse of the edge of a silver frame. Curious as to whose picture Alice would display, she lifted the flap of the carton.

"How's the game going?" Queenie heard Rex ask loudly, probably covering for her.

While the two men chatted, she looked down at two eight-by-ten glossies, both black and white, resting side by side. Both of Alice herself. Can't accuse Alice of being shy about who she admires, Queenie thought.

In the first photo Alice stood proudly, solemnly in cap and gown, the background—somewhere on the USC campus, Queenie surmised—blurred. In the second silver-framed photo, Alice was in profile, a light meter dangling from her neck as she leaned into a 35mm motion picture camera, presumably studying a shot.

Pride and Ambition, Queenie thought, supplying the captions—the qualities of herself Alice wasn't shy about displaying. Had Alice known Hammon Productions was dissolving?

"Hey, sis!" Rex called. He stood in the doorway frowning a warning.

"You want to see this place or not, miss?" their host said impatiently, trying to peek around the barrier of Rex's body.

On the sofa sat another box, also open, this one containing books on female deities and a boxed home-study French language course.

Queenie joined the two men in the kitchen, her mind far from the stove, dishwasher, and fridge. Was Alice a fellow traveler, a follower of the Goddess?

Their host whisked them through the remaining rooms, obviously anxious to get back to the ball game. However, Queenie noted nothing more of interest—until they reached the study.

Newly purchased, the receipt sticking out like a bookmark, was a copy of *Goddess Sites: Europe* next to the telephone/answering machine. Queenie also had a copy. Was Alice planning a trip?

"When will Ms. Baldridge be out of the house?" she asked when they were back on the porch.

"Movers are coming sometime this week. But if you're interested in buying, you could probably move in as soon as the papers go through," he said, locking the door.

"Why is she moving? I mean, is there something about the neighborhood—is crime a problem?"

"Oh, no! It's real safe around here. Guess she figures the last movie she worked on is gonna make her rich. Why not move if she's got the money?"

A loud cheer carried from his television across the courtyard. The man glanced anxiously at his bungalow. "Listen, I'm just helping her out for a day or two. If you're really interested give her a call."

"Will she be back soon?"

"Just a minute." He hurried to his bungalow then returned with a slip of paper. "You can reach her at this number."

"Well, thank you for your time," Queenie said, but he'd already gone back to the game.

"You think she might have seen something last night?" Rex asked as they moved toward the street.

"Might have," she replied absently. Had a call from "Lucifer" sent Alice, like Selma, running to friends? Further, had Lymon released Alice? The list was certainly growing: Hec Cerruti, Phil Sykes, and Chip Ingram.

Back in the car, she handed Rex the slip of paper. "Would you mind getting the address book out of my bag again and seeing if you can find a match to that number?"

"Sure. And how about stopping at the grocery store now?"

About the same time she pulled into the supermarket parking lot, Rex found the number.

"Got it, sis! And guess what?" he said excitedly. "It's Burke Lymon's home phone."

CHAPTER TWENTY-THREE

"Why is she staying at Burke Lymon's?" Rex asked as they grabbed a cart upon entering the cavernous food emporium.

"Alice must be a friend of the family."

Queenie began bagging fresh produce. Rex pushed the cart while she filled it.

"You work with her. Don't you know?" he asked.

"Her relationship with Lymon never appeared to go beyond the set. But she's worked for him ten years, and there's simply a lot I don't know. Too much, I'm afraid, especially about the man himself."

Rex looked in the cart, which was rapidly filling with fruit and vegetables. "Hey," he said, "save some room for the good stuff."

Within the hour they were carrying groceries and the new integrated telephone/answering machine Queenie had purchased at an electronics store into the St. Albans.

While Rex stocked Dick's kitchen with, among other items, pickled pig's feet, pickled okra, and Coors beer, Queenie installed and programmed her new telephone. After several awkward attempts at taping a friendly, clever message, she settled for: "At the beep leave your name and number." Not very cute, but in this town, in itself unusual.

For a moment she debated calling Alice at the Lymon's residence. Alice would want to know how Queenie knew where to find her, and Queenie preferred that Alice didn't know she'd been snooping in her bungalow. Of course she could simply ask Mrs. Lymon if she knew where to reach Alice. Queenie punched out the numbers. She still wanted to talk to Lymon's widow, discover more about her husband's past.

As it turned out, the answering machine at the Lymon residence was still on duty. She left a message and hung up.

She sat at the computer and, for several minutes, her fingers moved fluidly on the keyboard, entering the latest information into the BLM file.

Completely absorbed by what she was writing, she didn't hear the front door open and close.

Finally, pushing the Caps Lock key, she wrote FADE IN: WINDEMERE and was about to add the date when a loud *pop!* startled her.

"Holy Mother!" she bellowed, leaping to her feet.

"Easy, big fella," Rex said, startled by her reaction. He was standing in the doorway, having just opened one of two cans of Coors.

"Rex!" Placing her hand on her heart, she took a few deep breaths.

"Sorry, Q. Didn't mean to scare you." He moved up to the computer. "Think I should learn to use one of these things?"

"Why not? One day they'll be as common as cars and telephones," she said, and gratefully accepted the cold beer.

"What's that?" he asked, aiming his can at the monitor.

"Just some notes."

"Yeah but what about 'Fade in Windemere'?"

"Oh. That's the opening of a script."

"Really? One of yours?"

"No, Burke Lymon's."

"That's interesting. Was he going to make a movie about the witch trials?"

Queenie remembered the opening scene being something about a witch-burning. "Witch trials? How do you know that? Did Lymon talk to you about his script last night?"

"No. I was a history major, remember?" he said a little defensively. "It's just that I've been there. I think I even have a pamphlet on the town."

"Windemere?" she asked incredulously.

"Windemere, yeah. It's a real place."

"Where is it?"

"Let's see, I think it's a little over an hour west of Boston. There were witch trials there, you know, like in Salem. But they never got much attention."

Near Boston. She tried to keep her excitement in check. "Is there some sort of mental hospital there?"

Rex shrugged. "I wouldn't know about that. It's just a small town."

"How'd you hear about it?"

"I didn't; just stumbled across it. Back when I was in the minors," he said, as if that were eons past rather than just last year. "You know me, I like to travel around, soak up the history. That's one reason I love New England."

Queenie picked up her new receiver and called information

in the 508 area code. When she hung up she had two pieces of information. The area code for Windemere was 508, and there was no listing for anyone with the last name of Lymon. But that didn't stifle her excitement.

"I'd bet the farm he spent his Christmases somewhere around there—and Christmas means family," she said.

Then she showed Rex the sticker in *Independent Filmmaking.* "Ever hear of this bookstore?"

Rex raised his eyebrows in surprise. "Sure. Harold makes book on sports events."

"Harold of Harold's Cinema Books?"

"Yeah. He's an institution the cops conveniently ignore. I don't know him personally but I've heard about him. Does he figure in the murder?"

She eyed her brother thoughtfully. "We need to talk."

When they were comfortably settled in the living room, she asked him to recount his conversation with Burke Lymon.

"Well, we mainly talked baseball," Rex said, prodding his memory. "Let me think. . . . He asked about my arm . . . I know! When I told him I played for the Sox, that's when he gave me a drink. Said he couldn't believe I was *that* Rex Davilov—and you were in big trouble for not telling him I was your brother."

"Our relationship was strictly professional. Go on."

"Said he thought it must be a thrill playing at Fenway, so much tradition and all. We agreed its the most beautiful ballpark in the world. He really got hot when I told him some people want to tear it down and build a domed stadium." Rex shook his head in disbelief. "It's people who don't play the game, who think only of money and their own comfort, who screw things up for everyone.

"Anyway, he was at the seventy-five World Series. Saw Carlton Fisk hit the home run in the twelfth inning of the sixth

game that tied up the series with the Reds. He even remembered who threw the pitch. Pat Darcy. Hey! You got to be a fan
to remember stuff like that."

Queenie looked closely at her brother. "Did he say he'd lived
in Boston?"

Rex shook his head. "Like I said, we just talked about the
game."

"Did you see anyone in a blue jumpsuit, someone who looked
like a janitor?"

"A janitor? No. Didn't see anyone but your friend Joey. Mr.
Lymon fixed her a Coke and she hung around for a while. After
that, things get pretty blurry."

It didn't help that he'd been drunk earlier in the day, but she
didn't remind him of that particular embarrassment. Then suddenly she made up her mind.

"I'm going to Boston."

Rex was silent for a moment, then said, "You can stay at my
place."

"You don't want to go with me?"

"No . . . I, uh, not yet." He averted his eyes.

"Does Jane have anything to do with it?"

He ignored the question. "Listen, I know a guy at the *Star
News* might be able to help you out. Let me see if I've got his
number."

When he'd left, Queenie went to the phone. No time like
the present to commit yourself, she thought, and booked a seat
on a nonstop leaving the next day at two. That would give her
time to take care of local concerns, among them, a trip with
Rex to the Hollywood police station to give their statements.

She'd started to return Joey's call when Rex returned. He
gave her the name and number of the Boston journalist and
borrowed her car keys for a date in Venice.

200

"You know we still have to give our statements," she reminded him.

"Yeah, well, I'm busy now." He started toward the door.

"Rex! I mean it. And I have to be at the airport at—"

"Don't worry! I'll be back later." He was out the door like a shot, murder far from his mind.

Queenie then called Joey. Her mouth full of food, Joey answered from her room in the Ambassador Hotel. "Haven't seen sweat like that since I dated that Rams linebacker," Joey said after Queenie told her of Vitch's interest. "Sure. I'll go out with him. I'll go out with the murderer too, if you can fix me up."

Queenie imagined her friend, probably in her underwear, sitting in bed with a sack full of greasy hamburgers, last night's hairdo today's rat's nest.

"Look, Q, I'm waiting for a call from the editor at *World Abuzz*. Give me the guy's number and I'll get off the line."

Queenie had barely gotten the last digit out when Joey abruptly ended the conversation with a thick "Thanks, bye."

Next she called Callie Munday. "Callie, I need some help."

"Shoot."

"I.P.'s contact at the phone company."

"Hmm. Haven't talked to him since I.P.'s funeral last summer. Don't know if he's still with Pac Bell or not."

"Would you find out? And if he is, give him these numbers." The list included Selma's, Billy's, Alice's, and her own. "I'm looking for a common source of calls made to those numbers today." From Lucifer.

"I'll see what I can do," Callie said.

"Whatever, I owe you a dinner."

It took a few minutes, but finally she talked herself into calling Eric Diamond. Her palms began to sweat, her mouth went dry, and she felt dizzy. Then, after five rings, his answering machine came on. She hung up and pushed him out of her mind.

For a moment she stared absently out the window, her hand resting on the phone as if she'd just taken an oath. Following a hunch, even one seasoned by strong indicators, made her just a little uneasy.

"Goddess," she said softly, "am I doing the right thing?"

Outside, the palm fronds rustled and the rats chattered skittishly. She half expected a disembodied voice to say "At the beep, please leave your name and number. . . ."

Still, she had a strong feeling that something in Massachusetts would reveal the entity hiding in Lucifer's shadow.

Later, she turned on the local news, expecting Lymon's murder to open the broadcast. It didn't. What did sparked a memory of the dream she'd been awakened from that morning.

CHAPTER TWENTY-FOUR

FIRE!

She felt a rush of horror watching the broadcast open from the scene of a firestorm incinerating an area south of the Angeles Mountains. Firemen and police had risked their lives throughout the day evacuating people living in remote canyons, the inferno fanned by the unpredictable Santa Anas.

While earthquakes were a constant fear, fire was the greater threat. With diabolical speed, a single California fire could destroy more lives and property than tremblers. One only had to read Nathaniel West's *Day of the Locust* to bring forth a contemporary vision of Dante's *Inferno*—or recall the reality of fire consuming the hills of Berkeley, and fire raging along spokes to all points of the riot-torn city from south-central Los Angeles. Whether by arson, lightning, or riot, doom was written in flame and smoke.

The somber broadcaster rattled off names of areas affected.

Castaic was one of the first mentioned and had been one of the first evacuated when the fire erupted around midmorning.

"Holy Mother," she blurted. L. D. Barth's house was in Castaic. What if something existed in that house to either prove or disprove L.D.'s involvement in Lymon's murder? And what about L.D.? Had he been in the house? Evacuated? Dead?

Queenie dragged the phone, on its length of new extension cord, into the living room and tried every number she had for J.P., leaving her name each time, her eyes hardly shifting from the television screen. Wherever he was, the lieutenant wasn't answering.

She finally hung up, feeling an impulse to jump in the car and drive the forty or so miles north. Not that it mattered, since Rex had her car. The damage had already been done to Castaic. Besides, only a suicidal fool would make such a trip.

The fire was being covered from a distance, by helicopter and on the perimeter. The authorities were allowing only rescue and firefighting units into the danger zones. Even so, the drama was not diminished as Queenie watched fire pour down canyons as swiftly as floodwater, leap across ravines, and shoot up hillsides with devastating speed, consuming everything—brush, trees, and homes—wherever it chose to go.

An estimated eighty homes had already been destroyed (there would have been more had the areas been more densely populated), many more had been evacuated, and one firefighter was dead. One minute the winds were driving the flames and swirling black smoke to the north, the next minute southwest. Traffic, normally heavy on Sunday evening, was a nightmare. The highways were clogged in both directions by those trying to get out, those trying to get in, and those slowing down to look. Queenie felt foolish for even thinking of driving up there.

Finally the broadcaster said the three words sure to bring terror to the hearts of all Southern Californians: *Out of control.*

The devastation continued well into the night. It had to be serious when there were no commercial breaks.

Queenie headquartered in the living room, leaving the television set only long enough to dart around the apartment in preparation for her trip.

While the noisy printer chugged out her notes, Queenie decided to restock her satchel and dumped it in front of the television.

After adding, among other things, a change of clothes and requisite toiletries, she inserted her shooting script for *Lucifer's Shadow* in which each scene was precisely timed. It would help in establishing when people left and returned to their seats during the crucial first thirty minutes of the film. She would study it during the long flight.

She packed the Lenny Lipton book, her notebook, then hurriedly riffled through her desk until she found a packet of photographs.

Wanting to capture her passage from amateur to professional, she'd taken some candid shots while working on *Vampire Moon,* her first picture with Burke Lymon. When he saw her with a camera, he'd told her that only the photographer hired to shoot stills for publicity was authorized to take pictures on the set. She'd put her camera away and never brought it out again. But she did have that one roll.

She flipped through the photos until she found what she wanted, a picture of Burke Lymon talking to Harold Jonge, the late cameraman. Lymon's mouth was open, his arm clipped at the wrist as he pointed to the actors outside of the photograph. A light meter hung from a black cord at his neck.

Using a pink paper clip, Queenie secured the photo to the inside cover of the Lipton book. Finally she placed her lock picks in various pockets in the satchel in case in aggregate they would attract the attention of airport metal detectors.

Last she added her freshly printed notes.

Then, sitting in her cracked leather armchair, she watched the television for hours until her eyes felt burned and blurry. Queenie finally fell asleep in the otherwise dark room, bright flames flickering on her face.

monday

LIKE THE PREVIOUS morning, the telephone's insistent scream jerked Queenie awake. She reached down and grabbed the receiver, her eyes darting to the television. The image on the screen was one of aftermath. Finally the fire had been contained.

"I owe you one, Davilov."

"J.P.! I tried to call you yesterday," she said, her skin feeling greasy, her mouth full of *gradoo.*

"Yeah, well, I been busy," he said with a heavy sigh.

"You hear about the fire?"

"Did I? Hell . . . anyway, got good news and bad news. The prints faxed from Colorado and those on L. D. Barth's ax are a match . . . and there's been another murder." His words sounded like they were scraping across a gravel road.

Queenie's damp T-shirt suddenly felt like a cold rag.

"A body was discovered yesterday morning in Barth's house."

"Who?" she asked anxiously.

"White female."

"Nessa?" she whispered.

"At the moment, only the good Lord knows. Firemen broke into the house in the morning. They were evacuating everyone in the area. Same M.O., down to the message from Lucifer written in blood. The corpse was naked, found in the kitchen. About all they could tell for sure was that it was a blond female probably in her early twenties."

"Holy Mother."

"From the smell, they figured she'd been there a couple days—and that's the good news."

"If that's good, what the hell's bad?"

"No sooner did they find her than the house went up. The fire had already jumped across the road. These guys were only prepared to help the living get the hell out—not bag a body. No time, anyway. The fire moved too damn fast. One of 'em did have the presence of mind to grab the murder weapon."

"Another ax?"

"You got it. Sheriff up there was too busy to check out the house in time, after you gave me the address. Of course, no one had any idea what was inside. Vitch got up there—" He started to cough.

"Whose ax?" Queenie asked anxiously.

She had to wait for J.P. to finish coughing.

"Were you up there, J.P.?"

"Since about noon yesterday," he finally said weakly. "Once I got there it was obvious they needed all the help they could get. Shit. If I hadn't had to see the mayor . . . if I'd gone straight from your place . . ." He coughed again. "Fire's a funny thing." She heard him swallow hard. "The ax belongs to Billy Bright. So far, the press doesn't know. The firefighters have been too busy. Looks like I'll get to break the news on this one myself."

They were both silent for a moment.

The lieutenant spoke first. "Listen, Davilov, I got a real bad feeling about this case. Do me a favor."

"What?"

"Leave town."

She didn't tell him that's exactly what she planned to do. If she found anything in Boston she'd certainly share it, but for now, only Rex needed to know her plans. Hell, there was a murderer loose who might have an interest in her.

"We need your signed statements, so come in with your brother as soon as you can, then split. Go to Tahoe, someplace cool. Just let me know where you are. You have my permission."

"Well, I appreciate—"

"For once just do what I tell you!" he interrupted.

There was a *click* and the line went dead. "—your concern," she finished. She checked her watch. It was nearly nine A.M.

After showering, she braided her hair and dressed in comfortable clothes for the flight. She took the money Selma had given her, stuffed half in her wallet and jeans pockets, and put a couple hundred in an envelope to deposit in her bank account. The remainder she left in the strongbox, locked in her file cabinet. In these days of laundered drug money, banks were suspicious of anyone who made a large cash deposit.

Rex was up and dressed when she crossed the hall. She enlisted him to help transfer five gallons of water and the ice chest containing canned goods, a radio, flashlight, and sundry items for earthquake preparedness over to Dick's. He spoke little of his date with Jane, but his lack of grousing about going into the Hollywood police station told her that he could have broken his other wrist and probably not felt too badly about it. Love, in its early stages, was a marvelous barbiturate.

While Rex collected Clue's litter box and food, Queenie coaxed the cat from the closet with an open tin of tuna.

The domestic arrangements completed, Queenie gathered Clue for an intimate farewell. But Clue was having none of it. After squirming in Queenie's arms, she flipped onto the floor. With an angry twitch of her tail she began languidly exploring Dick's apartment. Probably deciding where to piss first, Queenie thought. But under the circumstances, she wanted Rex to stay away from her apartment. He'd be safe enough at Dick's. She just hoped Clue would not prove to be the guest from hell.

Finally they left the St. Albans for the police station, the first leg of her journey to Boston.

Around 1:45, Queenie joined the other passengers heading down the jetway toward the aircraft, her satchel slung over her shoulder, a baseball card in her hand.

When he dropped her off outside the terminal and had given her his keys, Rex had suddenly exclaimed, "I nearly forgot!" and pulled out his wallet.

"Honey, I don't need any money."

"Better than money," he said, handing over a laminated baseball card of former Boston left-fielder Jim Rice. Rex quickly related the story of a boy who'd survived a terrible plane crash in an Iowa field. When rescuers found him in the rear of the aircraft, he was clutching a Jim Rice baseball card.

If Rex believed Jim Rice protected the traveler, so be it.

Moments later, Queenie strapped herself in the coach aisle seat wondering what secrets, if any, moldered undisturbed on the eastern seaboard.

As the aircraft soared upward, Queenie leaned forward and glanced out the nearby window at the rapidly diminishing city. Seven million people, she thought. Seven million mysteries.

PART TWO

Everyone is a moon, and has a dark side which he never shows to anybody.

—MARK TWAIN

IT WAS RAINING when the cab dropped Queenie off at Rex's elegant old building shortly before eleven P.M. Monday night. Light poured down the steps from a chandelier in the lobby. Compared to the St. Albans, this was Versailles. No stained sofas, instead there was stained glass; no peeling walls, but dripping crystal; no human odors, only the rich perfume of waxed green marble.

After checking in with a guard built like a free-standing safe, she rode the quiet elevator to the fifth floor, painfully aware of the "open door" policy at the St. Albans that provided easy access to anyone, even someone carrying an ax.

She let herself into the apartment, then took a moment to orient herself.

The apartment was huge though sparsely furnished. In a living room large enough for a basketball game, a few pieces were huddled around the fireplace. The curtainless windows overlooked The Mall, a wide tree-lined promenade separating incoming and outgoing traffic on Commonwealth Avenue.

Rex shared with Tommy Cook, another rookie currently on a road trip. Tommy's rooms were down a hall just off the entry. Queenie found Rex's bedroom, study, and bath on the other side of the vast living room.

She switched on the bedside lamp and reached for the phone, suddenly needing reassurance. She dialed Dick's number. With each hollow ring her apprehension grew. Nervously she flipped through a pile of Polaroid snaps in a basket on the nightstand, barely noting they were all of baseball players and all auto-graphed. Though now a pro, Rex would always be a fan.

"Hello?"

"Rex!" she exclaimed with relief. "What took you so long to answer?"

"Just taking a shower, sis. Didn't think it would be for me."

Briefly they discussed her trip and Clue's behavior—good, so far.

"Seen any strange people lurking around?"

"They're all pretty strange around here—listen, sis, Jane's invited me to go surfing with some of her friends tomorrow."

"Surfing? Might be a little hard to do with one arm."

"Look at Jim Abbott."

"He's a pitcher, Rex. On land."

"Yeah, well, I'll find a kennel for the cat."

"What for? How far do you think you have to go to find waves?"

"Well, a place called Santa Cruz."

"Oh, right!" she said derisively. "Perfect. It's part of the Red Triangle."

"What's that?"

"A breeding area for great white sharks." Ax murderers in L.A., great whites in Santa Cruz. No one was safe in or out of the water.

"Don't worry, sis. I won't even look at the ocean until I finish *The Two Towers*."

"Well, that's a relief." At least he'd be out of L.A.

After concluding the conversation with Rex, she tried her new answering machine. An electronic male voice, sounding as if it had contracted the world's most monumental cold, repeated the number of "mettages," which totaled six. Then the first speaker came on. She was startled to hear Eric Diamond requesting that she be at his house at ten A.M. Friday morning. He would be in Hawaii until Thursday night. If she needed to cancel she could leave a message on his machine. The stuffed-up voice came back on and robotically announced the time of Eric's call: "Two. Tweddy-six. P.M."

Her body itched with excitement. Did this mean she'd been accepted as a client? Or did he merely want to tell her no to her face? Would the other writers be there too?

She scarcely heard the remaining messages, which concluded with one from Joey: "What's with the answering machine, Q? Thought you hated those things. Call me."

She hung up, reminding herself that Eric Diamond's invitation was not a confirmation of anything. Feeling weary and oddly depressed, she opened a window, thinking the cool damp air would revive her. Instead, the tranquil patter of the rain and the air's soothing caress began loosening the tight weave of her muscles. Then she realized that, as much as anything, she was suffering from emotional exhaustion.

After peeling off her clothes, she switched off the lamp and slid between the cool sheets, wrapped in the comforting smell of her brother. A prayer to the Goddess was still on her lips when she fell asleep, later to dream of swaying palms, green bottles sweating on pink linen napkins, and she and Eric Diamond shaking hands while Susan Fry sat in a corner, bound and gagged.

t u e s d a y

 QUEENIE AWOKE AROUND eight and called Rex's
friend at the *Star News*. He agreed to take her to the
newspaper's morgue but wouldn't be free until
eleven. In the yellow pages Rex kept in the nightstand,
she found an ad for Harold's Cinema Books, noting that
the store opened at ten. She jotted down the address.

While coffee brewed, she showered and dressed. Then, carrying a steaming cup, she entered Rex's study for a bit of snooping.

Clearly Rex had avoided the honeyed quicksand of sudden
celebrity and wealth. While he had chosen an expensive address, it was undoubtedly for location and the security the
building provided. He certainly had the money now to buy
upscale furnishings, but hadn't. She wondered how the coming
years, holding the prospect of multimillion-dollar contracts,
would affect his inherently modest tastes.

A small fireplace was squeezed between two bookshelves crammed with history books and various editions of Tolkien's trilogy.

After setting her cup on an end table beside a worn armchair, she sifted through the maps and pamphlets on a shelf beneath an eleven-volume set of Will and Ariel Durant's *The Story of Civilization*.

Finally she found the pamphlet on Windemere. She took it plus a map of Massachusetts and one of Boston and studied them while drinking her coffee.

At nine she left the apartment.

Last night the guard had said that anyone staying in a tenant's apartment while the tenant was absent was expected to meet Mrs. Warren, the building superintendent. Another security precaution.

Queenie knocked on the door near a bank of polished mailboxes in the lobby. Mrs. Warren answered almost immediately.

She was a tall woman in her late fifties dressed neatly in a crisp white blouse and twill slacks. Lining an upper shelf in her foyer were the sort of plates Queenie couldn't believe anyone really bought. Staring down at her from behind Mrs. Warren's neatly coiffed gray head was Tom Selleck, and flanking him, Elvis and Jean-Luc Picard of the Starship *Enterprise*. From celluloid to porcelain, this was immortality.

After introductions and Mrs. Warren's earnest wishes for Rex's swift recovery, Queenie asked for directions to supplement what she'd learned from the city map.

"Why don't you take a cab, dear? More rain's expected."

"I'd much rather walk. Don't get much chance to in L.A."

A few minutes later she hurried down the steps after refusing the offer of Mrs. Warren's umbrella. For now, the clouds were heavy but holding back.

Arriving at the bookstore before it opened, Queenie had a croissant at a café a few doors down from Harold's on Arlington Street. Then, promptly at ten, she entered the store.

In the narrow, high-ceilinged room books were stacked on rickety tables and filled towering free-standing shelves; some even resided, in a semblance of order, in the few glassed-in bookcases scattered randomly throughout the store.

The clerk looked far too young to have ever known Burke Lymon, so she asked for Harold.

He laughed. "You must be a tourist looking for relics of the Boston Massacre." Suddenly an old Leica materialized and he snapped her picture.

"If you ever get famous, we'll put you on Harold's Board of Fame," he said, and motioned to an enormous corkboard hanging by chains from the ceiling to about five feet above the floor. Covered with photographs, mostly amateurish shots, it served as the counter's backdrop. There were a number of publicity stills as well: head shots of well-known celebrities and street scenes from films shot in Boston. Her eyes locked onto a yellowed eight by ten of Steve McQueen and Faye Dunaway, a still from *The Thomas Crown Affair.*

"Just Harold," Queenie said.

The clerk leaned forward on his elbows, regarding her with mischievous eyes. "Let me guess—an obscure college in Kansas. Your film department consists of you, one Super-8 camera, three pimply students who drive you crazy quoting obscure film critics and no budget for film stock." He smiled. "Am I right?"

"Just Harold, please."

His eyes narrowed. "Hmm. Maybe I should put you a little farther west."

Queenie noticed stairs at the back and started toward them.

"Ah." He moaned. "Don't go. This was just getting fun."

Harold, the alleged relic of the Boston Massacre, sat behind a large desk in a dim, smoky office illuminated by a banker's lamp and grimy windows overlooking the street. Tufts of unruly silver hair bloomed from either side of a Red Sox baseball cap. The room reeked of mold, damp, and tobacco.

"Excuse me," Queenie said from the doorway. "Are you Harold?"

"I be he," he answered in a friendly manner, and waved her into the room. "What can I do you for, dear?"

Queenie moved up to his desk, guessing his age to be on the lively side of sixty, though he was probably older. She presented him with the Lenny Lipton book, back cover up, and the paperclipped snapshot.

"I'm wondering if you know the man in the photograph. Most likely he bought that book from you."

"Well, well," Harold muttered, his wooden swivel chair creaking loudly as he glanced from Queenie to the book and back again.

"Sit down." He waved to a chair in front of the desk. She felt encouraged but wondered why he didn't just come out and say if he knew Lymon or not.

He rubbed the gold sticker. "Hmm. Remember when I could afford these things."

"Do you know the man in the photograph?"

Instead of answering, Harold pushed the book back to her. They stared at each other for a moment while Harold pulled flesh from beneath his chin. Then he rubbed his forefinger and thumb.

Of course, she thought, feeling foolish. Well, it had been a while since she'd worked a case.

Queenie slipped fifty dollars from her wallet, used the bills as a bookmark, and slid the book across the desk.

Harold opened the book to the marked page. The money disappeared. He read, " 'Every filmmaker is independent at heart, as surely as each human being is alone, finally, in every activity that has any personal meaning.' Good choice," he said pointedly. Then: "Know who wrote that?"

"Stan Brackhage. The introduction."

"Yeah. Like I said, good choice."

She noticed a full ashtray, but as a Californian she still had to ask. "Do you mind if I smoke?"

"Now, what the fuck do you think?" he said, but without rancor. "Not from around here, are you?"

She began to roll a cigarette. "No. I'm—"

"Easy to guess. No one from around here would be asking about ol' Burke Lymon. Bet I'm the only one remembers him."

"I'd appreciate anything you could tell me about him," she replied.

"This got anything to do with his murder?"

"Yes, it does."

"You a cop?"

"Private investigator."

"Got some I.D.?"

After she produced the requisite credentials, he smiled, sat back, and immediately began a recitation. "You bet I remember him. Spent a lot of time in here—*reading* my books. Don't know how many times I had to tell him this wasn't a fucking library."

He held up the book for a moment then tossed it in front of her. "This is the only one the cheap bastard ever bought."

Queenie stiffened.

"Oh, you don't like that. Well, if you knew him like I did, you'd know what I'm talking about."

"I also worked for him," she said defensively, and lit her cigarette.

"Yeah? What'd you do?"

"I was his script supervisor."

"So how does a private dick get in the movie business?"

How does anyone? she thought. "I have a degree in motion picture production. You get what work you can in L.A.," she said politely but tersely. "You said—"

"My pop was a filmmaker," Harold interrupted. "Came out of the Chicago Art Institute—used silver emulsion like canvas, light like a paintbrush. In those days, no one was much interested in art films. Guess they still aren't."

"Are you a filmmaker too?" Queenie asked.

Harold laughed.

"See this hair?" He pulled on the wiry tufts. "Turned gray when I was twenty-six. That's what comes from living with artistes." Then he grew more somber.

"This," he said, looking around the room, "used to be my pop's film lab. He thought the bookstore would support the family and keep him in film. It didn't. I did. I started making book when I was just a kid. When Pop died I sold the equipment and moved my office up here. You know what keeps this place going? Basketball, hockey, football, and baseball. Not film. Film sucked this place dry, killed my dad and my mom. But," he added with a generous wave, "I'll never let their dream die. I'll always keep the store going. For some goddamn reason it works now."

She was about to turn the conversation back to Burke Lymon when the phone rang. Harold put his hand on the receiver, but before answering, he said, "Well, you've come to the right place, dear, because I've got an idea who might have offed Burke Lymon."

222

QUEENIE GOT UP and walked to the windows to give Harold privacy. Outside, it looked like a soaking gray blanket was suspended above the city. Thunder rumbled in the distance. She heard the *click* of a lighter and wished Harold would get off the phone.

Finally he hung up and she returned to her chair.

"Now, where were we?" He eyed her shrewdly from behind a veil of smoke. She immediately thought of the caterpillar in *Alice in Wonderland*.

"You said you thought you knew who killed him."

"Ah yes, well, could've been one of the druggies."

"What druggies?"

"The ones he worked with. Film was a hobby, see—as we both know, an expensive one. Course it paid off in the end, didn't it? Must have saved a little money when he worked at that place."

"What place?"

"Private, you know. Where rich people send their fucked-up kids. Real exclusive."

"Where is it?"

He frowned. "Huh. Don't think he ever told me. Just that he worked with drug addicts at some private institution."

"How about Windemere? That sound familiar?"

He shook his head. "It's been a long time. You gotta remember we mainly talked film. He asked a lot of technical questions. Funny."

"What's funny?"

"Him. He, well, didn't seem like the kinda person who'd work as an orderly or whatever. You know, menial shit. There was something classy about him.

"For all my bitching, I was kinda disappointed when he stopped coming in. He was bright—not like a lot of flakes whose only interest in movies is self-promotion."

The phone rang again. Harold spun around in his chair and spoke in a hushed tone. Queenie went back to the windows, this time having to wait over five minutes.

Quite unexpectedly, she felt a longing for a sweet-smelling wheat field, a hot afternoon barefoot and fishing under the shade of an oak tree, an overnight trail ride—shades of her childhood.

Harold hung up, scribbled a few notes, and, as she sat back down, looked at his watch. "Gonna start getting busy around here. What more can I tell you?"

Determined to get her money's worth, she said quickly, "Why do you think some drug addict killed him?"

"Who else? Probably someone who'd been released and went after him. Maybe he patterned one of his movies after them and they got pissed off."

224

"Was Lymon from Boston? Any family here?"

Harold shook his head. "Couldn't tell you. Never talked about any family. I got the impression he didn't have any."

"Friends? He ever come into the store with anyone?"

"Nah, he was strictly a loner."

Queenie took a notebook from her satchel and wrote down her name, Rex's home phone number, and her own in Hollywood while thanking him for his time.

"Well, Harold"—she handed him the piece of paper—"if you think of anything else, you can reach me at either of these numbers." Then she put the notebook and the Lenny Lipton book back into her satchel and stood up.

He studied the paper for a minute. "Davilov," he muttered a couple of times. "Where—hey! You wouldn't be related to Rex Davilov, would you? Plays ball for the Sox?"

"He's my brother."

"Son of a bitch!" Harold said merrily. He jumped out of his chair and walked her down the stairs and through the bookstore to the front door, all the while talking nonstop about Rex and how quickly he'd stolen the hearts of the ever-knowledgeable Boston fans.

Harold went outside with her. "Wait here, I'll get you a cab."

"That's okay. I'd rather walk to my next appointment."

"Where you headed?"

"The *Star News*."

"Shit! You can't walk there. It's in the Combat Zone." He whistled down a cab.

"But it's not that far," she protested.

"Nothing's far in Boston. But the Combat Zone, well, it's no place for a lady. Take the cab."

As far as she could tell, the Combat Zone consisted of derelict buildings housing bars and strip joints and dirty streets littered with unwanted winos and sharp-eyed hookers—not that much different than her own Hollywood neighborhood.

Arriving twenty-five minutes early, Queenie spoke to the guard, giving her name and that of the reporter she was to meet, expecting to be told to wait.

"I'm sorry, Ms. Davilov," the guard said. "But he was called out on an assignment."

She was about to ask if there was someone else who could take her to the newspaper's morgue when he pulled out a newspaper, some faxes, and a manila folder. "But he left these for you."

The folder contained a list of Burke Lymon's films and several bad reviews, apparently all the reporter could find in the morgue. She tried to concentrate in the cab back to Rex's but it was like reading on a speedboat. Finally she closed the folder and held on as the driver careened around corners, hitting straightaways with either a death wish or the courage of a test pilot.

See you in the obits, she thought, after she'd paid her fare and he shot away from the curb.

The dense storm clouds had lowered and thickened, shrouding the city in deepening darkness. The chandelier in the lobby had been turned on.

Once inside the apartment, she went to Rex's study, switching on the lamp to lighten the gloom. She sat down and reread the reviews, wading through the smug, gravelly prose, searching for some tidbit about the filmmaker himself. But these were no different from other reviews of Burke Lymon's films. Giving a sigh, she turned to the faxes, which were pertinent stories from this morning's *Los Angeles Times,* and the newspaper, yesterday's *Times.*

Publicity stills of Nessa and L. D. Barth smiled from the faxed front page above a photo of the charred remains of the house, the swimming pool in the foreground appearing to be filled with tar. Queenie remembered a hot tub near the pool. Apparently it hadn't survived. She noticed hedges above and behind the remains, indicating that the neighboring lot hadn't been touched. Such was the erratic nature of canyon fires.

She quickly read of the discovery of Nessa's body by two firemen who'd broken into the house thinking someone might be asleep inside. Alice Baldridge had come forward to say that she had gone to the house on Friday afternoon after L.D. and Nessa returned to L.A. to discuss the couple's "surprise" appearance at the premiere. When Alice left, Nessa and L.D. were arguing—a lover's quarrel, she'd thought. That apparently both confirmed the identity of the body and incriminated L.D.

An attendant story reviewed L.D.'s criminal past. His mother in Denver had been contacted but she didn't know of her son's whereabouts, nor had he ever mentioned being in love with his costar.

Since his name had been found on the murder weapon, Billy Bright was in custody, although he emphatically denied any involvement with Nessa's murder.

Scanning yesterday's newspaper, Queenie discovered, with no real surprise, that the LAPD was besieged by confessing "Lucifers" and the demands of terrified citizens, many of whom feared that the killer, or a copycat, might strike the film community at random.

In a story updating J.P.'s investigation, Queenie learned that Amanda Martin had been picked up—and released, for the second time in so many days. After attacking Queenie she'd gone after one of the religious freaks outside the theater, battering him with a discarded picket sign. The police had been called and took her to jail. Later her victim decided not to press charges, and she was subsequently set free. She'd been on her way to jail when Lymon was murdered. Damn good alibi, Queenie thought.

Finally she read two short notices, one about Lymon's memorial service, the other stating that *Lucifer's Shadow* was being released in Los Angeles and New York Tuesday night (tonight) followed by a list of Southland Theaters where it would be playing. Queenie felt a certain stab of regret that she couldn't attend the afternoon service for Lymon but reminded herself that her current efforts would cover paying her respects. Regarding the second notice, she felt a bit disgusted. The distribution company was wasting no time cashing in on the free publicity so generously provided by the grisly murders.

After putting the papers aside, she brought the telephone into the study and called information for Windemere, Massachusetts.

CHAPTER TWENTY-NINE

QUEENIE HUNG UP, trying to shrug off disappointment. The operator could find no listing for a drug rehabilitation clinic in Windemere. There wasn't even a hospital in the town.

Suddenly the phone rang, startling her.

"Hello?" she answered quickly.

"That you, Miss Davilov? This is Harold."

"Ah, Harold. What's up?" she asked.

"Well, you see I've got these files. Cards my customers fill out so I can send them ads about special sales or a book signing. You know."

"A mailing list."

"Yeah. That's it. Well, I looked through this old box of cards and, what do you know, I found Burke Lymon's. Got a pen?"

"Shoot!" she said, sitting straighter.

He gave her an address on Berkeley Street. "Now, that's where he lived when he first started coming in the store. In those days it was a rundown old building near the police station. That part of town's been gentrified, turned into expensive condos and town houses, so I don't know how much good it'll do you. And it's crossed out."

"At least it's a start."

"Hang on, I'm not finished," he said impatiently.

She scribbled on her notepad as he continued:

Burke Lymon
c/o C.O. Junior
P.O. Box 99
Windemere, MA

"Don't have a zip code number," he concluded.

She read it back and thanked him while reaching for the map of Massachusetts. She was just about to hang up when he asked, "By the way, is your brother around?"

In an instant she realized her mistake. *He's got Rex's home phone number!* "No, he's not."

"I'll try later."

"Uh, he won't be in, Harold," she quickly improvised. "You see, he's moving."

"Hey! I got friends in real estate could fix him up with a real sweet deal."

"It's kind of you to offer," she said. "But he doesn't need any help. Now I really must get off the phone."

"Tell him I called. I'll talk to him later."

Queenie hung up, tingling with excitement and self-directed anger. Because of her Rex would have to change his phone number. Well, she couldn't worry about that now.

She again called information for Windemere, this time inquiring after a C.O. Junior. But there were no Juniors in Windemere—at least with phones.

Then she had a sudden inspiration. Of course! More than likely, a private drug clinic would not be listed. And the town was small enough that locals must know of its whereabouts, the police in particular.

Calling the number provided by information, a youthful but stern-sounding sergeant answered. Her inquiry about a local drug clinic was met with a gruff rebuke. "Windemere is in the tourist business, lady, not the drug business!"

Next she tried the museum, the number printed on the back of the pamphlet. But each time she called, the line was busy.

For several minutes, she sat thinking. All along she'd planned to go to Windemere, but it had to be done properly. Even though this was only Tuesday, she wanted to conclude her business as quickly as possible. Friday might well be the most important day of her career, and nothing was going to keep her from that appointment at Eric Diamond's.

She came up with a simple plan. First, though, she'd need proper clothes and a high-dollar car. Rex's battered pickup truck wouldn't do for this particular trip and would have to stay berthed in the parking garage beneath the building.

She checked her watch. It was after midday. Rex had said Windemere was a little over an hour from Boston. Adding the time she needed to shop for clothes and pick up a rental car, she surely could locate the clinic before five. But if not, she'd find local accommodations and show up tomorrow morning.

Grabbing her satchel, she left the apartment.

Under the watchful eye of Tom Selleck in porcelain, Queenie listened as Mrs. Warren recommended several "good" dress shops on Newbury Street and an agency that rented luxury "automobiles" near the Common. Queenie wondered if Mrs. Warren ever used the plate, eating off Tom's face, as it were.

A few drops of rain splashed around her as she entered the first shop she sighted with a SALE sign in the window. She bought and changed into an elegant linen dress in a rich shade of green, a wide-brimmed hat, leg-flattering heeled sandals and matching handbag, and go-to-hell black sunglasses. She felt a little singed by the expense—to her the sale items had simply been marked down to retail—but the expenditure was worth it when the clerk at the car rental agency asked if she was in show business—exactly the image she'd intended to create.

Now prepared for the journey, she joined the cacophonous, stop-and-start traffic, slowed by what was now a downpour. She quickly learned that Bostonians pressed their horns when they couldn't press the accelerator.

This particular rental agency had added a tape deck in the late-model Chrysler and let her choose from a library of music.

Punching in George Winston, Queenie increased the volume and, while listening to "Rhapsody in Blue," shifted into the role of Mrs. Alan Smithee of Beverly Hills, a concerned mother looking for a discreet institution in which to place her drug-addled son. Few people outside Hollywood knew the name was used by those who, for one reason or another, didn't want their real name displayed in film credits. Queenie only wished she had some good jewelry to complete the image.

CHAPTER THIRTY

WINDEMERE WAS ABOUT ten miles north of the highway, nestled in lush, hilly country. Guided by the map in the pamphlet, Queenie drove to the center of town, arriving a little after three.

The rain had kept her company though diminishing in intensity the farther west she traveled. In Windemere it was reduced to a gloomy drizzle.

Quaint shops, bars, and restaurants surrounded a small common. Centered on the carpet of bright green grass was a coven of naked witches kneeling around a hooded, satanic-looking creature, their bronze bodies slick with moisture.

The library and museum were at the north end of the common in a building under restoration. Queenie parked the Chrysler and climbed the worn steps, hoping either the librarian or the museum curator would be more forthcoming than the police had been. She passed under scaffolding to the whine of a sandblaster.

Wearing earphones, a man in his late twenties sat behind the counter facing the door. No one else was around; the library's patrons probably had been driven off by the noise.

"Museum's closed for repairs," he said in a raised voice, pulling off the earphones as she approached, obviously taking her to be a tourist.

"Actually I'm in town to see about the clinic," Queenie said loudly. From somewhere beyond the bookshelves came the sound of hammering, then suddenly all the noises stopped and they brought their voices back to normal.

He frowned. "Pardon?"

Queenie pulled off her sunglasses and smiled richly. "I've come from Beverly Hills to see about the drug rehabilitation clinic. Perhaps you could help me with the address."

He gave her a sharp look. "Lady, you're a little late. It's been closed, uh, seven, eight years."

She suddenly realized how silly she must appear: a moneyed, well-connected woman having such terribly dated information. "Actually," she went on smoothly, "I called around locally but no one told me it was closed. The police were most unhelpful."

He smiled sympathetically. "People around here would rather pretend it never existed. Town fathers were furious when Mr. Oldfather opened the drug clinic—they figured he should be more civic minded and open the estate for tours. But after his daughter died of an overdose he had other things in mind. More power to him, I say. Sorry you came so far for nothing. I'd take you through the museum but it's being remodeled." He jerked his head toward the back. "Just making it tackier, if you ask me."

"Oldfather, you said." She recalled reading something about an "Oldfather" in the pamphlet.

"The clinic was on the Oldfather estate. 'Bout five miles out

234

of town. Might make you feel better just to drive by, though there's not much to see from the road. Just take Oldfather Road, right off the common."

On the off chance he might recognize Burke Lymon, she showed him the photograph.

He looked at her quizzically and shook his head. "He recommend the place to you?"

"Doesn't matter. But thank you, you've been most kind."

Queenie left, her step more sprightly now that the existence of the clinic was more or less confirmed. Even if it was no longer in operation, someone might be around who remembered Lymon.

Queenie found herself traveling beside a high stone wall in what was otherwise deserted country. Finally she came to an open gate. Having seen no other human habitation since leaving the town center, she assumed this was the place.

She passed between two massive pillars and stopped at the gatehouse. The windows were dirty and ivy crept up, close to covering the panes. Though far from falling down, it had the sad look of abandoned buildings. She drove on, following a gravel road that wound between thickets of sycamore, English walnut, and maple trees. Finally a Florentine mansion came into view. As she approached, statues of Winged Victories flanking the steps to the front door grew larger and larger. The road curved around the front of the house. Just beyond was a small, graveled parking lot.

Emerging from the Chrysler, it was Queenie Davilov who hurried up the steps, the masquerade now superfluous. She thought ruefully about the money now wasted on Mrs. Alan Smithee.

At the door she inhaled deeply, feeling anxious and excited. She pushed a button in the wall and heard a shrill buzz on the other side, then overwhelming silence, not even the sound of a leaf falling.

She rang again, the peal reassuring. She stared at the door for a long moment, then looked around.

After the third try, the door abruptly opened. An older gray-haired man with a robust body and a sad, jowly face stood on the other side, his expression quizzical.

"Yes?"

"Hello. My name's Queenie Davilov. I've come from California and was wondering if there's someone I could speak to about a former employee. Perhaps you remember him. His name's Burke Lymon."

The name didn't seem to register. She reached into her new, overpriced handbag and passed him the photo. "Here's his picture."

Quite unexpectedly, his vitality drained. His face paled and he swayed, about to fall. Queenie automatically moved forward.

"Are you all right?"

Without waiting for an invitation, Queenie stepped into the wide foyer of pale Italian marble. He nodded and, still clutching the snapshot, fell back into a chair beside the door.

He took a moment to compose himself while Queenie hovered. "Are you all right?" she repeated.

He waved his hand and took a few deep breaths, his eyes closed.

"Just give me a minute," he whispered.

Across the foyer she noticed double glass doors opening on a courtyard where nymphs cavorted in a pool of water lilies. On either side were what appeared to be east and west wings. Was this the former clinic, or had it been housed beyond the flat plain of green lawn she could see flowing from the edge of the courtyard?

"Who are you?" he asked, bringing her back.

By his reaction to the snapshot, she felt confident this man knew Burke Lymon and obviously had considerable feeling for him—whether good or bad remained to be seen. "I used to work for Mr. Lymon."

He opened his eyes and studied her for a long moment then rose from the chair. Without relinquishing the snapshot, he moved forward.

"Come with me," he said.

She followed him to the left, down a long corridor, his slippers whispering, her sandaled heels loudly stabbing the floor, disturbing the peace of a place she sensed was normally closed to noisy reality. She felt strongly that drug addicts had never roamed freely in this house.

They passed a staircase on the right and then he turned left again, leading her into an office with a view of the circular drive. He motioned to a leather armchair in front of a massive dark walnut desk. She removed her sunglasses and sat down, looking directly at the painting hanging behind the desk, feeling the spur of excitement. It was a rocky seascape similar to the one she'd seen in Lymon's study on Saturday night. Though she was too far away to make out the signature, she felt certain the same neatly printed name would grace the lower right-hand corner: Holly.

With his back to her, he stood at an antique sideboard choosing one of several decanters and poured a drink. She wondered if he'd offer her one—shared drinks meant shared confidences—but he didn't.

He moved around the desk carrying the snifter. After taking a tentative sip, he leaned across the desk and handed back the photo.

"So you remember Burke Lymon?" She slipped the photo in her handbag.

"No. I've never known anyone named Burke Lymon."

She looked up at him, startled. "But the man in the picture is Burke Lymon. You recognized him!"

He took a deep breath and said in a low voice as he sat down, "That's Junior."

Her heart did a little flip. "You mean, that was his nickname?"

"No. That's Charles Oldfather *Junior*."

CHAPTER THIRTY-ONE

NEITHER SPOKE FOR a moment while Queenie absorbed this extraordinary news.

"You'll have to excuse me," he finally said, "but I've had a number of shocks lately." He stood and offered his hand across the desk. "I'm John Wakefield. I'm sorry but I've forgotten yours."

Queenie shook his hand. "Queenie Davilov, Mr. Wakefield." She thought of the address Harold had given her: Burke Lymon, c/o C.O. Junior.

"What's your interest in Junior?"

"I'd heard Lymon—Junior—worked here at one time. You see, Mr. Wakefield, I'm a private investigator." Not knowing if one of those shocks he'd experienced included news of Lymon's murder, she waited for him to reply.

"You're investigating his death?"

She felt relief. "Yes. Are you a relative?"

"I'm the caretaker," he replied somewhat curtly.

Though polite, she sensed he did not trust her. Without trust, she couldn't get answers—at least truthful ones.

"Maybe I should tell you what led me here," she said.

"Yes," he said.

For the next ten minutes or so, she gave him an abbreviated account of her work for Hammon Productions, the murder, and her reasons for coming to Massachusetts. He sipped his drink without interrupting and appeared genuinely surprised to learn that Lymon had been in the movie business.

". . . then his secretary gave me the phone number he always left when he went away for Christmas. She and I have both tried to call, getting no answer."

"It's his private line," Mr. Wakefield told her. "The ringer's turned off unless he's home."

"At one time he had a postal box number, care of C. O. Junior in Windemere."

"I don't know anything about that."

"This is his home, then?"

"Of course. He inherited the estate when Charles Senior— his father—died in 'eighty-seven."

"I heard he'd worked at the drug clinic."

"Oh yes," Mr. Wakefield said softly, staring past Queenie. Then his eyes slid over to meet hers. He seemed to want to tell her something but at the same time was reluctant.

"Anything you remember, Mr. Wakefield, might help me find who killed him."

When he didn't answer, she changed her tack. "How did you learn of his death?"

He took another sip of the brandy. "His wife. No details, just that Junior had been killed by some madman and she wanted me to prepare the house, said she'd be arriving any day." He paused to finish the brandy. It seemed to be loosening him.

"That's why I've been leaving the gate open. She told me not to contact the lawyers, that she'd take care of that." He suddenly sighed. "My fear is she's planning to sell the estate."

"Another of the shocks?"

"Most definitely. Wakefields have worked for Oldfathers for over one hundred and fifty years; myself since I was fifteen."

"When did she call?"

"Sunday noon."

"Is there no one else to inherit?"

"Unfortunately, no. . . . My God, what could he have been doing to attract such a killer?"

"That's what I'd like to know," she said pointedly.

"Movies," he said flatly and shook his head. "Who would have thought . . ."

"You never knew?"

He continued shaking his head.

"Why not?" When he didn't answer, she asked, "Do you think I could see his rooms? Maybe there's something there that'll help me."

He looked away, debating with himself. Finally he stood up. "Well, all right. But just for a few minutes. If his wife arrives, I'm sure she wouldn't appreciate my opening the house to a stranger."

"I *am* looking for her husband's killer, Mr. Wakefield."

"Yes. Well, come along."

Together they exited the office and walked toward the staircase.

"Junior did work at the clinic. It's about a half mile from the main house. He lived in staff quarters, was paid minimum wage. It was penance, you see."

He continued as they mounted the stairs. "Charles Senior

started the clinic in the seventies after Holly died of an over-dose."

"The painter?"

"Yes," he said, and gave her a quizzical look.

"I've seen her work in Lymon—Junior's—office in Holly-wood."

"She was his younger sister. They were very close. Their mother died when Junior was ten, Holly eight. Charles Senior ran the multimillion-dollar family shoe business. With that kind of money to tend to, he had little time for the children. And he never had an inclination to remarry. Junior and Holly more or less raised each other until they were shipped off to various boarding schools. Neither fared too well, got mixed up with drugs. Instead of going to college, they lived together at the family summer house on the Cape—Holly was going to be a painter and Junior, well, Junior was going to find himself or something. . . . Holly did paint but they both got more involved with drugs."

At the landing, he moved down the wide corridor of the west wing. A solid bank of windows overlooked the courtyard and into the east wing.

"Anyway, when Holly died," he went on, "the old man finally took notice. He refurbished the outbuildings, hired the best people, and pretty soon there was a waiting list. In the mean-time, he got Junior into Emerson College in Boston, set him up in a cheap apartment, and gave him barely enough to live on."

"That must have been when he created the persona of Burke Lymon," Queenie said.

"Maybe so, but it was Charles Oldfather Junior who flunked out his first semester. Charles Senior brought him back here to work. Like I said, he was paid a minimum wage and lived in staff quarters. The experience seemed to straighten him out.

After a couple of years, his father invited him to go into the family business, but Junior declined. There was a terrible fight and the next day he was gone."

Wakefield stopped in front of a door and sighed. "Charles Senior considered hiring a private detective to find him, but Junior was a man now so he just let him be. Junior did come home every Christmas but never told his father where he'd gone or what he was doing. And he never asked for money."

He pulled keys from his pocket, picking through them to find the proper one.

"Did you ever meet his wife?"

"Frances? Oh, yes. I knew Frances very well. Very well, indeed."

After unlocking the door, he stepped aside for Queenie to enter.

She was momentarily taken aback, for the room was almost identical to Lymon's private sanctum in Hollywood. And here was the fireplace and hooked rug Queenie had imagined, though no Irish setter was sleeping before the hearth.

Wakefield switched on the nearby brass lamp and opened cranberry-colored linen curtains positioned on either side of the fireplace. Outside Queenie could see a giant willow weeping into a small pond.

Scattered here and there were books and magazines on fly-fishing, but that was all, nothing to announce his profession as a filmmaker.

"The bedroom and bath are through here," he said, opening the door to an adjoining room.

They entered the bedroom. Off to the left and in front of another window that looked out on the pond and willow tree was an antique rosewood writing desk, a small portable type-writer on the floor nearby.

Wakefield watched her search the cubbyholes that revealed nothing more noteworthy than a few stamps, ballpoint pens, and envelopes. The old man moved up beside her.

Queenie pulled out the single drawer, but he quickly shut it before she could see more than the edge of a folder.

"I'd prefer that you didn't disturb his things."

Loyalty to the family probably made her snooping offensive.

"The bath is this way."

She followed him past a huge walk-in closet, noting some women's clothes hanging inside alongside men's attire.

"Does Mrs. Lymon share these rooms?" she asked as he entered a tiled bath.

"No," he said. "She hasn't been here since they were married."

She glanced inside the medicine cabinet but found no pills, not even a bottle of aspirin. "I noticed some dresses in the closet," she said casually. As she closed the medicine cabinet she saw Wakefield's reflection, his color rise, his facial muscles tighten.

"You must be mistaken. Now, I think you've seen enough," he said, exiting the bathroom.

He was closing the closet door when she reentered the bedroom. She followed him out of the apartment.

"You said before that you knew Mrs. Lymon, Frances, well," she remarked as he locked the door.

"At one time she was Charles Senior's nurse—but that's another story."

"I'd like to hear it," she said, trying to keep up as he moved briskly down the stairs.

"Maybe some other time." He moved quickly to the front door.

"My sunglasses. I left them in your office."

They retraced their steps to the office. Queenie picked the sunglasses off the desk. "Just one more thing."

Wakefield appeared annoyed.

"May I use your rest room?"

Obviously relieved, he said, "You'll find it at the end of this hall. Just before you reach the conservatory." She left him refilling his brandy snifter.

Taking up nearly half the space in the lower west wing, the conservatory loomed ahead like some dark cave. She passed a large bedroom and, coming to the bathroom, stepped inside to pull off her shoes. Then she slipped out, after making certain Wakefield wasn't watching, and entered the conservatory.

On all three sides heavy drapes were drawn. A grand piano was at the far end of the room, the center of attention in a grouping of comfortable furniture.

Queenie moved quickly to her left and, reaching behind the first set of drapes, unlatched one of the tall French windows. Then she silently hurried back to the bathroom, flushed the toilet, and put on her shoes before she returned to the study.

Wakefield walked her back to the foyer. "You must like living here. It's so beautiful," she murmured.

"Yes," he said mournfully.

"That's a beautiful piano in the conservatory. I love piano. Do you play?" she asked conversationally.

"Oh, no. Not musically inclined, I'm afraid."

She hoped that meant he never entered the conservatory. She wanted to ask about security, if guards or dogs patrolled at night, but to do so might give her away. She'd have to find out on her own.

At the door they shook hands. Then she left the estate and drove back to Boston.

CHAPTER THIRTY-TWO

A RED LIGHT blinked in the gloomy bedroom, reminding her of a winking evil eye, though it was nothing more than the message light flashing on Rex's integrated telephone.

Ignoring it for the moment, Queenie hurried to the bathroom, her bare feet making squeegee noises on the hardwood floor.

After dropping her packages by the door, she switched on the light and peeled off her sopping dress. The bun she'd made of her braid had come undone and hung down her back, the hairpins sticking out, making it look like some prehistoric centipede.

She kicked the door shut and was momentarily stunned when she caught sight of herself reflected in the full-length mirror on the back. There she stood, naked, the dress at her feet reduced to a puddle of the richest green. Dry Clean Only. She now understood the reason for the instruction attached to the dress label. The same hue stained her body, as if she'd been haphazardly spray-painted.

"Holy—I . . . I'm Gumby!"

Keeping in mind Harold's advice that nothing was far in Boston, she'd declined the rental agent's offer to call a cab for her after she returned the Chrysler. The prospect of a walk had appealed to her and, besides, she had plenty of time.

And then she'd been caught in a squall of such intensity that Boston drivers actually reduced their speed. Stumbling blindly, her packages clutched to her breast, she'd found the Mall but it seemed to expand as she trudged on. Her attempts to stop taxis proved fruitless. Either they were already engaged or they didn't want this bright green woman staining their backseats.

She tossed the dress in the tub then joined it, wishing she'd taken up Mrs. Warren's offer of an umbrella. She plucked the hairpins from her braid as she showered.

Once reasonably stain-free and dry, her hair turbaned in a towel, she dressed in the black sweatsuit she'd bought at Filene's Basement before returning the car. Following her emerald trail, she began to mop up, finishing at the elevator. As he said he would, the guard had taken care of it and, she imagined, the lobby too. He'd been altogether understanding.

Back in the bathroom, she wrung out and bagged the dress. Now she would take it to the dry cleaner's.

In the bedroom, she played the message tape while rolling a cigarette.

Rex's voice came on first, informing her that Clue was "staying" at The Cat House on Wilshire Boulevard. "The key to your friend's apartment is under your door. Your car keys are in his place. Uh, talk to you later."

She hoped he'd finished *The Two Towers*.

Harold had called twice, his second message the last on the

tape. She now had his last name, Mann. She barked at the machine. "Listen, Mr. Mann, you can get in big trouble harassing people on the phone!"

But it reminded her of something. She called Callie Munday. An array of odd high-tech noises told her she'd interrupted a computer game.

"Did you get in touch with the Pac Bell guy?"

"Haven't you figured out how to work your own answering machine? I left a message."

"Oh. Well, what did he say?"

"He started the search after I talked to him yesterday, but he wants a top-of-the-line car for a week."

Quid pro quo. "Fine. I'll take care of it. Thanks, Callie, that's all I needed to know," she said, surprised when the woman continued rather than ended the conversation.

"What do you think about all this crap?"

"What crap?"

"Come on. Don't tell me you haven't heard?" Then Queenie heard a slight intake of breath. "Ah, you're not in L.A. Where are you?"

"Doesn't matter."

"You okay?"

"I'm fine, Callie. What's going on?"

"For starters—oh, before I forget. Vitch stopped by last night. Said if I saw you to tell you they found carpet fibers on the Chinese shoes. I guess you know what he's talking about."

"Yes," she said softly. So, the Chinese shoes had been worn—and surely not by L. D. Barth.

"—wouldn't believe the testimonials," Callie was saying. "Anyone who can pronounce his name has made some sort of vacuous statement about how much they loved Burke Lymon, how close they were. The people in this town! Can't turn on the radio or the TV without hearing ten, twenty people gush about 'Burke this, Burke that.'"

"No one who knew him ever called him Burke. It'll fizzle out soon enough. Another life, another sound bite."

Queenie heard Callie snort. "Not this time, hon. Did you know the film's being released tonight?"

"Yeah, I read something about it."

"Well, people have been waiting in lines all day. And listen to this, some deejay started a rumor that the movie itself is riddled with clues to the murderer's identity; that Burke Lymon produced the film for the sole purpose of exposing this person."

Queenie lit her cigarette.

"*And*," Callie continued, "whoever sends in the best scenario describing who did it and how wins five thousand dollars and a part in a schlock horror movie some opportunistic producer is shooting in the desert called *Lucifer's Curse* or *The Curse of Lucifer*. It's about—"

"A filmmaker axed at his own premiere?"

"Gee, how did you know?" Callie remarked. "Anyway, another radio station's already started a call-in contest centered around all of Burke Lymon's previous films. They play a snatch of a theme song or bit of dialogue and the first person to call in and correctly identify the film its from wins free tickets to *Lucifer's Shadow*.

"Then there're the video sales and rentals of all his old films, and this morning two theaters, one in the Valley and one in Hollywood, started Burke Lymon retrospectives. They're showing his films back to back and will continue to do so twenty-four hours a day until the perp is caught."

"Which, of course," Queenie said with a sigh, "they'd prefer didn't happen. At least not while sales are brisk. How's J.P.'s investigation?"

"I'll get to that," she said. "There was a near riot at the memorial service this afternoon in Palm Isle. Couple thousand people showed up. The police arrested two men with axes and one woman for throwing tomatoes."

Had to be Amanda Martin, Queenie thought, wondering if the woman had been looking for her. "Did the widow show up?"

"Apparently her limo did. But the crowd scared her off."

"And J.P.?"

"Not a good time to be a cop . . . Beverly Hills P.D.'s working for once. Some gang invaded, all armed with axes. Lots of movie people have been getting threatening phone calls—even on car phones. From the sound of it, Satan spends all of his time on the telephone. And, of course, every lunatic in town's a Lucifer wannabe. They're lining up at the Hollywood police station! Cops are smothering under piles of confessions. Hardware stores are sold out of axes, airlines leaving L.A. are packed, private protection agencies are making a bundle . . . and everyone blames the cops. Heat's on, believe me."

Queenie whistled.

"Never seen anything like it. Of course, the winner in all this is the movie. Talk about your free publicity. By the way, you have points?"

"No."

"Too bad." Callie paused. "Well, this movie's gonna make *someone* rich."

"Just so," Queenie said absently. "Just so. . . ."

"Sounds like you've got an idea who."

"Maybe. . . . I'll touch base with you when I get back, tomorrow if I'm lucky."

250

She fixed a sandwich and, while eating, unloaded and then restocked her satchel with just the essentials: lock picks, editing gloves, a new penlight, her Swiss Army knife, and wallet. She spent the rest of the evening studying her notes and shooting script. Then at ten P.M. she left for Windemere in Rex's pickup.

CHAPTER THIRTY-THREE

QUEENIE PARKED THE truck in a ditch opposite the open gate and shielded by a couple of English walnut trees.

There was no traffic on the isolated road but, as a precaution, she raised the hood and left a note under the windshield wipers: CAR TROUBLE. GONE TO GET HELP. It might discourage any patrol car from investigating further.

Passing quickly through the open gate, she stayed well in the trees parallel to the gravel road.

It was a fairly clear night with broken clouds scuttling across the waning moon. Every few yards she stopped and listened but heard no dogs, humans, or tires crunching on the gravel.

Suddenly she started. The mansion had come into view, the Winged Victories shimmering like apparitions, casting huge threatening shadows against the facade. Then she realized they were illuminated by floodlights at their pedestals. She took a deep breath. They're stone, she told herself. Even so, they looked dreadfully supernatural.

She crept farther west then north, to within a few yards of the weeping willow. One window on the ground floor glowed faintly. Must be Wakefield's bedroom, she thought. She'd counted on him being asleep by now. She'd have to be even more cautious.

At a crouch, she ran from the shelter of the trees to the conservatory, praying that Wakefield hadn't checked the windows. There she stopped for a moment to put on her editing gloves.

The window she'd unlatched opened smoothly and with barely a sound. She allowed herself a sigh of relief, then stepped inside. After pushing the curtain aside, she entered the shadowy conservatory, then moved quickly to the hall.

Just ahead, light bleached a rectangle on the floor.

She tiptoed to the door and peeked in. Wakefield's gray head was just visible above the back of an armchair. He looked to be reading a book. She passed through the light stopping once to listen. There was no sound of anyone else in the building.

Taking the carpeted stairs two at a time, she hurried on to the door of Lymon's apartment. It was still locked. With the penlight in her mouth, she found the proper pick. The old-fashioned lock succumbed easily and in seconds she was inside the room.

Moonlight trickled in through the still-open curtains. Otherwise, the room fell into caves of darkness. Passing quickly through the sitting room, she entered the bedroom and went straight to the desk. There she took the folder from the drawer, set it on the writing surface, and, holding the penlight over the contents, began to read.

She shivered slightly while quickly scanning the five typewritten pages of what was a business plan, an outline of Winged Victory Productions. Lymon was planning to build a studio on the estate, using the main house for his offices and living space, the outbuildings for production.

So, she thought, he hadn't planned on getting out of the film business—just out of Hollywood!

Behind the business plan was a single sheet of lined notebook paper on which were two columns of handwritten names. The column on the left, and by far the longest, began with Alice Baldridge and ended with Phil Sykes. Hec Cerruti's name was in the left column. In the right column Queenie found her own name after Sooch Bauer and Billy Bright; last was Selma Steinberg.

Apparently the two columns represented those he was releasing and those he was considering bringing with him to start the new production company. To avoid conflict among the crew, he must have decided not to ask those in the second column until after the premiere.

The business plan also explained why he'd done his postproduction work on the East Coast: to set up contacts for his future operation.

She tucked the folder in her satchel then opened the closet door and stepped inside. After gently closing the door behind her, she pulled the string, turning on an overhead light, and switched off her penlight.

Checking out the dress labels, she discovered they were all size 6. Much too small for Mrs. Lymon—and Lymon himself, for the thought had crossed her mind that maybe he liked dressing in women's clothes. Otherwise why would Wakefield have acted so embarrassed?

Nessa was small enough to wear size 6, but still the dresses revealed no real identification of their owner.

Noticing a step ladder leaning against the back wall, she set it in the center of the floor and stepped up to examine the shelves. Other than a few empty boxes and a lot of dust, there was nothing. Then she spied an area where the dust had been rubbed away. Above it she saw a latch. Her heart began to beat a little faster.

Since there were no exposed hinges or knobs, she reached out and pushed. A door swung inward.

Moving the ladder closer, she hoisted herself up on the shelf. She pushed the door until a *click* told her it was flush with the interior wall.

Switching the penlight back on, she worked herself through the door and into the space. She found herself in an attic barely illuminated by shards of moonlight coming through a shuttered north window. An electric heater and a coiled extension cord rested on the floor immediately to her right. She stood up and flashed the light around the room.

The stale air was oppressive and the lack of light made the space feel close around her.

A barrier had been set up cutting this area off from the rest of the attic, which she figured must have run the length of the west wing. Probably enclosed for heating, she thought.

She bumped something and reached to catch it before it fell. Sweat broke out beneath her shirt. On closer examination she found it was a photographer's light on a stand aimed toward the window. In front of it, on a tripod, was a sophisticated-looking camera. She swung the penlight around. Beneath the shuttered window a large sheepskin was draped across what looked like a built-in cupboard.

After dropping the sheepskin on the floor and mentally crossing her fingers, she opened the lid of the cupboard. Inside were stacks of contact sheets and strips of negatives in protective wrappers. She sat down and spent the next ten minutes examining them all.

For the most part, the tiny printed images were nudes posing on the sheepskin, though a few others had been taken in Boston. And the featured model was Nessa.

Queenie looked around her and pondered the setup, thinking the hidden room and the clandestine nature of it must have appealed to Lymon's secretive nature.

Suddenly she jerked up. Had she heard a sound crack the eerie silence? Or was it her imagination?

One of those interior voices that speak loudly but are often ignored urged her to leave—and quickly. She stuffed the contact sheets and some negatives into her satchel. Then she closed the lid of the cupboard and replaced the sheepskin.

She had just poked her head into the closet when she heard voices nearby.

Her heart leapt in her throat. Someone was opening the closet door. She grabbed for the string to turn off the light but it was just out of reach.

CHAPTER THIRTY-FOUR

SHAKING, SHE SCOOTED farther back while reaching to pull the door shut. It was stuck, wouldn't budge. Someone entered the closet. She closed her eyes as if that would make her invisible. Then she remembered the ladder positioned close to the shelf. But there was nothing she could do about it—except pray while her heartbeat changed from a canter to a full gallop.

"Don't forget to call the police and report that truck I saw." Holy Mother! It was Mrs. Lymon, her voice coming from the bedroom.

Queenie silently cursed. Now she had the police to think about. Unless she could get back to the truck before—

"Soon as I'm finished, madam." Wakefield's reply was much closer. Queenie opened her eyes and saw him pushing the dresses into the back of the closet and pulling Lymon's things forward. For the moment he was too preoccupied to notice either the ladder or the open crawl space. She prayed his eyesight was weak, that he hadn't thought about the light being on.

"Finished doing what?"

"Making room for your clothes . . . madam. I didn't expect you'd want to stay in his rooms."

He vanished from Queenie's field of vision, half shutting the door behind him. Had he entered the closet simply to hide the dresses? She counted the seconds.

"Now what are you doing?"

"Unpacking for you," Queenie heard Wakefield reply.

"Don't bother. I want to take a bath."

"Yes, ma'am."

"Go call the police *now*. I don't like the thought of prowlers around. Oh, and Wakefield."

"Yes?"

"You can pack your own bags. I'd like you out of the house in the morning. My own people will be coming in."

Queenie heard a heavy silence then Wakefield's weak "Certainly." His heart must be broken, Queenie thought, sympathy cutting into her own fears for a moment. But just for a moment. She had to get to her car before the police arrived. And the fastest way out was through Lymon's apartment.

She heard water begin to pound in the bathtub. Now or never, Davilov, she thought. She pushed her satchel onto the shelf and quickly followed it. Uneasily she noticed the door was open.

She was half out of the crawl space, her hands on the edge of the shelf and poised to slide one leg out, when Mrs. Lymon entered her line of vision. Her naked back to the closet, she was poking around in a suitcase opened on the bed.

Awkwardly balanced, Queenie froze. By the looks of it, Mrs.

Lymon was going to hang up her clothes. She was less than six feet away. Any errant noise would alert her.

Take your frigging bath! Queenie silently entreated, her arms beginning to shake. Sweat rolled off her nose, dropping onto the top of the ladder, sounding to Queenie like rocks *pinging* against glass. But so far, Mrs. Lymon hadn't heard.

Finally, pulling out a silky robe, Mrs. Lymon moved off to the left. Queenie scrambled down the ladder then pulled her satchel off the shelf. Hiding behind a row of suits, she moved to the door, crushing pair after pair of shoes. She waited at the door and listened.

Several long seconds passed. Mrs. Lymon must have taken today's afternoon non-stop flight out of LAX, then hired the same test-pilot cabbie to drive her to Windemere. Callie had said Mrs. Lymon's limo showed up at the memorial service. Obviously the woman hadn't been in it. While the press and everyone else assumed she'd been frightened away from the service by the crowds, she'd been on her way to Boston, the flight arriving at Logan Airport around ten-thirty P.M.

Finally Queenie heard the creak of faucets being twisted. A moment later the water stopped pounding.

Now she listened for splashing sounds while sweat coursed from under her breasts and down her back. The wait seemed interminable.

Then she heard Mrs. Lymon scooting around in the tub.

Time to boogie.

Controlling the urge to run, she first checked to be sure she wouldn't be seen from the bathroom. Then, holding her breath, she tiptoed through the bedroom and sitting room, and finally out the door. After closing it softly behind her, she stood staring through a window into the lily pond below, regaining her breath.

Now she had a decision to make: Leave through the front door and run to her car—or enlist Wakefield. Where was his loyalty now that he'd been dismissed? Survival instincts screamed for her to run. But curiosity urged her to take the risk.

Like a silent shadow she hurried down the stairs. The front door was straight ahead.

Without hesitating, Queenie turned to the right.

"The pickup's mine. Call them back and tell them not to bother," she said from the doorway of the office just as Wakefield put down the receiver.

For a brief instant, she thought her sudden appearance might have frightened him into a heart attack. He teetered momentarily then recovered himself.

"Seems to me your loyalty should now be to Lymon alone."

They stared at each other for a long moment.

Finally he picked up the receiver. Only then did it occur to her that he might tell the police he'd caught an intruder.

They both angled into slots across the street from the Common and a few doors down from the only business that appeared open on the entire street, a tavern called the Blue Devil. Queenie locked the pickup and then joined Wakefield beneath a sign hanging from an iron rod depicting a blue demon dancing with a high-stepping witch. She thought ironically of herself earlier, tinted from head to toe.

They shared a table in a dark corner after he'd paid for the drinks, Wakefield nursing a triple brandy, Queenie sipping a Rolling Rock. He was either holding back tears or still shell-shocked by his abrupt dismissal. In either case, she had to get him talking. Maybe another shock would do the job.

Feeling a bit heartless, she tossed one of the contact sheets on the table. He peered at it then suddenly reared back. "It was her! She killed him!" he said unexpectedly.

"Nessa? She was murdered before Lymon." She put the sheet back in her satchel.

"My God. She's dead too?" he whispered.

"You knew her?"

Finally he met her eyes, his indignation unmistakable. "I suppose I should be sorry. But I'm not. She was"—he cleared his throat—"his fiancée."

Like John Wakefield's, Queenie's shocks were compounding.

"They were going to be married as soon as his divorce was finalized. She, Vanessa that is, lived on the estate for a while. We never talked except when she asked for something. Junior must have instructed her not to mention him. Otherwise I might have learned of the name he was using."

"Vanessa. That was her name?"

"Vanessa Glass. Junior met her in Boston two Christmases ago. She was an actress. He saw her in *A Christmas Carol* in Boston. She played the ghost of Christmas past."

"Go on."

"There are people around here who think the Oldfathers live under a curse. I'd always thought it nothing more than silliness . . . until she came along." He cleared his throat again as if the words had claws.

"The first Oldfather was a Puritan, a lay preacher and cobbler by trade. He started a witch hunt in the village, bringing terror to anyone who was the least bit different. There were a number of deaths, mostly by drowning, but one young woman was burned at the stake. Supposedly, she put this—this curse on the family. There are drawings of her in the local museum. The resemblance to Vanessa is uncanny."

Queenie had read much the same story in the museum's

pamphlet, though without the reference to Nessa. "Was she from around here?"

Wakefield waved his hand impatiently. "Who knows where she came from? All that mattered was that she'd ruin his life! I just knew. But Junior was—" He stopped as if searching for a word. "Enchanted. Yes, that's exactly it. *Enchanted.* She spent a few days with him before he left. . . .

"Then he called July of last year telling me to open up one of the cottages. Apparently Vanessa had contacted him and needed a place to stay.

"When he was home last Christmas, she moved into the house with him. At the end of the holiday, they left together. He told me when I saw them again it would be as husband and wife. I thought maybe he was appeasing me since he knew how much I disproved of him having, er, such a relationship while he was still married to Frances."

He stopped sipping, now *drank* his brandy.

"Earlier today you said you knew Frances well."

"Hmm, yes, but I haven't seen her in ten years, since she and Junior were married." Abruptly he clammed up.

"Wakefield, she just tossed you off the property. Who in the hell are you protecting? Her family? Her family money?"

"What are you talking about?"

Queenie related what Frances had said to Lieutenant Fitzgerald in the theater, that she had money of her own.

John snorted. "That's a flat-out lie—unless she's talked herself into believing the Oldfather fortune is hers. She was Charles Senior's nurse. He had a number of infirmities—and I don't think you need to know their exact nature," he said, giving her a stern eye. "Suffice it to say he required a nurse and, well, he wasn't exactly an easy patient."

"Go on."

"None stayed very long. And then we found Frances."

"Found?"

"Through an agency. She came for an interview. Charles Senior, well, liked her immediately and wanted to hire her right then. I told him he shouldn't make an exception."

"How do you mean?"

"Anyone who worked for him had their backgrounds thoroughly checked by a private detective agency in Boston."

So, she thought, Lymon had acquired that precaution from his father. "And she checked out?"

"Oh, yes. He was just afraid she'd take another job while we waited for the report. As it was, she had little background to check. No references, since she'd just graduated from nursing school. Lower-middle-class upbringing in Cambridge. An only child. Father left when she was an infant, mother a waitress." He looked accusingly at Queenie. "All the trappings of a gold digger."

"Other than that, no complaints?"

"Let's see, it was ten years ago, May, when she started. That Christmas, when Junior was back for his yearly visit, he met her and well, they married in January." He fell silent again.

"And that's all?"

"I said she was a gold digger."

"That's hardly a felony."

He finished his brandy. "It's late and I have to pack."

Suddenly she flashed on whom he'd been protecting and why. "I suppose you caught them in the act."

"What?"

"Frances and Charles Senior. Having sex."

CHAPTER THIRTY-FIVE

HE BLINKED TWICE, then opened his mouth but nothing came out. He appeared either astonished that she'd said it or relieved that he hadn't had to.

"This is no time to be prudish," Queenie admonished. "Sex can be a dangerous weapon."

Ignoring her, or maybe cued by her comment, Wakefield left his seat and stalked outside.

She quickly joined him in a brisk walk past the closed shops, their lighted fronts featuring occult oddities local Christians sold for enlightened profit.

"You said Hammon was the name of his company?" Wakefield asked.

"Yes."

"Maybe I should have paid more attention to the movies. Hammon is an old family name, on his mother's side."

"Great. But that doesn't tell me—"

"Holly's death estranged them, you see," he blurted. "I think Junior blamed his father—for neglecting them. And surely Charles Senior blamed Junior for not looking out for Holly."

"But he always came home for Christmas," Queenie added to Lymon's defense.

"In Holly's memory. He tried hard to make Christmas special out of his love for her. Her grave's in the family plot. No matter the weather, he spent time there every day he was home. Who knows, he might have seen something of Holly in Vanessa. I'll give her that. Frances was different. No, he married Frances purely out of spite."

Now the truth was coming. "Why do you say that?"

He sighed. "One night during the Christmas holiday he met Frances, I went up to take Charles Senior his nightly toddy. As I approached the bedroom door I heard strange noises. To be honest, I thought they were, well . . . but with an older man you can never be sure—he could have been having an attack—

"The door was ajar so I peeked in—and immediately regretted it. She—Frances—was engaging Charles in, uh, a certain—"

"Graphic descriptions aren't necessary."

"No, what horrified me was that Junior was in the room! Hidden behind a curtain, watching. I had seen him several times listening at his father's door, but he quickly moved away at my approach. How I managed to keep quiet, not to drop the toddy, I'll never know, but I slipped away without anyone knowing I'd been there."

"And you never told anyone," Queenie said.

"Absolutely not! The very next day what had been a mild flirtation between Junior and Frances began to get serious, Junior the instigator.

"You see, Ms. Davilov, despite her motives Frances did make Charles Senior happy. She was a beautiful girl . . . I knew they'd been engaging in, er, relations. The bedroom door was sometimes locked and the sounds were, well . . . I always knocked just to be sure—it would have been remiss of me not to. Anyway, several weeks later Junior married Frances in the family chapel. I don't need to tell you Charles Senior was not pleased."

"Did he plan to marry her?"

"Oh, no. He treated her more as a plaything. When she married Junior, he was like a boy grieving for a lost pet. For her part, I think she was pleased to at least have her claws in one of them, though with Junior she was putting some distance between herself and the money. Of course, it's all moot now. Everything's hers."

"You saw Lymon—what, the week before last?"

"Oh yes, but he kept to himself. Spoke to me only about mundane matters—what he wanted for dinner, that sort of thing. But, of course, it was not my place to pry."

"No one came to see him?"

He shook his head.

The drizzle turned to rain and Wakefield picked up his pace until they were next to his car. "I have to go back and pack now."

"I'm sorry," Queenie said sincerely. Hunched over her notebook, she gave him her home phone number then jotted down the number where he could be reached at his sister's home in Boston, promising to let him know how everything turned out.

While driving back to Boston, the rain on the roof of the pickup reminding her of prolonged applause, she understood where Lymon had acquired his taste for the occult. In Windemere. But would it help solve his murder?

She recalled the word game she'd played Saturday night: *Ly-mon—my lie*. Had Burke Lymon's subconscious subtley influenced his choice of a new name? He certainly wasn't the man she'd thought him to be. He must have thrown L. D. Barth and Nessa together purposefully and both had played their parts well. And Chip Ingram had been right about money being hidden away.

Now Lymon's death had meaning. As did Nessa's. But L.D. no longer seemed the most likely villain in this scenario. Even if he had fallen in love, had learned the truth, and felt he'd been made the fool, Queenie no longer believed he'd killed them both.

At about four A.M. Wednesday, Queenie got up from Rex's desk and stretched. She'd managed to get a seat on a flight leaving at six-fifteen, and it was time to think about heading for Logan Airport. It would have been easy to stretch out on Rex's bed for an hour or so but she didn't want to risk missing the plane.

She gathered her notes, excitement overpowering fatigue. After returning from Windemere, she'd tackled Vitch's list, fitting coveralls, baseball caps, boots, and plastic exercise suits on a number of people as if she were playing with paper dolls. More mentally taxing was finding purposes for such items as the tarp, plastic bags, clean popcorn and drink containers, and the clothesline. On the surface, Burke Lymon had gone to the bathroom and met a brutal fate. She knew now, though, that that wasn't quite the way it happened.

After neatly stacking the notes, she placed them in her satchel along with Lymon's business plan and photos of Nessa, the faxes and *L.A. Times*, and the copy of *Independent Film-*

making. Last, she added the shooting script, which she needed to study further. It was crucial to figuring the timing of the murder; she'd study it on the plane home.

After changing clothes, she dumped everything into her satchel, including the wet dress. Then, finding three envelopes in Rex's desk, she slipped a twenty into each and left the apartment.

In the lobby, the guard called a taxi for her. She handed him the envelopes, telling him to keep one for himself and to give the others to the day guard and Mrs. Warren. She hoped they wouldn't find the amount too paltry.

Finally she took several deep breaths and then hurried down the steps to wait for the cab, the perfume of elegance locked securely in her memory.

CHAPTER THIRTY-SIX

LUCIFER HAD A shadow and it was all too human. Queenie leaned back, turning her head toward the window. With only a sprinkling of passengers in coach, she'd managed a row to herself from which paper trailed to the aisle seat.

Miles below, the Midwest displayed its fruitful plains in fitted pastel rectangles, reminding her of a rug she'd once made of carpet remnants and duct tape.

The world is so symmetrical and tidy when viewed from a lofty perch, she thought. Maybe that's why the deities often ignore us. From where they sit, everything looks fine.

She got up and went to the aft bathroom. She used the stainless steel toilet then splashed water on her face. Her eyes reminded her of a couple of carelessly dug holes. It's painful to know the truth, she thought. It's even more painful to keep it to oneself.

She returned to her seat, considering calling J.P. from the airplane, to tell him she knew who killed Burke Lymon. But he probably couldn't spare the time for a long conversation. In fact, he probably wouldn't even listen until she gave him proof—the one thing that still eluded her.

The plastic window shade made a slight scraping sound as she pulled it down. She almost expected to hear the same sound as she lowered her eyelids and began to empty her mind of bloody green garbage bags, skulls smiling from ax handles, popcorn containers, soft drink cups . . . and demons with familiar faces.

"Excuse me. Excuse me!"

Queenie's eyelids sprung open. A flight attendant leaned forward so closely that Queenie could smell the woman's fresh makeup.

"You need to clean this up. We're getting ready to land."

"Oh. Yeah," Queenie mumbled, trying to reorient herself, exit the dream in which she and Rex had been leaping for—jeweled cones? No. Hats, cloche hats. Rex even wore one.

"Bring your seat back to the upright position and be sure to fasten your seat belt."

The crisply delivered instructions fully awakening her, Queenie began stuffing the papers in her satchel, the murder's details now firmly organized in her mind.

Lifting the shade, she watched the aircraft cut into the cobbler-thick sky crust covering a rich filling of baked humanity.

"Which cat house?" the cabbie said outside the terminal, turning to get a better look at her.

Later, when he braked in front of the St. Albans, Queenie

270

figured the kennel was one cat house he wouldn't soon forget. Clue hadn't stopped yeowling since Queenie collected her, having to wear a heavy rubber mitt to drag her clawing and spitting out of her "hotel room."

"Thanks," the driver snapped as she paid him fifteen dollars over the fare. "If I was you, I'd get tropical fish." Leaving rubber, he shot up the street.

Sensitized by cleansing rain and the olfactory diet of a more refined environment, Queenie smelled the St. Albans before even entering the courtyard.

Hearing her name called, she turned around abruptly. Inside the elaborate gingerbread house/carrier Rex must have purchased, Clue's shrieks intensified as if, like Gretel, she was about to be toasted in the witch's oven.

J.P. looked both ways then trotted across the street.

"What are you doing here?" she asked in surprise.

He gave her half a smile. "Aren't you glad to see me?"

"As a matter of fact, I am."

"Jesus. What have you done to the cat?"

"Come on. Let's just get her upstairs," she said as they entered the building.

The elevator shuddered then jerked violently.

"You look tired. Where've you been?" J.P. asked.

"Boston," she said sharply, all too aware of the luxury she'd left behind. J.P. didn't seem affected by Clue's wails and the noisy, foul-smelling elevator.

"Huh. Then I guess you haven't heard. Late yesterday I was taken off the investigation."

"What? But why?"

"Good question. I called Callie to see if she'd heard anything. She told me you might be in to see her today. I've been staked outside your place all morn—"

Interrupting J.P. with a loud clang, the elevator jolted to a stop. J.P. opened the two doors and they both stepped out.

"—all morning," he finished. "I was wondering if you'd heard anything. And, well, I wanted to talk."

"Why would you be taken off the case?"

"*And* put on vacation. They said I'd never been assigned the case in the first place."

Once inside her apartment, Queenie took Clue into the bathroom, opened the carrier, and quickly closed the bathroom door. Then, using the key Rex had left beneath her door, she went across the hall and brought back Clue's things.

"Your brother around?" he asked as she carried the cat litter toward the bathroom. She eyed him sharply.

"Hey! I just thought he'd like to know the lab found methaqualone in Burke Lymon's blood," the lieutenant said in an injured tone.

"I'll tell him." As Queenie opened the bathroom door, Clue dashed out and vanished into the bedroom.

"Just don't shit on my pillow, okay?" she called out, setting the litter on the bathroom floor.

"What'd you say?" J.P. asked as she entered the living room. He stood at the TV holding the cloche hat.

"I was talking to Clue—" Queenie stopped, watching him: *that hat ... the dream on the plane ...*

"So you've got one of these too. Suddenly they're all the rage. Never thought of you as keeping up with fashion."

Ignoring the comment, she continued to stare, her mind working.

He pulled out the hat pin, examining it. "Lethal piece of jewelry," he said, then stuck it back on the hat.

... Sunday morning: the tape ...

272

Queenie's eyes widened. "Holy Mother!"

"What is it? You look like you've seen a ghost."

Queenie launched herself across the room. The tape of the Saturday night news was still inside the VCR. She switched on the machine. When the tape began to rewind, she grabbed the hat and looked at the large pearl hat pin.

"It's been staring right at me. . . ."

"What're you talking about?"

"You've got to see something—rather it's what you *won't* see that's important."

The rewind completed, Queenie jabbed the play button. The broadcast introduction projected on the television. Queenie fast-forwarded, stopping the tape when the broadcaster stood outside the Mikado. Then she hit the play button.

They watched and waited.

"Now!" Queenie said when the image appeared. Mrs. Lymon exited her limo and walked up the Astroturf to the Mikado's entrance. Queenie paused at a close-up and pointed to the hat.

"Look at the hat," she said. "Look closely." She pointed out the large black opal gleaming on the matte black hat.

"What the hell's going on, Davilov?"

Queenie held up her hand. "Just wait."

The scene cut to Mrs. Lymon, the policewoman, and Queenie leaving the theater. The three women approached the camera, Mrs. Lymon the focal point.

"Now what do you see?" Again she pointed to the hat.

"The same hat."

"But the hat pin's missing!"

She replayed the sequence.

"You see? The hat pin was there when she arrived but it wasn't there when she left."

He looked puzzled.

Queenie took a deep breath. "When I played the tape Sunday morning something seemed wrong but I couldn't place it."

"Davilov. What are you talking about?"

"The murder, J.P.! All we needed was proof." She tapped the hat on the screen. "Don't you see? *That's* our proof—we've got to get into the Mikado!" More to herself, she added, "I need my stopwatch and a flashlight."

She started to move away. J.P. grabbed her arm. "Davilov! Slow down. What are you saying?"

"We've got to find that hat pin," she snapped impatiently, forgetting that he didn't know what she did.

"Why?"

She blinked. "To prove that Frances Lymon murdered her husband." Then she added, "It must have dropped when Alice changed into Frances' clothes."

CHAPTER THIRTY-SEVEN

"JUST WAIT TILL we get to the theater," she said when he asked her to explain. "First I need to tell you what I learned in Boston."

J.P. drove, his tape recorder rolling. He didn't say much, appeared to be concentrating on the traffic, but she knew he absorbed every word, mentally collating each bit of information.

"Wait here," he said, pulling up to the theater.

Yellow police tape still cordoned off the entrance. She watched J.P. speak to an armed guard wearing the brown uniform of a private security firm. Queenie reasoned that Mrs. Lymon had beefed up security by bringing in outside help. At one point both men glanced in her direction. Then they separated, the guard disappearing into the theater, J.P. jogging back to the car.

"Gotta keep a twenty-four-hour watch on this place," he

said, and, putting the car in gear, drove into the alley. "There've been bomb threats. I told him you had crucial evidence and you needed to get in to see the layout one more time. He knows I'm not heading the investigation anymore but I said there was no one else available to bring you over. We've got fifteen minutes."

The guard had left the west exit door ajar and then resumed his post. J.P. stopped in front of it. He and Queenie both put on gloves and entered, going directly to the projection booth.

They hurried up the narrow stairs. Just outside the booth, J.P. stopped. "Give me the flashlight."

Queenie took it from her satchel.

"Stay here."

"But—"

"I won't risk two of us mucking up evidence."

The wait seemed interminable, giving her enough time to tear apart her scenario. What if Mrs. Lymon had simply taken her hat off in the bathroom and not bothered to secure it to her hair again with the hat pin? What if the hat pin was simply in her purse?

"Find anything yet?" she called out anxiously.

As it wasn't on public display, the projection booth hadn't been remodeled. Only the plumbing in the tiny bathroom had been updated. Queenie remembered the booth's scuffed and warped floorboards, the metal shelves against the wall where cans of film collected dust. . . .

"Davilov!"

Queenie jumped up. J.P. appeared in the doorway, his shoes illuminated by the flashlight dangling in his hand. His expression was grim.

"I found it."

Her heart fluttered. She took a deep breath to calm herself. "Where? Where'd you find it?"

"In the corner under some shelves, wedged between loose floorboards. Must have gotten kicked aside or something. I'll leave it for Frank Baird, he's in charge now. Great, Davilov! Evidence at the scene."

She felt confidence return in a rush.

"Any popcorn and a soft drink up there?"

He left. After a moment, he returned.

"No food."

Back in the lobby, Queenie checked her watch. She only had about eight minutes rather than the full twenty minutes for an exact replication of events. She wouldn't need the stopwatch now.

"Come on, then," she said, taking the flashlight and moving toward the open doors of the auditorium. "The timing won't be perfect but when we get back to my apartment, I'll give you the notes I made on the plane and the shooting script. Part of my job as a script supervisor is to time each scene. . . ."

Like an usher, she aimed the flashlight at the carpet, stopping when she located Mrs. Lymon's seat. An empty cup and a popcorn container were beside it.

"Mrs. Lymon sat here. At about ten minutes after seven, she left her seat."

"How do you know the time?"

"By recalling what was on the screen when she got up," she said quickly. "Anyway, she went up to the projection booth. Both she and Alice wore dresses that were easy to slip in and out of. Alice puts on Frances's clothes and, bringing the popcorn and soda she'd taken to the booth before the film started, pulls the net veil down over her face and hurries into the theater to take Frances's seat. Mrs. Lymon had brought a silk coat she left on the seat beside hers. That way Alice would know exactly where to sit. I saw Alice taking refreshments to the booth—if she'd stayed up there they'd still be there.

"That takes care of Alice for the time being," Queenie said, and hurried back into the lobby, switching off the flashlight.

"Meanwhile, Mrs. Lymon dresses in the janitor's jumpsuit, jams her hair up under the baseball cap, slips on the Chinese shoes, puts on the editing gloves then the household rubber gloves, and leaves the projection booth."

"How did you know about those clothes?" the lieutenant asked suspiciously.

"Just let me get on with this, J.P. We don't have much time. She goes to the garbage bin that was inside by the west exit. I saw it there when I went to clean up after we arrived. Everything she needs is hidden in the bin underneath what passes for garbage—in case anyone happens to look—though it's simply clean refreshment containers inside a garbage bag.

"First she takes the OUT OF ORDER sign and tapes it to the men's room door."

Queenie moved into the lobby, the lieutenant beside her. Outside they could see the guard and passing traffic. A car slowed and someone leaned out the window to snap a picture.

"She pushes the garbage can into the lobby. The baseball cap's pulled low over her face. If anyone had entered the lobby, they'd not give her a second thought, would just think the janitor was cleaning up."

Queenie hurried behind the candy counter. "She takes out the new bottle of Scotch and pours some out. Do you have the key to the manager's office?"

"Not anymore."

Queenie made a face. "Oh, well . . . the door would have been unlocked so Lymon could get to the supplies. He's pretty zonked by now on the Scotch with the Quaaludes in it. She gets his prints on the bottle then moves him inside the office. If he's already passed out, she just drags him in. Then she closes and locks the door.

"She was a nurse. In his current state, it's my guess she simply presses the right vein and cuts of the blood supply to his brain. Or maybe she knows just what nerve to hit in the back of his neck. In any case, he loses consciousness.

"In the office she spreads the tarp on the floor. She drags Lymon onto it then slips several layers of Hefty bags first over his torso, then over his legs, and secures them with the clothesline. Once he's tied up she puts on the plastic exercise suit and the rubber boots. Then she takes the ax and, using the blunt side, bashes in his skull."

"Why the blunt side?" the lieutenant interjected.

"She didn't want to split the bags and spray blood in the room. That's also why she used so many bags. And the plastic suit and boots protected her clothes just in case blood did splatter. She couldn't risk being seen back in the lobby with blood on the jumpsuit. After all, the murder was supposed to look like it occurred in the men's room."

Queenie took a deep breath. "By the way, did you find blood in the manager's office?"

"No."

"So far, so good. No blood splatters in the office. And Lymon's probably dead now. She rolls him in the tarp, ties it up with the clothesline, lifts and dumps him in the bin."

"You think she's physically capable of lifting a hundred-fifty-pound man?"

"She's in good shape, J.P., and you can bet she had the added boost of adrenaline. But, for the sake of argument, she could lower the bin on its side and push him in, then use the wall for leverage to bring it upright.

"Okay, now she takes off the protective suit and boots, drops them in the bin, then puts the bag of prop garbage back on top. She unlocks the door, checks to make sure no one is around, and wheels the trash bin out of the office. Then she locks the door, rinses out his cup, and pours in clean Scotch, taking away the old bottle and leaving the untainted one in the bag. Finally she wheels the bin through the lobby."

"Why bother locking the door?"

"For one thing, Alice has to be missing her keys. If the door is locked, it's going to be noticed."

"That's funny," J.P. said, his expression anything but amused. "I brought her purse to her Sunday morning. She looked through it, said all her keys to the theater were missing."

"The locked door and missing keys support the story that she was knocked out and her keys stolen."

Queenie checked her watch. Only about four minutes remained before the guard would kick them out.

At a half trot, she and J.P. crossed the red and black Oriental motif carpet and moved into the alcove. While the vomit had been cleaned up, Queenie thought she could still catch a faint whiff of sickness.

She started to enter the men's room, the OUT OF ORDER sign still taped to the door.

"Better not," J.P. cautioned. "We don't want to disturb anything."

Though seeing the scene again would have helped, if Queenie could figure out the sequence thousands of miles away, a few more feet wouldn't matter.

Her mouth felt cottony. She could have used a drink of water. She licked her lips and began, her face rigid with concentration as she relived the mutilation.

"In the men's lounge, she pushes the bin up to the edge of the bathroom. First thing, she removes the 'prop' garbage and sets it in the lounge. Then she takes the bottle of Scotch and empties it in the sink, rinsing it out. For the moment, she puts it back in the bag with the prop garbage.

"Once again she steps into the protective gear—plastic suit and boots—but this time she removes the yellow gloves and slips the surgical gloves over the editing gloves.

"Now she tips over the bin and unrolls Lymon from the tarp. She unties the clothesline, folds the tarp, and removes the bags from his legs. She puts the tarp and clothesline in one of the bags then takes the other bags off his torso.

"Using whatever blood that's accumulated in the bag after the first blow in the office, she writes her message from Lucifer on the mirror, then splatters the rest around the walls. If he'd been hacked to death in there, the blood would have geysered all over the place. As a former nurse she knows this but it doesn't worry her. The scene will be horrifying enough that a detail like that could easily be overlooked—in the beginning anyway. In fact, it was what led me to believe he was dead by the time he reached the men's room.

"Now she slips Alice's keys in his coat pocket—"

"How'd you know th—"

"An educated guess," she said quickly. "She takes out the ax and, well, chops up her husband's body, leaving the ax imbedded in his skull. That done, she carefully removes the protective clothes, which are now bloody. I think she must have stood just inside the bathroom so she could reach the clean bags and not drip any blood on the carpet. She peels off the silver plastic jumpsuit and drops it in a bag. Then she removes one boot and steps on the carpet, drops it in the bag, then the other bloody boot, puts her other foot on the carpet, drops that boot in the bag. The blood pools where she'd been standing."

"Lieutenant Fitzgerald?" someone called out.

"Damn," Queenie hissed.

J.P. raised his hand for silence, then, peeling off and stuffing his gloves in his pocket, he hurried into the lobby. When next he appeared, he wasn't alone.

"—appreciate it," he said. Taking Queenie by the arm, they left through the west exit, the guard watching.

J.P. opened the car's passenger door for her. She slid onto the hot seat, immediately rolling down the window.

"Just finish," J.P. said as he got in the car. "We'll hang here for a minute." He turned on the engine. Cool air immediately blasted from the air conditioner.

"Let's see," she said, recalling where she'd left off while rolling the window back up. "Oh, yes, the gloves. . . . She takes off the surgical gloves, drops them in the bag with the plastic suit and boots, then slips the yellow rubber gloves back on. Finally she tosses in the prop garbage and leaves the bathroom. Talk about good timing. This is where she really got lucky. . . .

"She hurries out the west exit—the first time Billy goes to meet L.D., she's probably in the manager's office—and checks to see if she's alone. Then, using the garbage bin for cover, she takes off the yellow gloves, the jumpsuit, hat, and Chinese shoes and puts them in another of the Hefty bags. That all goes into the bin under the 'prop' garbage, from which she now takes the rinsed Scotch bottle and heaves it far down the alley. Street noise would cover the sound of smashing glass. She closes the lid and hurries up the accordion stairs, which Alice lowered for her just after the movie started.

"She quickly hoists the stairs back up, rips the fingers of the editing gloves, and simply tosses them behind the bin. She had to keep them on to prevent leaving prints on the fire escape.

"Back in the booth," Queenie continued, "she bumps the projector." She turned to the lieutenant. "The image on the screen jumped. At the time I half expected the film to melt—you know, a bad splice, a caught sprocket, or something.

"But it must have been her signal to Alice. Maybe a minute or two later, L.D. enters the alley to meet Billy Bright. Once Billy returned to his seat, Alice pulls down the veil and goes back up to the projection booth. The two women quickly change clothes.

"Probably wrapping her hand in the full skirt of Alice's dress to prevent leaving prints, Mrs. Lymon knocks Alice unconscious with the lead pipe then returns to her seat. She had to do it so the police would believe an intruder knocked Alice out.

"From beginning to end, the murder took just about twenty minutes. And they'd barely finished when my brother got sick and stumbled onto the body."

J.P. turned to look at her. "They were lucky they weren't caught in the act."

"Lymon bought the theater several years ago and had it refurbished. Alice had a key. She and Frances had time over the summer to rehearse. Still, as the saying goes, 'Fortune protects the bold.' " Queenie said, then explained the normal clean-up arrangements. "So, had everything gone according to plan, the evidence in the garbage bin could well have ended up in the incinerator."

They didn't speak for a moment. Then J.P. turned to her. "Hell, at this point I guess it doesn't matter—along with other shit, an empty Johnnie Walker Red bottle was found on the roof. Don't know yet about prints or lab tests—since I was pulled from the case. Looks like she tossed it up there."

After putting the car in gear, he began to back out of the alley. "Not bad, Davilov. Damn. They just might have gotten away with it."

"Yeah, but like my mother says, 'No matter what you do, there's always shit in the corner.' In this case, a hat pin."

CHAPTER THIRTY-EIGHT

BEGRUDGINGLY, J.P. COMPLIMENTED her on her sleuthing as he headed south to Callie's, Queenie to discover if the phone company contact had come through, J.P. to see if Callie had heard anything new about why he'd been taken off the investigation.

"I was at Palm Isle Monday with a warrant to collect those files from Lymon's office. Still don't know if there's anything in them. But she could have destroyed anything incriminating. She was quite accommodating until I went looking around the grounds."

"For what?"

"Squirrel traps. You know I always suspect the spouse. But, frankly, I thought she'd hired someone. Anyway, it was true Amanda Martin had been camping out around there, but her sending those dead squirrels was ludicrous. The setup was too complicated for her to manage, especially in her state. Mrs.

Lymon must have sent the one to her husband and the other was a fabrication. If she was concerned she would have given it to the police, not burned it.

"And I did find traps in the gardener's shed. But I also learned there was a plague of the critters in the area.

"She also told me she needed to go out of town on urgent business. I said if she left L.A., I'd get a warrant for her arrest. She didn't like that either."

J.P. pulled into the lot full of cars. Queenie glanced around quickly but didn't see the Jaguar. Had the Pac Bell contact come through?

The bells jingled as they entered the cool office. Callie, absorbed as usual in a computer game, looked at them, seemingly taken aback.

"Together again?" Callie asked.

"Just business," J.P. said quickly. "Heard anything?"

"Just a sec," she said, and scribbled a figure on a slip of paper. "That's what you owe me for the Jag, hon."

Queenie brought out her checkbook. She'd have to put more money in her account to cover the cost of the week's rental of the very car she'd lusted after. Got to be careful what you want, she thought while Callie and J.P. chatted. You just might end up paying for it.

"... and Mrs. Lymon did bring in a private firm to guard the theater, which frees up you guys," Callie was saying. "After that, I guess it was easier to convince the right people to take you off the case." Callie shrugged. "Sorry, J.P. All I've heard is that she's been sweet as pie."

J.P. didn't say any more.

Queenie tore out the check, hoping she'd get her money's worth. "Heard anything from the Pac Bell guy?"

Callie went to her desk and brought back a piece of paper

with the four telephone numbers Queenie had given her last Sunday. Three were ticked off: Selma's, Billy's, and hers. Alice's wasn't.

"The calls were made from a car phone."

Queenie frowned. "A car phone?"

Callie's eyes sparkled. "Yeah. Burke Lymon's."

Deep in thought, Queenie was quiet as J.P. drove back to her apartment. Something didn't fit but she couldn't name it and now she was trying too hard, freezing it out. *What was it?* Maybe she just needed sleep, but she didn't want to give in to fatigue just yet.

While coffee brewed, Queenie handed him the bound shooting script and the folder containing Nessa's photos, Lymon's business plan, and the sheet of paper with the two columns of employees' names. Then she began collating her notes: those from the computer in one pile, those she'd written in longhand on the airplane in another.

"Why don't you pour us some coffee," she said.

"Better yet, why don't I buy you a beer?" he said, dropping the papers on the coffee table.

"Don't you want to go into the station?"

"I said a beer, Davilov, not a night out. Besides, I need a bite to eat."

Why not? she thought. And a beer might free her mind of the missing piece. Whatever she was trying to recall, she felt it was related to Nessa's death.

Seeing the bag with her dress in it, she asked, "Mind if we stop at the dry cleaner's?"

"No problem."

Remembering her good linen suit, she went into the bedroom closet, plucked it off the floor, and threw it over her arm. In a town that made it possible to fly somewhere over the rainbow, surely a dry cleaner could rid her suit of tomato stains and restore her new dress to its original beauty.

On the way out she noticed Clue watching from the pillow. "Just be nice, sweetie. No surprises when I go to sleep tonight."

They left the apartment.

"Where to?" he asked, turning on the ignition while she cleaned out the jacket's pockets, in the process finding Hec Cerruti's business card.

"Huh."

"I said, where to? Which dry cleaner?"

An image flashed in Queenie's mind of the faxed *Times* photograph of the remains of the house in Castaic. Hec had remodeled it for *Neptune in Scorpio,* the second Burke Lymon film she'd worked on. She remembered the charred landscape, the sludge-filled swimming pool in the foreground. Above and in the background, almost completely—but not quite—cropped from the picture had been a row of hedges.

Hec had also built a hot tub, which having been destroyed by the fire, didn't appear in the photograph. At the moment though, she traveled back to one particular day when a shot was being set up with the two principals drinking wine (rose-colored water) and sunning themselves in that hot tub. Lymon had spent an hour setting up the scene while the actors turned to bleached raisins beneath the water line.

"Davilov?"

Staring out the window, Queenie held up her hand for silence.

"And . . . action!" Lymon declared.

Not twenty seconds into the scene, Lymon suddenly cried, "Cut!"

"I didn't flub my lines," the principal actress protested.

"No, no. Not your fault. Let's take a break."

That said, he immediately took Queenie to one side. "Don't look now, but up the hill there's some clown with a video camera. I want you to go up there and stop him from shooting any more film of us. The sooner it's done, the sooner we can get back to work."

Her job depended on being able to fulfill such ancillary requests.

Trudging up to his house in the hot sun, she reminded herself that Lymon's rights in no way allowed him to dictate where anyone aimed a camera.

Still, she'd tucked her hair into a baseball cap J.P. had given her with LAPD in bold letters across the crown that she kept in her car and buttoned a shirt over her white T-shirt. The house above was set apart from the others around it and so was not difficult to locate as she traversed the canyon roads in her car, parking below the house. At the man's door she flashed her P.I. I.D. before he could read it. She told him in a stern tone that the cops were looking for a rapist believed to be in the area, some guy with a camcorder . . . using resident's backyards . . . mid-twenties, tall, dark hair, glasses, about twenty pounds overweight . . .

By the time she returned to the set, the camera was gone. The next day, thick hedges surrounded the patio.

"Queenie?" J.P. was looking at her, his arms wrapped around the steering wheel.

"Have you been up to Castaic since the fire?" she asked softly.

"No reason. The girl's murder isn't in my game plan."

Suddenly she fixed her dark blue eyes on him. "Have people been allowed back in yet?"

"Yesterday, I think. Residents only."

"And firemen, cops . . . some media people."

"Well, yeah, they don't want looting."

"Let's bypass the beer and dry cleaner's for now."

"You want to see the house, don't you?"

"If you give me a hard time, I'll go on my own."

"You'd need me to get you in."

"I'd use my old press card."

He sighed then pulled out into the street.

"Just let me use you as a backboard, J.P., and we might get this thing figured out."

During the trip, J.P. listened, his tape recorder rolling again. Queenie started by repeating what Hec Cerruti told her about Jim Hernandez having a crush on Nessa and hanging around outside her window while they were on location.

"Well, the night he died—falling off scaffolding—he told Hec that Nessa was someone important. Apparently he'd overheard her on the phone. Alice was supposedly asleep, but I'll bet she wasn't. During that conversation, Nessa must have revealed that she and Lymon were going to be married."

J.P. punched the lighter and stuck a cigarette between his lips.

"Alice, then, told Frances. Lymon and Nessa certainly had everyone fooled. We all thought L.D. and Nessa had something going. But now that I think about it, there was something artificial about their relationship. Something forced."

The lighter popped out. J.P. lit the tip of his cigarette. "How do you know Alice and Frances are friends?"

She told him about Alice's neighbor showing her and Rex the house on Sunday and, believing them to be prospective buyers, giving them the number where Alice could be reached.

"The number was for Lymon's residence." After taking her tobacco and papers from her satchel, Queenie began rolling a cigarette, speaking all the while.

2 9 0

"Like all of us, Alice must have heard the rumors that Hammon Productions might go under. We were all concerned for our jobs—nothing new in Hollywood. Alice had been with Lymon ten years. She had a lot to lose. All sorts of fears would assail her: She was too much in the Burke Lymon mold and no one would hire her because of that; she's in her mid-thirties when people in their mid-twenties are considered has-beens; name the fear, it's there. So she decides to tell Frances about Nessa.

"Then we have Frances's fears—her husband is planning to marry another woman and she'll never have a chance to lay her hands on the Oldfather fortune. Maybe she threatens to expose him, tell everyone he's never been poor after all, that his sister was a drug addict . . . but maybe he doesn't care anymore. He's in love and preparing to start over in Massachusetts. So there she hangs without leverage. Enter Alice."

"And," J.P. interjected, "Frances starts to consider killing him and the girl."

"With Alice a perfect assistant. My guess is, she promised Alice Hammon Productions. With that incentive, Alice outdoes herself, determined to make this movie a blockbuster. Anything to sensationalize the murder ups the ante at the box office. Everything fits so well, even down to arranging for Nessa and L.D. to disappear. That's when the free publicity started. And they get a patsy in the bargain—L. D. Barth.

"At the wrap party, Alice finds out where certain people will be during the summer. Billy Bright tells her about the weekend poker games at his girlfriend's house."

"Besides coke, he confessed to selling Quaaludes to L. D. Barth," J.P. said.

Queenie felt a little angry that Billy had lied to her, but it didn't matter now. "Alice must have taken the pills from L.D.'s place while he was gone, stolen his ax, stolen Billy's, doctored the Scotch, and switched the bottles after Lymon arrived at the theater . . . wait! That's it!"

"What's what?" J.P. asked, glancing over at her.

She reminded him about the calls from Lucifer. ". . . I've been trying to remember . . . last Saturday night I met with Selma Steinberg. She mentioned that Alice had borrowed Lymon's car to check on the restaurant where the after-party was being held. Alice had said something about her own car giving her problems. Well, J.P., she used *Lymon's* car. She must have taken his car phone and put it in the trunk of her own car. Sunday, after she left the hospital, she went back to her car and made those threatening calls on Lymon's car phone! Later she probably just tossed it. On the phone, Alice was Lucifer!"

"Jesus," he said. "Movie people."

J.P. showed his badge to the policeman at the barricade. The only people allowed in the area were police, fire units, escorted news crews, and, of course, local residents with identification— some to collect what they could, the majority to gawk at fried and unrecoverable lives.

Conversation tapered off as J.P. drove through the scorched terrain, a landscape in black and ash gray, the air rank with the stinging smell of charred earth and timber. Great clouds of ash charted their passage in this backcountry where people had chosen isolation instead of the cramped life of the crowded city.

Every once in a while, they spotted a house remarkably untouched. More often though, solitary chimneys marked blackened plots like gravestones.

At least the wind had spent itself, as if quietly retiring from the fight to regard the hushed battlefield. Otherwise, they wouldn't have been able to see or breathe.

Queenie had driven this route many times during the filming of *Neptune in Scorpio*. Even thinking of a watery god in this environment seemed pitiful. She remembered the trees dressed in autumnal reds and golds, the sand-colored arroyos, the simple houses blending with the environment—all reduced to a gray desert dotted by scorched brick monoliths and black spears that were once living trees.

J.P. slowed, preparing to turn right into the drive of the burned out house. Below was the muck-filled swimming pool, the house nothing more than a rectangular black cutout.

"No. Not here. Up farther. See those hedges?"

"I thought you wanted to see the house—what's left of it anyway," he said, nonetheless driving on. They went down a dip in the road, then up and around a bend.

"Stop here," she said.

On this side of the hill they could see the stone house. The hedges in the news photo had alerted her that the house might have been spared. She was relieved that it had. Still, the occupant might not be home, or he might not be able to help. Coming up here had been betting on a hunch and the memory of a single day last fall.

J.P. pulled off the road just beyond a NO TRESPASSING sign chain-linked between a new mailbox and a freshly cut post barricading a gravel drive. It was a ridiculous caution as there was no fence to prevent further entry.

Queenie got out of the car. J.P. shut off the engine and followed.

The name on the mailbox was Arnold Popi. They trudged up the narrow drive.

"Who lives here?"

"If he's home, you'll see. Just let me do the talking."

There was no birdsong, no rustling leaves, no skittering of small animals. Only their shoes crunching bits of charcoal sounded in this stunned quiet.

At one point Queenie stopped and picked up a piece of paper, the edges singed. It was a page from someone's recipe book. She dropped it, feeling suddenly overwhelmed by sorrow. Unlike the person they were calling on, many more people had lost everything, down to a recipe for chicken soup.

The front door opened before they arrived and a large bookish-looking man in his late twenties stepped out, hands inhospitably fisted on his hips. She figured the rising ash had alerted him to their approach.

He had dark hair and was still twenty pounds over-weight.

"Mr. Popi," she said, extending her hand like an acquaintance. "I'm Queenie Davilov. This is Detective Fitzpatrick."

J.P. automatically held up his badge.

"We'd like to ask you some questions," Queenie said.

"Am I supposed to know you?"

"We met last fall. There was a rapist—"

"Oh, that. Yes." He then folded his hands in front of himself almost as if protecting his genitals.

"May we come in?"

He hesitated, then stepped back for them to enter.

"Guess that sign was pretty effective," J.P. commented.

"Hm?" Popi closed the door.

"No trespassing. Kept the fire out, didn't it?"

"Oh, that. Put it up yesterday. The fire stayed away because I keep the dry brush off my property and the earth damp. That, and no wood shingles on the roof to fuel flying sparks. . . . You got to respect nature if you live out here. Build with stone, not wood. Use water to protect you. Most people will probably go back to the city. Should have stayed there in the first place. With the Santa Anas starting up early, people should know better. If you want to live around here, you gotta take care of your place."

They followed him into a large living room filled with computers and electronic equipment, including a big-screen television, all wearing plastic dustcovers. A large window on the right afforded a view of the drive. On the opposite wall, sliding glass doors opened onto a wide patio surrounded by high hedges. A film of ash covered everything.

"You want to see my I.D., make sure I really live here?" he asked, and began digging in his back pocket. "Fine with me. I'd just as soon know the police are on their toes."

"Mr. Popi, we're investigating the murder of your neighbor," Queenie said abruptly, taking him off guard. "The young woman who lived in the canyon just below you."

She saw his Adam's apple bob.

"Look, I already talked to the police. First thing yesterday, I went into the station."

"How did you know about the murder?"

"Read it in the newspaper. *Yesterday's* newspaper—first time I saw the story. At my parents' house in Moro Bay. That's where I went Sunday morning when they evacuated us."

"Us?"

He shrugged. "Me, the people who live around here."

"You're single?"

"Yes. I live alone." His Adam's apple bobbed again. Queenie could feel the heat shimmering off his body. "I'm a game designer. Computer games."

"Did you like Nessa?"

"Who?"

"Your neighbor. The girl who was murdered."

"She was all right. But I didn't really know her."

"Pretty girl, wasn't she?"

"Yeah."

"How did you know that?"

He started breathing more rapidly and licked his lips.

"Mind if we get some air?" Queenie asked. Before he could answer, she moved toward the patio. Just inside, a camcorder on a tripod leaned against the wall.

The two men followed. She went straight to the ash-laden hedges. In one spot the branches were broken in a circle.

She turned around.

"Uh, the view's pretty grim," he said anxiously.

"I imagine it used to be pretty spectacular. Especially when Nessa was around." Her eyes were now cold as deep space. Popi appealed to the lieutenant with a look. J.P. regarded him without emotion.

In the distance she could hear the rumble of the highway. "You work from your home, Mr. Popi?"

"Yes."

"Communicating through computers, modems, fax machines . . . must be lonely."

"I'm free to choose the way I live."

"The videotapes must give you a sense of companionship. You can play them over and over on that big screen. Have Nessa right here with you."

His face turned a dusty rose. She had him.

"We'd like to see them. Particularly the last tape you made of her."

"You have no right—"

"We're talking *murder*," she interrupted, nailing him with her eyes.

He held up his hands. "Now, look, I never talked to her, never even went near her!"

"What about Friday?"

"I didn't—"

"The camera was here," she said, pointing out the broken branches in the hedge. "Did you go down there after you saw her come home?"

"Of course not! I heard her singing."

"So you came out here and started the camera rolling. What time was it?"

"Four something. She was in the hot tub, playing with the toy whale and singing something from *My Fair Lady*. After a few minutes I got a phone call. I left the camera running and went in the house. It was my dating service. They called to say someone liked my video and wanted to meet me. Said if I could come in to their office before five I might be able to set up a date for that night."

"And?"

"So I got my keys and went. Their office is in Newhall. I'll give you their address. You can go talk to them."

"First, we'd like to see that tape."

Back inside, Queenie and J.P. stood waiting while Popi pulled a tape from his camcorder. The hum of equipment punctuated the uncomfortable silence.

Without offering them a seat, he removed the dustcover from a VCR on top of a seventeen-inch television. He wasn't going to project on the big screen; perhaps he thought the smaller version would somehow diminish his sins.

At the moment, Queenie didn't care that he was a high-tech peeping Tom. She wanted to see that tape.

Putting himself between them and the screen, he punched in the tape.

"Mr. Popi—"

"You wanted to see last Friday. I'm fast-forwarding," he replied angrily, his back to them.

Queenie and J.P. exchanged knowing glances. Popi must have been taping Nessa all summer. Well, that's what Queenie had counted on.

Finally he stepped to one side. "You're lucky I have my own generator."

"No, Mr. Popi. You are," J.P. said sharply.

Digital numbers appeared on the lower right of the screen; last Friday's date and the time: 4:17 P.M. Nessa stood beside the hot tub, her face animated, her lips moving in silent song. She began to strip, first unbuttoning her blouse, then pulling off her jeans.

Then she stopped and abruptly turned to her right. Someone had just stepped out of the house.

CHAPTER THIRTY-NINE

QUEENIE MOVED CLOSER to the screen. All eyes focused on the unfolding of the silent drama as L. D. Barth entered the picture. Queenie imagined the screen door to the kitchen banging behind him.

L.D. stopped at the tub and frowned, looking angry. He said something. Nessa lowered her naked body into the tub then looked up at him.

"Damn. I wish I knew what they were saying," Queenie said as L.D. spun around and reentered the house. Nessa began to sing again.

"Shit," J.P. said. "Stop the tape."

The screen went blank.

"I need to use your phone."

Popi smiled slightly, as if he'd won a minor battle. "Sorry. No service yet."

"How about phone books, the yellow pages?"

"Might take me a few minutes to find them."

"Never mind. Just give me the tape. Come on, Davilov."

They stopped in Saugus to use a pay phone. Forty minutes later J.P. parked in a lot in front of a well-known school for the deaf located on an estate in Pasadena.

The secretary of the school's director led them into an impressively furnished sitting room where, Queenie figured, parents were probably interviewed. Outside a set of open French doors, a beautifully tended rose garden flourished.

"The director will be with you in just a moment," the secretary said, and left them alone.

J.P. looked around uncomfortably. Neither were dressed for their surroundings. "Pretty impressive for a bunch of deaf kids," he said.

"They're not blind, J.P.," Queenie remarked.

At that moment, a tall, very fashionable woman in her mid-forties entered and introduced herself as Ms. Andrews. Both Queenie and J.P. stood up and shook her hand.

"Let's make this quick, shall we," Ms. Andrews said. "Normally, I would have sent a teacher to help you, but, since you said on the phone that this is part of a murder investigation, I thought it best to take care of it myself."

She opened a cabinet built into the wall, revealing a television and VCR. J.P. handed her the tape and the three of them moved closer to the monitor, Ms. Andrews controlling the remote so as to turn the tape on and off as necessary.

Nessa and L.D. were as they'd last seen them at Popi's, she in the tub, he looking down saying something to her.

"The young man ... something about taking his 'ludes.

300

She says no way and asked him to bring her a glass of wine."

Mrs. Andrews stopped the tape. "You realize, of course, that it's difficult to be totally accurate here because of the positioning of the people, the lighting, and such?"

"Just do your best," J.P. said, and she started the tape again.

As time scrolled in the right corner, Nessa sang, splashing water on her torso. L.D. reentered carrying a full wineglass. Nessa took it, looking up at him.

" 'I left a couple joints on the table,' " Ms. Andrews said. "She asked if there's any more coke. He says he tried to call Billy but he's not home. He'll try and get a hold of him so they've got some for tomorrow night."

On the screen, L.D. began to move to the right.

" '. . . see you tomorrow night.' Then something about being famous. She says no big deal . . ."

Ms. Andrews fell silent as L.D. moved to the right of the house. They saw the rear of a motorcycle, a helmet on the seat. In a plume of dust, L.D. left the screen.

Nessa drank wine and sunned herself. The minutes ticked away. So far the only thing the tape determined was the time Nessa had been alive Friday afternoon.

Finally Nessa set her glass on the ground and leaned forward, her attention on something on the opposite side of the tub. Then they saw little jets of water shoot upward at about five-second intervals.

A moment later a plastic whale swam in front of her, water spurting from a blow hole. Nessa suddenly tensed, glancing to her left. A few seconds later they saw part of the front grill of a car at the far right edge of the screen.

Ms. Andrews piped in. "She's calling out, uh, 'Who's there?' "

Nessa then appeared to relax and turned back to the toy

3 0 1

whale, talking to it. " 'It's only Alice.' Then 'Come to baby-sit' and something else . . ."

The time recorded was 4:27 P.M. Then Alice appeared, glancing around nervously. Nessa mouthed something.

"She says 'hi' and 'what's up?' "

Alice jerked her head back in the direction from which she'd come. Nessa frowned. Then Alice moved quickly behind the tub and to the screen door. She stopped.

"The woman says 'Hurry up, she's only got a minute' and the girl asks, uh, something 'Want to see me?' The woman says something about 'bringing you a dress for tomorrow night.' "

Nessa made a face and spoke to the whale.

Ms. Andrews translated: " 'Frances? It's probably a flour sack.' Uh, something, something, then 'shock the bitch.' "

Wearing only water from the hot tub and a smile, Nessa waltzed toward the house, then disappeared behind the screen door.

Ms. Andrews had nothing more to say.

For a minute or two more, the three of them watched Moby Dick sail round and round the hot tub, spraying a spume of bright water.

CHAPTER FORTY

QUEENIE AND J.P. were well on their way back to Los Angeles before either spoke.

"Christ. That was almost worse than seeing the actual murder," J.P. commented, lighting his third cigarette with the second.

Queenie concurred. Seeing Nessa so girlish and playful, a bright future destroyed with the closing of the screen door.

When Nessa visited Lymon that Monday night, it was simply to see her lover upon his return from New York. Whether or not L.D. had known of the affair didn't matter now. At least he'd be able to come out of hiding and derive some pleasure from his work on what was fast becoming a box office smash.

Queenie thought about Arnold Popi. When they were first viewing the tape at his house, he'd said that he hadn't seen anything out of the ordinary—which was why he hadn't turned it over to the police. What with the fire and all, Queenie gave him the benefit of the doubt, though it was one of those freaky things—like the snaps Joey took of Lymon's body—that would always appeal to certain collectors. And quite possibly the authorities would never have known of the tape's existence had Burke Lymon not spotted the camera that day last fall and, without a word to anyone else, sent Queenie to Popi's house. In a sense, Lymon himself had bridged the canyons of death to avenge the woman he loved. At least, that's what she wanted to think.

"My guess is that Alice picked up Frances from the airport last Friday and drove her to the office—Selma told me she'd come to leave some packages for Lymon. Could have been to establish an alibi. Alice probably rented the same model and make car as Nessa's so if a neighbor saw it, they wouldn't give it much thought. Alice and Mrs. Lymon drive out to the house, situate themselves so they can see L.D. leave, then go in. Alice had already told L.D. to drop off Nessa and leave; she must have known what time he'd be there."

"Oh, yeah," J.P. said, "that coverall probably came from Barth's. Though it had been washed, grease and oil were imbedded in the fabric—like it had been worn to work on a car or motorcycle. Boy, did they have that poor bastard by the short and curlies."

Queenie leaned back and took a moment to rest her eyes. Her body tingled unpleasantly. Soon she would have to sleep.

Back in Hollywood, after stopping at the Korean dry cleaner's near her apartment, J.P. pulled up across the street from the St. Albans. Queenie ran upstairs and gathered the papers J.P. would now take into the Hollywood police station to use in writing a detailed report. Frank Baird would probably get the accolades, but, to his credit, J.P. didn't seem to mind.

He rolled down his window and she gave him the papers.

"Good luck, J.P. Mrs. Lymon's probably still in Windemere securing the Oldfather fortune. Alice might be harder to find." She mentioned the French language course and book on sites of the Goddess in Europe.

J.P. was quiet for a moment, then he grabbed her hand. "You know, you'll need to come into the station again. Just get some sleep first."

She extracted her hand and slapped the car.

"Hey," he said. "I still owe you a beer."

She crossed the dirty street to the St. Albans hardly aware now of the gritty neighborhood. She wasn't thinking of Mrs. Lymon, Alice, J.P., Rex, or Dick. The overload had dumped everything from her mind. Only Clue concerned her.

There's always shit in the corner. Queenie just hoped there wasn't any on her pillow.

friday

 FRIDAY MORNING AT a few minutes before ten, the same diminutive servant ushered Queenie through Eric Diamond's house and out to the flagstone veranda where he seated her at the glass-topped table. As usual, she was unfashionably punctual.

With a flourish, the man brought the familiar sweaty green bottle of water, which he set carefully upon the pink linen napkin. She thanked him, then turned her attention to the lovely garden where the Japanese gardener, as if he'd never left, tended the yellow roses.

No other writers were there; no Susan Fry fouling the air with her acerbic glossolalia. But for the servant, Queenie was quite alone. That didn't mean much, she was always on time. The others weren't.

Somewhat bemused, she drank some of the designer water. She'd spent Thursday in Joey's hotel room rehashing the details of Lymon's murder for *World Abuzz*, her efforts to be rewarded by half of Joey's payment for the article. She'd decided that it would take a more morally disciplined person than herself to find fault with a friend who, in one day, elevated her to a new tax bracket.

While she and Joey labored in a plush room crowded with room service trolleys, the extradition of Frances Lymon was under way. From a cell in the Windemere jail, she staunchly defended her innocence. Her efforts, though, were thwarted by Alice Baldridge, who, soon after being picked up at the Lymons' Palm Isle estate, confessed all.

As Queenie had speculated, Alice had been promised Hammon Productions for her efforts in the murder. Her final act in the drama was to appear on occasion as Frances Lymon, duly veiled, in the back of the limousine, while Frances quietly took care of business in Windemere. Naturally enough, whenever the police or press wished to speak to her, she'd be "under sedation." Both women had counted on L.D. being caught quickly, after which Alice would leave on an extended trip to Europe.

The news whiplashed Hollywood. Almost instantly, producers and writers were talking deals to make *The Frances Lymon Story.*

In all the excitement, and unnoticed for the moment, L. D. Barth slipped into town and appeared at the Hollywood station. J.P. had called Queenie with the news.

Being an ex-con, L.D. knew he'd be suspected immediately and felt it safest to get out of town. He'd hopped on his cycle and taken off for the mountains where he'd been holed up since early Sunday. As soon as he heard about Alice's arrest, he headed back to Hollywood.

Then, last night, she'd celebrated with Joey, staying over at the house now that Joey had left the Ambassador Hotel. They'd been out all night, finally returning to Selma's for breakfast. About an hour and a half ago, Queenie had gone home for a quick shower and to feed Clue. She'd stopped to play her messages: Rex would return Sunday, and Dick would try to reach her next week—he just wanted to let her know he looked forward to seeing her again.

Consequently, feeling a little fuzzy, she wasn't immediately aware of the Filipino servant taking a seat to her right. Peripherally, she noted movement and turned.

Then, to her amazement, he grabbed the top of his head, pulled off his hair—a wig, she realized—and set it on the table between them. Next he popped a pair of tinted contact lenses from his eyes and placed them in a small container taken from his pocket. He completed the transformation by peeling off his nose.

Queenie's speechlessness seemed to please him enormously.

Eric Diamond's pale green eyes twinkled as his small mouth stretched to accommodate bellowing laughter. His thinning, matted white hair and bald nose contrasted comically with the dark pancake makeup on his face.

"Used to be a character actor, a short-lived career," he said while putting the familiar horn-rimmed glasses on his pink-white, aristocratic nose. "Like to have some fun now and again. It was I who greeted you and the others last Saturday. Funny how people react to servants. You were the only one to thank me when I served refreshments. The others didn't even notice. And I did enjoy listening to the idle chatter."

"Mr. Diamond," Queenie replied weakly, still dazed by the transformation.

"Servants make wonderful eyes and ears," he went on crisply. "Frankly, I was a bit shocked . . . how ridiculous suggesting that

I'd sign a client only after taking her to bed!" He shook his head and pursed his lips as if such a thing were beyond belief—which it wasn't.

"Susan did write a good script, but I felt that, after all, it might have been her only one. And that, that *suggestion*, well, that proved she's really without wit. And then, of course, you gave me that second script. I decided to read it before making my final decision. It was between you and Clayton Myer—your second script settled it."

"And?"

Diamond regarded her thoughtfully. "Rumor has it you had something to do with Burke Lymon's widow being charged with his murder."

"It was part of a job. Does this mean that I'm—"

He cut her off. "The other woman too," he went on. "Getting ready for a holiday in France. I guess they felt confident that actor would take the rap. Dear me, one way or another, actors are always getting screwed."

"Mr. Diamond. The script? Does this mean I'm—"

Again he didn't let her finish. "Oh, yes! Salable. Just as good as the first one I read. Different too. I like that. You've got many scripts in you. And that's what it boils down to, doesn't it?"

"You mean—I'm a client?"

"Good heavens, of course. I expect you to help maintain my extravagant lifestyle."

Her heart soared.

"Down to business, then. I might have a job for you. At least it would bring in some money while I peddle your scripts." He paused.

Barely able to contain herself, Queenie waited for him to continue.

"Producer I know needs a script doctor. The film's a murder mystery. You up to that sort of challenge?" His eyes twinkled.

Off to her left, the palms rustled. She glanced over, wondering if rats nested in Beverly Hills palm trees. Probably not. Then she reminded herself Beverly Hills had once been a lowly bean field.

"No problem," she said excitedly. *Murder seems to suit me.*